CIRCLE
OF
CHESTERFIELD

GARY L. KREIGH

AIA PUBLISHING

Circle of Chesterfield
Gary Kreigh
Copyright © 2023
Published by AIA Publishing, Australia
ABN: 32736122056
http://www.aiapublishing.com

ISBN: 978-1-922329-56-1

PROLOGUE

"I'm too hot."

"Do you need to stop?"

"No!" the young man replied, panicking at the thought of stopping. Steam swirled through his confusion.

"But you're not sweating anymore. You're overheating."

"I'm okay. I can keep going."

A man's voice bellowed from outside the tent. "Quiet! Meditate!"

They remained silent for a while, then the dazed student whispered into his concerned buddy's ear, "I just need to concentrate."

"But you haven't. You're mumbling. You haven't been making any sense."

A sharp breath inward. The young man grasped his friend's arm. "I'm better now."

"No, you don't have to do this, Conner."

Conner squeezed harder. "Yes, I do!" He turned to face his friend, unable to comprehend why he didn't understand.

"You can stop anytime now. It isn't worth it."

"But it is, Logan. I have to go on."

"I still hear talking," the man said, only louder. "You're being irreverent."

"Don't listen to him," Logan whispered, leaning closer. "If you're feeling faint, you have to stop this right now."

Conner didn't answer. He couldn't. His breath deep, labored; his heart raced. Sweat no longer dripped from his temples. His eyes searched through the misty darkness for relief.

"What is it you want?" Logan asked.

"Water. Is there water here?"

Logan exhaled frustration. "No, Conner, there's nothing. That's what I'm trying to tell you. He won't let you have anything. It's all part of the cleansing." Incandescent stones cast an eerie glow upon his partner. Logan gave him a once-over. "And look at you. You're not being cleansed. Not like this. He's killing you. Tell him you want to stop."

Conner shook his head vehemently. "No, I can't. I won't."

"But you can, you must."

"No! Don't you see?" he asked, gasping, sputtering. "I have to go on. I'm the chosen one."

CHAPTER ONE

Professor Callan Morrow glanced at his watch. His evening *Introduction to Fraud* lecture had ended. The seats in the theater were empty, his every move echoing in the stillness. Students from other classrooms shuffled in the hall outside the door. He grinned. The day was over.

Classroom lectures were getting easier. Current events changed the dynamics of each class daily. No lecture routine, no question predictable. Bright. New. A relief. Finally, easier, almost fun.

He turned to gather his material when something white caught the corner of his eye on the gray tile flooring. A five-by-seven-inch card, folded in half, lay between the first row of the theater seats and the door.

Callan stepped to the card and picked it up, flipping it in his hand to open the flap. A large black insignia of the copyright symbol dominated the inside. The front cover had nothing more than a name in deep, bold, black letters written in calligraphy: *Marissa Reynolds.*

He glanced to where she'd sat just minutes before, five rows up and to the right. Her big, empty eyes reflected interest, but he suspected her thoughts had been somewhere else, somewhere other than class.

Marissa Reynolds struck Callan as a quiet, rather reserved individual, easily impressionable but sharp and studious. She rarely offered her opinion; when she did, she spoke with confidence. Her words were often overlooked though. Her voice was soft and high-pitched, a tone difficult to listen to without her classmates gritting their teeth. Marissa was dependable and practical, another reason people overlooked her. Predictability wasn't interesting. But this evening was different. Callan couldn't put his finger on exactly why, but tonight Marissa had intrigued him. Different. Yes, tonight Marissa was something she wasn't ordinarily.

Callan placed the card with other items he had to take home, hoping to run into her on the Vermillion College campus the following day. The West Central Indiana college was compact and intimate, and people often did run into each other. If not, she may even call his office to retrieve the card herself once she realized it was missing.

Marissa didn't retrieve it, however. Callan received no phone call the next day, no visit, and he didn't run into her by chance. She didn't attend class the following evening either. Callan made inquiries to other students and professors, but no one had seen her.

He took the card that he'd placed inside his briefcase and studied it more closely, staring blankly at the bold insignia for several minutes. A cold, uneasy apprehension shivered across his back.

Was the card dropped on the floor of his classroom as a message to him that Marissa was in danger?

Callan had no reason to believe that she was, but years of professional fraud experience had taught him one thing: While the world embraced differences and unconventional behavior, to Callan, an abrupt change of lifestyle or behavior was a red flag. A fraud examiner like Callan didn't take to variances. Variances weren't to be celebrated; they were to be examined further.

He didn't have much to go by for such an opinion, however. All Callan had was a card—a small, nondescript card with a copyright insignia on the inside and his student's name on the cover. That was it. Not much on which to base a hunch, except that her absence from class and her lack of relations with other students and professors was an anomaly.

But something else did happen off campus. Callan heard that a student had died, a young man. A quiet one at that but well liked. Another young man was injured too. Near death, he gathered, under unknown circumstances in an isolated valley known locally as Bal Hinch. *Sad, very sad,* Callan thought, *especially for the parents of the two men.* He had two sons of his own. But it had nothing to do with Marissa as far as he could tell. The mystery of Marissa's absence was all he could fathom at the moment.

Callan drove through the warm mid-September air with his car window down, hoping the fresh air would bring new energy to the repetitive thoughts that mulled through his mind. He dropped his briefcase in a chair just inside the entrance of his Victorian home and strode into the kitchen.

His wife, Terese, leaned against a counter, a light sweater and purse in hand, listening intently to a news anchor from a stereo system across from her.

"Heading out?" he asked, noticing only the sweater

and purse.

Terese placed an index finger to her lips for silence then pointed to the radio, listening until the news anchor completed her story. "Was there a hazing incident on campus?" she asked, frowning.

Callan shook his head and shrugged. "A student died. I heard about it today, but it was ruled accidental. A camping accident."

Terese glanced back to the radio. "I don't think so. They're ruling it hazing now, involving something called a lodge of some kind. Quite frankly, I didn't understand it."

"A lodge? You mean at one of the conservation clubs in the country? You're talking about those two boys, right? I thought they were camping."

"Made to look like camping," Terese said, "because it wasn't a *lodge* lodge."

Callan's eyes narrowed; he didn't understand.

"I don't really know what I'm talking about, Cal," Terese admitted. "It wasn't a lodge as we'd think of one. Authorities are calling it some sort of a sweat lodge, I think; yeah, a sweat lodge. I thought you might've heard a little more about it today on campus."

Callan pleaded ignorance.

Terese turned away. "Well, it's disturbing to say the least. I can't imagine why you hadn't heard anything."

"I've heard," Callan said, defending himself, "but what I've gathered is that two VC students were out in a pasture somewhere in a tent. One of the students, a male, died, and the other student, another male, was sent to a hospital in Terre Haute. I haven't heard how he's doing though."

"The news said he was released."

"Released? Well, that's good, I guess. I'm surprised he was, but I'm glad. What else did the news say? Do they know what killed the other student?"

Terese hesitated. "Yes, they did say. Sweat."

Callan's eyes narrowed again.

"You heard me right, Cal. The young man sweated to death."

He turned away to think. "You mean like through steam?"

"Exactly."

Callan thought some more. "And it was hazing, not camping?"

"That's what they're saying. I can't believe you haven't heard this on campus."

Callan leaned against the kitchen island, shaking the cobwebs from his head. "Yeah, me too, but I've been preoccupied with my own student mystery. So did they say what club or fraternity was involved?"

"They don't know yet." Terese readjusted the sweater on her arm as if she was now ready to take off. "It's so odd. They gave a name of Conner White or Conner Wait, something like that, as the boy who died."

"And the one who lived?"

"I didn't catch it completely. Logan, I think. Surely, someone on campus would know. What about your student assistant? Would she know anything?"

An image of Leah Carver popped into his head. "Yes, I'm sure she's heard more than I have, but . . ." He looked at his watch. "Yeah, she should be out of her study group by now."

Callan reached into a pocket, pulled out his cell, and punched in his assistant's number. Leah answered promptly. He asked if she had time to meet him at a small café near campus.

"This must be important," she said, sounding reluctant.

"It is rather."

Leah agreed if Callan gave her twenty minutes to change clothes. Callan beat her to the café by only a couple of minutes. She waltzed in, wearing a faded VC sweatshirt, short-shorts, and flip flops. Her eyes were red and slightly swollen. Leah plopped into a chair across from him and yawned, combing her fingers through scraggly, shoulder-length chestnut hair, while she glanced at the menu board over Callan's head.

"Would you like something?" He paused a moment, studying her weary expression. "Were you sleeping? Crying?"

She smiled. "No—reading. Principles of insurance. These are tears of boredom you see. Yeah, a double shot of anything would be great."

Callan rose and returned from the counter with two lattes, one a small, the other the largest and strongest they offered. He handed the latter one to Leah.

"Do you know a Marissa Reynolds?" he asked, scooting his chair closer to the table.

"We're not friends or anything."

"But do you know her?"

"Yeah, sure, I know her."

Callan leaned forward. "Do you know her well enough to know where she is?"

Leah took a sip of her coffee, licked her upper lip, and brushed a clump of hair that clung to her cheek out of the way. "No, why?"

"Then do you know her well enough to call her?" he asked. "Just to see how she's doing."

She hesitated but nodded. "Sure, but I've been your assistant long enough to know she's not fine if you're asking, Professor."

Callan pulled the card he found on the floor of his classroom out of a side pocket and slid it across the table. "Ever see something like this before?"

Leah rubbed an eye, yawned again, and opened the inside flap. "No, but"—she studied it closely—"it's strange, isn't it? What is it? An invitation?"

"That's what I was hoping you'd be able to tell me."

Leah paused to squint. "She was in a few of my business classes when we first started out at VC, but she changed her focus. That's about all I can remember."

"Changed focus. You mean, like she changed her major?"

"I dunno; she just quit taking so many business classes and began taking subjects like geology, anthropology, astrology, even biology. Not sure if she officially changed her major."

A different focus clearly. "So . . . what can you tell me about her?" Callan asked.

Leah shrugged. "She's not really someone you can describe very well. I mean, she's in my dorm on a different floor. Sweet as can be, cute as a button, that sort of thing, but she doesn't connect with a lot of people. Not someone I gravitate toward, but I do know her, and I've talked with her."

Callan thought back to Marissa's presence in class. He had the same impression. "She hasn't been in class lately. I want to be sure she's okay. I'm going to check at administration to see if they know something, but thought I'd try you first."

"They'd know how to contact her parents, for sure," she replied, grasping her coffee for something to hold. "But if you want to know something less official, I may know of someone who can help. Marissa has a friend. Mitchell Dells. Nice guy, good looking, kinda cocky, into martial arts. I think his dad was in the Marines or something and taught him. Likes to show off sometimes, but he's not bad, got a good head on his shoulders."

Callan nodded. "Good. Look him up for me, will you? Ask him how she's doing. No need for alarm. Act like you're just curious then let me know where I can meet him."

Leah nodded, downed more of her coffee, then scooted away from the table.

"Not yet," Callan said, anticipating her leaving. "There's one more thing. You've heard about that incident in the country, haven't you? What they're calling hazing? A student died. Do you know anything about it?"

"Not really. Only rumors going around."

"Did you know the guy who died?"

"Yeah, but not well." Leah looked down to avoid eye contact. "The stuff being said is all across the board. It's odd."

"That goes without saying if he died from sweat. Anything else?"

"No, I'm telling you, Professor. It's odd. I mean, this Conner fellow was kinda quiet and to himself, and Logan, well, Logan . . ." Leah turned away again. "Yeah, it doesn't make sense if you knew them, especially Logan."

"What are you talking about?" He sensed evasiveness.

"You do know they were found in their underwear."

Callan shook his head.

"Yeah, I mean, well, I just say that because that's what I'm hearing; I mean, what kids are saying on campus, mean things . . ."

"It was sexual?"

Leah sighed. "Yeah, but that's why I said it doesn't make sense, especially if you knew them both. What I thought of Conner was that he was straightlaced and conservative. Logan was, well, he was known to have a crush or two on us now and then."

"By *us,* you mean . . ."

"Yeah, me and my friends."

Callan paused. "So do you think this guy who knows

Marissa also knows these guys found in the sweat lodge? Think he'll talk to me about them?"

Leah drew a breath and held it for several seconds before nodding. "Yeah, I'll give it a shot."

CHAPTER TWO

Mitchell Dells agreed to meet Callan in the old wing of the college library. Callan entered into a hall lined floor to ceiling with reference books on dark, walnut shelves built in the early 1920s, reminiscent of the Municipal Law Library in Munich—stately, large, and intimidating. He passed through an arcade to another hall, mostly of tables lined with massive arched windows on one side of the room, more shelves on the opposite wall.

Callan spotted a group of students, some studying, others chatting, mostly coeds at a table, surrounding an animated young man, smartly dressed in a crew neck sweater. Piercing gazes from the group followed Callan's approach. Whispers subsided completely the moment he reached their table. Mitchell acknowledged Callan and steered him to a secluded corner away from his colleagues. They sat in chairs as old as the building itself that Callan found to be surprisingly comfortable.

The young man appeared just as Leah described. Confident and handsome, with strands of wispy, sand-colored hair that tapered to a clean-cut neckline. His designer jeans and cream-colored sweater snugged his athletic build. He sat poised, pressing his fingertips together as though he was about to begin a scholarship interview.

"This is a pleasure, sir," Mitchell said when settled.

"Oh, really?" The opening comment surprised Callan.

"Yes, sir, you're a celebrity of sorts on campus with the crimes you've investigated. It's not often a person associated with the college makes it into papers outside of Vermillion, what with the airline scandal you solved in Chicago and the extortion murders last spring in Broad Ripple."

"Then you know of my career."

"Know of it, Professor Morrow? Why, you're our own Sherlock Holmes, Hercule Poirot, and Philip Marlowe wrapped into one if you ask me." Mitchell lowered his hands and leaned forward. The patronizing smile he carried since Callan's arrival dissipated. He took a deep breath then sighed. "Which is why your presence concerns me," he said. "Something's wrong, isn't it? It's about Marissa."

Callan cocked his head, confused. "Why would you say that?" He could've just as easily been there to talk about the boys found in the country.

Mitchell glanced through the beveled window to an outside courtyard and shook his head. "Because I haven't seen her in several days. I've talked with her, but I haven't seen her. That's not like her."

"When was the last time you spoke with her?"

"Maybe two or three nights ago." Mitchell didn't blink. "It was a phone call," he added.

"Where was she calling from, do you know?"

He shook his head and looked away in thought. "No, I can't say that I do. It was a normal conversation. Short.

Marissa's not much of a talker for a young woman."

Callan didn't respond. Silence was often a great prompter.

Mitchell took the cue. "She wanted to know if she'd left something when our study group met last, or if I'd picked it up by mistake."

Callan became more interested. He leaned forward just as the young man sat back in his chair as if his response was self-explanatory. "Did she say what it was?" Callan asked.

"No, I can't say that I understood what she was talking about."

"Was it a card, by any chance?"

Mitchell's eyes widened. "A card?"

Callan pulled the mysterious item with the copyright insignia from his pocket and handed it to him.

Mitchell flicked back bangs that'd fallen onto his face with a jerk of his head. He studied the card then stared expressionless into Callan's eyes. "What's this about, Professor?"

"The way you asked the question indicates that you recognize the card."

The young man scoffed. "No, it means I'm as confounded as you. I don't know what to make of it."

Callan told him how the card came into his possession. When finished, Mitchell softened and took another look at the card, inside and out.

Rather than offering a new perspective or additional information, he simply shook his head and frowned. "I'm sorry," he said softly. "I'm not sure I can help you. I wish I could."

"Did your last phone call with Marissa indicate that she was going somewhere or planning to be somewhere?"

"Not at all," Mitchell said, "except that she did tell me about an invitation she'd received."

"An invitation? What did she say about it?"

"Not much."

"Didn't you ask?"

"No," he said, sounding annoyed. He handed the card back then rested his elbows on his knees. "She didn't say anything, and it wasn't any of my business. Besides, the card doesn't look like much of an invitation now, does it, Professor? I mean, does it to you?"

Callan shrugged. "I don't know. It could belong to a secret society on campus or something similar."

Mitchell chuckled at the thought. "A secret society? At Vermillion?" The young man laughed again and shook his head. "With all due respect, Professor, VC is so small, I can't imagine any society staying secret for very long. At any rate, I've not heard of any, and I can't imagine Marissa of all people getting involved in something like that."

"Why not?"

"She's not the type."

Callan hoped his silence would again prompt Mitchell to elaborate.

"She isn't one that falls for clubs or secret societies," Mitchell said, his voice sharper. "She can be naive sometimes, sure, but she's not gullible. Besides, she pretty much stays to herself. She's not a joiner."

Callan paused again.

"She's not, Professor."

"I'm not doubting you," Callan replied. "I'm sure what you've said about Marissa is genuine, but not everything you've just said to me is true."

Mitchell leaned back and glared at Callan. "What are you saying?"

"I'm saying that your comment about secret societies on

campus isn't entirely true. I believe there *are* such gatherings on campus."

Mitchell shrugged. "Maybe there are. I wouldn't know."

"Wouldn't you?" Callan asked. "Did you know the student who died in that incident in the Bal Hinch? I believe his name was Conner."

"Conner Whaite?"

"Then you did know him."

"Yes, of course I knew him," Mitchell replied. "We all did. It's a small college, Professor."

"Then you must've heard some scuttlebutt around campus."

Mitchell stared blankly, shook his head, and lowered his voice. "Not really. Conner was a loner too. A thinker."

"But students talk."

"Not about him." Mitchell repositioned himself in his chair. "Conner was into contemplation, self-analysis, high-order thinking, stuff like that," Mitchell said. "He wasn't a Mensa or anything, just a bright guy."

Callan's expression didn't change. Mitchell stopped talking. They stared at each other for several seconds.

"If you think I'm lying, ask anyone," Mitchell said.

"I didn't say you were. What about this Logan fellow? Did you know him?"

"Yeah, of course. Good guy, for the most part."

"And for the other part?"

Mitchell smiled. "A little full of himself."

Callan smiled back.

Mitchell caught what Callan was thinking. "Hey, takes one to know one, Professor. Know what I mean?"

"Yeah, I'm afraid I do," he said. The conversation lulled. Callan ran out of topics to discuss. "Look, I won't take up any more of your time, Mitchell, but I must ask you one more question in all seriousness. Do you believe Marissa is safe?"

Mitchell's eyes darted about the room as though he hadn't given the question prior thought. "Safe from what?" he asked. "What do you know that you're not telling me?"

Callan shook his head. "That's just it. I don't know anything. No one else does either, it seems. That's what bothers me."

CHAPTER THREE

Callan returned to his campus office. His conversation with Mitchell Dells did little to lift his spirits about Marissa Reynolds's safety. His eyes shifted to the shelves of reference books on fraud he'd collected over the years. Surely, there was something he'd studied or read about that could give him insight to the enigma that faced him, but he was hard-pressed to know where to look. In fact, as he scanned his domain, everything he'd collected and stored in his office seemed pointless, practically useless now. He'd never faced a situation like this before. A sudden chill frightened him. Not for himself but for Marissa.

He sighed, realizing he hadn't finished preparations for his next class. The phone rang, offering a diversion, at least momentarily.

"Professor Morrow?" Leah asked, urgency in her voice. "Mr. and Mrs. Reynolds arrived in town from South Bend."

"Who?"

"Marissa's parents."

"Ah!" Callan exclaimed, remembering, now excited. "But why? Has something happened? Have they received word from her?"

"No, nothing," Leah said. "That's why they've come to Vermillion, to see and talk with her. She wasn't in her dorm room, and her roommate, Dana Weiss, didn't have much information. They're worried sick."

"How did you find this out?"

"Mr. Reynolds asked Dana if there was someone they could talk to. Mitchell must've let her know about your meeting with him, so she gave Mr. Reynolds my number as your assistant so that he could get ahold of you."

"Have they been to administration?"

"Yes, but I'm not sure they got any information that was of much help," Leah said. "They received a standard administrative reply that their daughter was over eighteen and entitled to privacy. That just added fuel to the fire."

"Where are they now?"

"Campus Inn. That's where they're staying."

"Good. Have them meet me in the lobby in ninety minutes if that works for them. My next class should be over by then."

~

Sunlight through the atrium windows of Campus Inn accentuated the somber faces of Marissa Reynolds's parents as Callan walked toward the couple. Leah stood off to the side. Her expression appeared as eager as her voice on the phone, but she reserved comment except for a casual greeting. She led him to the couple sitting nervously on a divan away from the reservation counter.

Greg Reynolds rose when they approached. His strong,

solid features complemented his professional appearance. Greg's handshake was firm and confident, even though his eyes told a different story. He introduced his wife, Nancy. In comparison to her husband, Nancy Reynolds appeared pale and drawn, as if she hadn't slept in several days. Her hair, though professionally styled, was unkempt in the back but presentable around her face, as though she only cared to fix what she could see in a mirror. Callan waited patiently for Nancy to extend her hand before he reached out to shake it gently. She didn't meet his eyes, glanced away as soon as she caught sight of them. She dabbled her nose with a white hanky and pursed her lips in an effort to remain strong, but Callan believed she wanted nothing better than to return to their room to resume sobbing.

Callan took an occasional chair from the side of the divan and placed it so he could sit across from the couple.

Greg thanked Callan for agreeing to meet with them. "Ms. Carver, here, tells us that you may have some news about our daughter. We've just been to administration, but they've heard nothing, or, at least, that's their official word. I'm fairly certain their response, regarding my daughter's right to privacy, was a deflection, indicating that they haven't a clue. My daughter's been missing for several days, Professor. To hell with her privacy. We're her parents. We're paying her tuition. We want to know what's going on."

"I understand," Callan said, "but I'm afraid news about your daughter is premature."

Greg's nostrils flared. "Is that another way of saying you're not going to tell me because she has a right to privacy?"

"No, by all means, I'm as concerned and as interested in Marissa's whereabouts as you are. I've been asking questions myself but haven't gotten very far."

Callan's comments didn't appease Marissa's father.

"If Ms. Carver hasn't told you," Greg said, "Mrs. Reynolds and I drove down from South Bend to determine if her lack of communication with us is something the authorities should investigate. We listened to the news this morning in the car. Apparently, other strange events have occurred at Vermillion that can't be explained and may be associated with the college." Greg noticed Callan and Leah's lack of reaction and added, "A student's death has been all over the news in case you're trying to keep us from worrying. We even heard it in South Bend. That's why we've come."

"What did you hear exactly?" Callan asked.

Nancy reached for her husband's arm, urging him to change the subject. The expression on her face indicated that she couldn't bear repeating what they feared.

"Then tell me the last time you spoke with your daughter," Callan said.

"Was it four days ago?" Greg asked his wife.

She nodded reluctantly. "But we talk every day," she said, emphasizing that four days without word was abnormal for Marissa.

"How was the conversation when you last spoke?"

"It was fine," Nancy replied. "Nothing out of the ordinary. Marissa sounded like herself. I thought nothing of it."

"Does she have friends back home that could shed some light?"

Nancy shook her head and looked away. "They haven't talked with her in a while. I've checked."

"Is that unusual?"

"Yes, some, but not entirely. You see, Marissa is a very private individual in many ways. She enjoys having a few close friends rather than many acquaintances. Her friends are quite a bit like her—private, that is."

Callan drew the card with Marissa's name on the front from his pocket. He handed it to Nancy Reynolds.

"Have you seen anything like this before among any of Marissa's belongings?"

She took the card and studied it carefully, then shook her head. No expression. Nancy extended it to her husband as if he, too, would find it as meaningless as she did.

"What's this symbol?" he asked immediately.

"Have you not seen it before?" Callan asked.

"No, why should I have? Looks like a copyright symbol."

Callan agreed but shook his head.

Greg turned to Leah. "Have you seen anything like this around campus?" Before Leah could answer, he turned to Callan and asked, "Where did you find this? Why is Marissa's name on it?"

"That's what I was hoping you could tell me," Callan said.

Greg lowered his head and sighed, wiping his face with the palm of his hand as if in an attempt to wipe away his frustration. "Yes, yes, I'm sure you did. I apologize for being so abrupt. I'm out of sorts, you see. We both are. Please keep us informed if you find out anything."

Nancy's phone buzzed. She glanced at the display, gasped, and lifted the phone to her husband. Her hand convulsed, nearly dropping the phone as she did so.

Greg caught it midair, eyeing the number across the screen. "Good God!" he called. "It's Marissa. She just texted you."

"Read it, please," Nancy said, still shaking. "I don't think I can."

"It just says, *I'm okay Mom, will talk soon.*" Greg Reynolds flushed with anger and snapped, "By damn, she'll talk to us now!" He punched a callback number to talk rather than text.

Callan couldn't hear what was being said on the other end of the line, but he assumed the call went to voice mail.

Greg rocked anxiously, leaving a curt and pointed command to his daughter to call him immediately. The phone buzzed again. *In a meeting, can't talk. Will talk soon. Promise. Love you.* "Meeting?" he spouted. "What sort of meeting? What happened to her classes? I'm not paying her to go to meetings."

Nancy implored him to calm down. "She's safe, Greg. You heard her. Let's just praise God that she's safe. That's all that matters."

Greg shook his head, fear mixed with anger radiating from his eyes. "Safe?" he asked. "I want more than safe, Nancy. I want to hear her voice. I don't believe for one second that she's in a meeting." He turned to Callan. "Do you, Professor? How do we know these texts are even hers unless we hear her voice?" He trembled and turned back to his wife. "Don't tell me she's safe, Nancy, until I see her in front of me, and I can see for myself that she's alive and well."

The sudden realization her daughter could be in harm's way brought tears to the woman's eyes. Leah sat on the small sofa next to her, took her hand, and tried to console the broken mother.

His wife's reaction ignited Greg once again. He punched Marissa's number into the phone one more time and waited for voice mail. "Marissa, please call us," he said, this time in a fatherly tone. "We're worried sick about you. Please, get out of the meeting just long enough so that we can hear your voice and know for sure that you're safe. We're in Vermillion. If you're in Vermillion also, we want to see you. Please call me back right away. I love you. We both love you very much."

Nancy gave her husband an approving nod.

Callan took a deep breath and looked away, his jaw set.

Greg Reynolds noticed. "What are you thinking?" he asked. "I know when a man's wheels are turning, and you have something on your mind."

"It's nothing, just thinking about next steps," Callan said. "I was thinking that while the two of you wait for Marissa's call, I'd like to spend my time interviewing her roommate." He turned to his assistant. "Do you know Marissa's roommate very well? What's her name?"

"Dana Weiss," Leah said.

"What about her?" Greg asked. "Are she and Marissa close?"

"Not sure how close, but they're roommates. That makes them close enough for me to talk with her," Callan said.

Nancy agreed.

Greg turned toward his wife. "Why do you say that? Do you know her?"

She nodded. "They're not like real friends, but Dana should know enough to be helpful, I'd think. I called her earlier, but she seemed tight-lipped. I wasn't sure what that meant." She hesitated, lifting a finger. "Then there's this other boy," she added. "He may know something as well."

"A boyfriend?" Greg asked impatiently. "By God, he better not have . . ."

"Who is he?" Callan interrupted.

"A young man by the name of Mitchell somebody," she said. "I can't recall his last name in all this confusion. We've met him. You've met him, Greg. You said you liked him."

Greg snarled. "I remember now. I said he gave me a good first impression. That doesn't mean I like him. If I find out he's hurt our daughter in any way, my second impression will be my fist into the middle of his gut."

Callan raised his hand. "I doubt that will be necessary," he said. "I've met Mitchell. His last name is Dells. Nice kid, but he wasn't much help."

"So you've talked with him?"

"Just this morning."

Nancy slumped. Sadness returned to her eyes. "Oh, I thought for sure he could shed some light."

Callan leaned closer. "Why do you say it like that, Mrs. Reynolds?"

"Well," she said demurely, "because he called me just last night."

Hearts stopped. Silence.

Greg gasped. "What?" he blurted.

"It was accidental, I'll grant him that, but Mitchell rang my number just the same."

Greg Reynolds paced nervously. "I don't understand. Why would this kid have your cell number?"

Nancy shifted on the divan and shook her head in contemplation. "Oh, I don't know. You remember, Greg. He and Marissa went to that concert at the performing arts center back home. He picked Marissa up so they could go together." Nancy looked up at Callan to explain. "We live just outside the city, up near Granger, Mr. Morrow. Mitchell wasn't sure he could find us. He joked that he didn't want to find himself in Michigan, so Marissa gave him my cell as an extra number to have just in case."

"But you said it was accidental that he called you," Callan replied. "How so?"

"He was trying to reach Marissa."

"But he called you instead?"

"Yes, by accident."

Leah glanced at Callan. "Butt call, I'd guess."

Callan nodded. "Did you talk at all or did you two just hang up when you realized it was a mistake?"

"We had small talk. We laughed about the mix-up. He apologized and asked how we were, then hung up. I figured after he talked to me that he'd call Marissa right after. That's why I'm disappointed he didn't have better news to share with you."

"Didn't this Mitchell kid tell you about the call?" Greg asked, glaring at Callan. "I would've thought that if he really wanted to be helpful he would've mentioned it."

Callan focused on the swaying tree limbs through the atrium's expansive windows as he reflected on his conversation with the cocky young man whose sandy hair dangled about his face. Ire grew from within. Callan swallowed reflux rising from his gut. He agreed with Greg Reynolds. He thought Mitchell would've mentioned it too.

CHAPTER FOUR

"Where do you think I can find him?" Callan asked Leah. The two rushed out of the inn and scurried across the campus mall.

Leah glanced at her watch and winced.

"Will he be studying?"

"I dunno. I doubt it," Leah said. "He may have class. If not, he'll be back at the library."

Callan eyed her expression and noticed a smirk creeping across her face.

"You don't have to study while you're at the library," she said, "unless it was different back in your day."

This time, it was Callan who smirked.

Leah's hunch proved accurate. Callan entered the main hall of the library and found Mitchell Dells at a long wooden conference table, talking to a coed who chewed gum with an open mouth and a protruding tongue. Two other women were at the other end of the table. One twirled strands of her long brown hair with frosted ends as she eavesdropped to Mitchell's conversation, while the other texted and laughed, engrossed in her own world.

Mitchell caught a glimpse of Callan when he entered the building—just long enough to lean closer to the woman to whisper a few words. She started to turn around but stopped abruptly when he made a covert gesture for her to not do so.

He thinks he's sly, Callan thought. He wasn't in the mood for any more of the young man's attempts to interfere with his inquiries, still aggravated that Mitchell had lied to him about not hearing from or talking with Marissa. Although Mitchell nodded when Callan approached, he didn't say anything. Callan didn't either. Instead, Callan glanced down at the woman's belongings for any identifying marks. *DW* was scribbled on the cover of a spiral notebook.

DW was a petite, young woman with thick, straight hair, dark as chocolate, and skin that appeared to be of Mediterranean descent even though he believed her surname to be German. Her eyes, equally dark, lacked vibrancy. She gnawed her gum with increasing effort and stared at Mitchell for his reaction.

"Are you Dana Weiss?" Callan asked, taking a chance.

She chewed, unwilling to give him the time of day.

Callan didn't bother introducing himself, figuring Mitchell had already briefed her when he entered the room. "May I ask, do you know where Marissa Reynolds is?"

She shook her head.

He glanced to Mitchell, catching him in the middle of a facial gesture Callan believed was a prompt on how she should respond. "Is that the truth," he asked her, "or is that what he told you to say?"

Dana shrugged. "I don't know where she is. She's not been

to the dorm."

"When was the last time you talked with her?"

"I don't know," she said, softening. She focused on a nail that was slightly chipped and reached inside her purse for a file. "I'm not good with dates and times. Why are you asking me these things? Mitchell, what is this?"

Mitchell grimaced. "I already told you. Just answer him. When did you talk to her last?"

She sighed. "Oh, I don't know, like I said. That's just it. I don't know. It's been a while. Honest."

Callan paused to study her eyes, still dull and elusive. Even so, he believed her.

"It's not like she's my best friend," she added.

Callan believed that too. Dana seemed to be the type of person to have a lot of acquaintances and very few close friends—the exact opposite of Marissa Reynolds as told by her mother. Nevertheless, Callan didn't hesitate to say, "You don't seem concerned that she hasn't been around."

She clacked her gum. "Why should I? We give each other space. I like space."

Callan side-glanced at Mitchell before returning his focus to Dana. Was Dana naturally cold and insensitive about others, or was she intimidated by what Mitchell may have said to her as he approached their table? Callan couldn't decide, but he believed the coed knew more than she was letting on.

"Give us a minute, will you?" he asked her.

Dana packed her things and shuffled toward the other two women who had moved from the table to near an exit doorway.

Mitchell pretended to organize papers while keeping one eye on Callan, standing motionless but irritated in front of him.

"I took you at your word when you said you didn't know

where Marissa was," Callan said.

"It was my word. I wasn't lying."

"I'm going to ask you once again: when was the last time you talked to Marissa?"

Mitchell turned away. "I can't tell you."

"Why not?"

"It wouldn't be right."

Callan's eyes narrowed, trying to determine what he meant. "Help me to understand. What wouldn't be right?"

"Telling you where she is." His scoffing tone insinuated that Callan was a buffoon for asking.

"How's that?"

"You don't get it," he said. "She's not missing, Professor. She's not missing at all. She just doesn't want to be found. I think everyone should respect when a person wants to be left alone. She wants that respect right now."

Callan set his jaw and let the young man simmer.

Mitchell shifted his weight but said nothing more.

"Then tell me this," Callan said. "Is she safe?"

He nodded.

"Is she with someone who can be trusted?"

Mitchell nodded again.

"I need a name."

His head jerked up. "I can't give you a name," he said boldly.

"Can't or won't?"

"Won't. I just told you. It wouldn't be right."

"Dammit, Mitchell." Callan stepped closer. "I need a name, or your word is no good with me. I can tell you right now that her father doesn't give a flying rat's behind about what you think is right or wrong when it comes to the safety of his daughter."

Mitchell shook his head. His lips tightened. "That's because he doesn't understand either. She really wants this time alone, Professor. You must believe me. It's vital that she gets a little more time. I don't understand why she can't have it."

"Because I need a name to believe you."

The young man sighed and for the first time, Callan could feel him relenting to pressure.

"Logan Allister," Mitchell said, in a tone too low for Callan to hear. Mitchell repeated the name, only louder. "She's been with Logan."

Callan didn't take the time to thank Mitchell for the information he received. Instead, he marched out of the library, pulled out his cell phone when he reached the sidewalk and punched in Leah Carver's number. She answered right away.

"Logan Allister," he said, first words out of his mouth. "Where have I heard that name before?"

Leah stumbled for words. "Why, Logan, don't you remember, he was the one in that sweat lodge when Conner died."

Callan paused. That didn't make sense. "I thought Logan was in the hospital."

"No, remember? He was released."

Callan's knees nearly gave way. He took several seconds to steady himself. Jumbled thoughts clouded his mind. He wasn't sure if it was fear or anger that welled inside him. Conner, Logan, Marissa, Mitchell, Dana, sweat lodges—their significance blurred together, information came at him faster than he could process.

A voice called through the haze. "Professor Morrow?"

Callan realized he'd let the phone drop to his side. He lifted it slowly to his ear.

"Are you okay?"

"Yes, yes," he said, his voice fading. "Logan Allister. I need something."

Leah told him she'd get whatever he needed, whenever he needed it.

"Good, because I want to know everything you can tell me about him."

CHAPTER FIVE

Leah sat on her bed, legs crossed, staring through the slats of the blinds covering her dorm window to a world that didn't make sense to her anymore. The sun filtered through the branches of a tree just outside, casting opaque shadows upon her bedspread but emanating a warmth that reminded her that not everything was muddled in the confusion of recent events.

Except for Logan Allister, that is. She thought she knew Logan. Her recollection of him wasn't muddled. She'd shared a couple of classes with him, partnered with him on a business investment project, even studied in a small group one semester. He wasn't only personable, he was open and compassionate. The circumstances surrounding the sweat lodge in the country were confounding and sometimes contradictory, but Leah was certain of one thing: Logan wasn't hazing; he was Conner Whaite's friend. He would've been supportive. Nothing she'd heard on the news, in the classroom, or in the dorm could convince her otherwise.

But what was Logan thinking to get involved in such a

club or organization that condoned such behavior? Was he lured . . . or worse, forced to participate? Leah didn't believe he was gullible or naive. At least, she didn't think he was, but she, too, wasn't so naive to believe that she knew everything about a person, even someone as genuine and transparent as Logan Allister.

And what is a sweat lodge, she wondered? She reached for her phone and scanned the first article that popped up on her display, but the description didn't make sense to her. A sweat lodge sounded more like a spiritual Native American ceremony or ritual than a college hazing ploy.

Was he with Marissa as Mitchell told Professor Morrow he was? If not, then where was he? Where would he be with her? Why wasn't Mitchell more helpful?

Her head spun. A welling sadness made it difficult to breathe. The shadows on her bed disappeared when the sun cowered behind the mid-September clouds. They reappeared minutes later but were different. The sun had moved, shadows changed. She stared at the altered outlines in such a mesmerizing way that she nearly missed the vibrating buzz of her cell beside her on the bed. Startled, she thrashed about the covers until she found it, then gazed blankly at the screen that identified the caller. Leah blinked rapidly to be sure she saw the display properly, then clicked the button to answer the call.

"Marissa?" she asked.

The silence alarmed her.

"Marissa!"

"Leah?" a voice finally asked.

"Yes, Marissa, it's me." Leah hardly recognized the voice, but she called her name with the hope that it really was her. "Where are you? Are you okay?"

"Yes, yes, I'm fine," she said, sounding more like herself.

"Your parents are worried sick, Marissa. Have you talked to them?"

Marissa hesitated on the other end.

Leah feared they'd lost connection. "Marissa?"

"Not yet," she said. "I received a voice mail from them, but Dad sounded too angry to talk just yet."

"That's not true. He's just worried about you."

"Okay, good." More hesitation. "I'm fine, Leah. I really am. I called . . . I shouldn't be calling . . . no, I called . . . to find out about Logan. How is he? Is he *really* okay?"

"What?" Leah asked. The connection garbled Marissa's voice. Leah switched ears, hoping to hear better. "Isn't he with you?"

Silence.

"We thought he was with you, Marissa," Leah said, alarmed. "Mitchell told us that Logan was with you."

"Us?"

"Yes. Professor Morrow has taken an interest. He said he would on your parents' behalf."

"But why?"

"Well, because he found a card on the floor of his classroom the other night," Leah said. She spoke clearly and slowly, unable to comprehend why Marissa would find his involvement hard to believe. "It had your name on the outside of it and a copyright insignia on the inside. You didn't show up for class after that. He got worried. He still is."

"A card?"

"Yes, a card you had; surely you know what I'm talking about. It had your name on the front and a copyright symbol on the inside."

"Oh," Marissa said. "So that's what happened to it."

Leah's head spun some more. "Then you know what I'm talking about."

"Yes, of course, but, oh, I wish Professor Morrow hadn't been the one to find it. Of all the people, Leah. He won't leave this alone. Oh, Leah, this is terrible."

Leah arched her back, shocked at her friend's response. "Of all people? Are you kidding, Marissa? Professor Morrow is the best of all people to find the card."

"But I wish he hadn't."

Leah paused and drew a breath. "Marissa, what does it mean?"

"Oh, Leah, you wouldn't understand," she replied, whining softly.

"Please give me a chance."

"No, I meant that you wouldn't approve."

"But you're still not giving me a chance."

Marissa's voice sharpened. "Trust me on this, Leah. That card and my absence is something I want, something I need to do on my own. I don't want you to talk me out of it."

"Then at least tell me that you're safe."

"Of course, I'm safe," she said. "I'm not a fool."

"I didn't say you were, but I don't have to remind you that Conner is dead, and Logan was in the hospital."

"You make it sound so horrible, Leah." The soft whining returned.

The comment astounded Leah. "Marissa, it *is* horrible," she blurted. "Why is anyone to think otherwise? Now, tell me about Logan."

Marissa regained strength. "What about Logan?"

"Is he involved in the same thing you are, whatever it is?"

"Logan will have to speak for himself." Her voice hardened, then softened. "Is he all right?"

"I don't know," Leah responded, unwilling to divulge any news even if she had some. News about Logan appeared to be the only leverage she had. "All I know is what I hear on campus."

"Oh, Leah," Marissa cried, "I just don't understand how this could've happened."

"But what happened, Marissa? If I only knew what happened, maybe we could understand together. Will you tell me, please?"

"No, no, I should go," she said. Panic welled in her voice. "I shouldn't have called. Please don't tell anyone I called. I was just heartbroken about Conner and . . . Logan, and I . . ."

"Marissa, what were they doing in that field? In that tent? Please tell me. They say it was hazing."

Marissa didn't answer.

"Was it hazing?"

Still no response. Leah called her name, but the call disconnected abruptly.

CHAPTER SIX

Across. Seven letters. Joyful noise.

Terese curled her nose. Ecstatic had eight. Cheerful had eight. Elated was six. There was nothing joyful with seven. She turned to Callan, but he wasn't there. He had been sitting in his chair a moment ago. Had she spent that much time contemplating a crossword clue that she didn't hear him leave?

She set her book and pencil on the cushion beside her and walked into the kitchen, expecting a pot of coffee to be brewing or his decanter of brandy out of the cabinet and his nose planted deeply into the pantry, searching for a salty snack.

Nothing.

There was one other place. She strode to the stairwell and looked up. A soft light cast a golden hue across the upstairs hall. Terese returned to the kitchen, prepared two cups of coffee, decaf for her, and inched her way up the steps to the doorway of his office.

She didn't ask if she could set the beverage on his desk. When it came to hot coffee, freshly brewed, permission was never needed. He smiled but offered no additional gratitude. Terese took a seat nearby in a chair he used to read. She knew her husband well enough to know he never read at his desk. That was reserved for thinking.

This evening, however, Terese received a different vibe. She wasn't so sure he was thinking. The hard lines across his forehead and the drawn look upon his stubbled face indicated something deeper wrestled inside.

"Take a sip," she said, reaching over to push the cup closer to his hand.

Callan did so but said nothing.

"I thought you'd be glad to hear that Marissa called Leah," Terese said. "I can see it did just the opposite." She hoped he would respond and elaborate.

He didn't.

"She's safe, Callan."

This time she drew a breath out of him. "Physically, yes. Mentally, I'm not so sure," he said. "Based upon how Leah described their conversation, she sounds . . . detached."

Terese frowned. "I don't know what you mean."

"Detached," he repeated. "Emotionally, physically."

"Could be stress, Callan. Some kids handle college better than others."

He shook his head. "There's the matter of the card and her unwillingness to tell Leah about it. The card has nothing to do with stress, but it has everything to do with detachment."

This time, Terese had to agree. "But from what?" she asked.

"That's not what concerns me. The bigger question is, To what?"

"Oh, I see. Then it's not about hazing on campus at all, is it? A secret society of some sort?"

"Mitchell Dells says there isn't one."

Terese scoffed. "Well, from what you've told me about Mitchell Dells, I wouldn't put much credence in what he says, and if I know you, you haven't either."

"No, but it doesn't make it any easier. I haven't found anyone on campus who knows otherwise."

"Aren't you in contact with any professors who may have heard something—anything— that could be of help? Surely, some information has leaked out somewhere that a person of authority has overheard. Who's that business professor you often speak of?"

Callan shook his head as though no one came to mind.

"The woman," she said. "Dry sense of humor, dumpy-looking husband."

"Professor Fordworth?"

"I suppose. I've only met her once or twice. Glynis. I thought her name was Glynis."

"Yes," Callan said, strumming his fingers on the top of his coffee cup. "Glynis Fordworth. She might know. She has a good rapport with students. Glynis could've very well heard something."

Callan took another sip of coffee and sat back in his chair. The lines on his forehead and the drawn expression on his face didn't fade, however.

Terese gave him several seconds with his thoughts before adding, "There's something else. What is it?"

"Nothing," he said.

Terese smiled playfully. "No, hon, husbands aren't allowed to say nothing and get away with it. I reserve that right."

He returned the smile. "Okay, then nothing . . . except I fear we're running out of time even if Glynis can tell me something."

Terese reached to touch his arm. "But you can't think like

that. You're doing the best you can."

"But I do think like that," he said. "It's not enough. I can't help it. I know her father is out there, looking for her, but he's too close. He's not objective, and he doesn't know the campus and the kids like I do—or Glynis for that matter."

Terese took his hand and caressed it. "But for some reason, Cal, I'm getting the feeling you're too close as well."

Callan tried to pull his hand away, but she wouldn't let him.

"You know what it's like to suffer loss, to feel the unknown. I believe for some reason, this experience with Marissa Reynolds is bringing all of that back. You know what I'm talking about, Callan. The night your parents were killed. I can see it on your face."

Callan shook his head. "No, this is different," he said. "Marissa's situation is different."

"How so?"

He pulled free this time. "I can't explain it."

Terese frowned. If that was his way of not trying to, she wouldn't accept it. She prompted him to try.

"I can't," he said, frustration rising in his voice. "I mean, I don't know what I'm talking about. It's a feeling I had back then. I was never so scared and alone in my life, but I always had . . . I always knew . . . I was going to be okay."

"Because your aunt and uncle were there for you?"

"What?" He turned abruptly toward her, confused. "My aunt and . . . what? No. No, something different, something completely different." Callan looked away, back into his memory. "Yes, they were always there for me, but it was something else. Something hard to explain. There was a presence with me. People. Energy. Life. Always there. Always when I needed them. A presence. I can't explain it."

Terese nodded, trying to comprehend but finding it difficult to empathize when she didn't completely understand.

"You don't believe me."

"Yes, I do," she said earnestly. "There's nothing not to believe."

"But you don't know what I'm talking about," he said.

Terese sighed. "No, but I haven't been through what you've been through either. What about your sister? Did she feel the same way at the time? Does she still feel the same way now?"

"No," he said sadly. "She took a different path. She's bitter about life. She's angry our parents were taken away, and she's let the world know she's pissed about it. I can't explain her experience either."

They sat in silence before Terese finally said, "How is what you went through similar to how you're feeling now about Marissa?"

"It's not just Marissa," he said. "It's Conner, and Logan, and the other students on campus affected by this incident. What's similar is how instantaneously it seemed to happen. My parents' car crash happened in an instant. Conner's death, the sweat lodge, and Marissa's absence seems just as spontaneous to me. Out of thin air, just as abrupt. In an instant."

Terese shook her head. "It appears that way, Callan, but I suspect when you get it all sorted out, you'll find there was a lot more going on before the incident than you ever imagined. It's been like that with every case you've been involved with. On stage, it's organized and comprehensible to the audience, but behind the curtain, it's chaotic with activity no one can see."

Callan reached for his wife's hand. "And that's why you caught me in the state I'm in," he said. "I hope someone, or something, has been watching over her like they did me. Because I hate to think what will happen if Marissa chooses the wrong path."

CHAPTER SEVEN

The next morning, Callan sat in his campus office and scanned his desk. It's true what they say about the morning, he reminded himself. Everything is brighter. Things have a different perspective. There's renewed hope, fresh ideas. He could feel a new resolve in his spirit, and he brushed aside dark thoughts from the night before. In fact, the whole conversation with Terese was rather embarrassing, mulling it over now. What a funk he was in to babble on so. Terese must've thought he'd gone mad or worse yet . . . made up his experience of long ago. After all, he was ten years old when his parents died. Perspectives differ as a child.

Callan took a deep breath and scanned the top of his desk. He shuffled teaching plans and notes, and pushed reference books off to the side so he could think. He needed room for a new outlook if such an outlook was in store for him this morning.

Besides, Marissa Reynolds's whereabouts weren't his concern. Not really anyway. Of course, he had a vested interest, finding the card that started the whole thing, but the card was only a small part of what he feared was happening on campus. There were others in authority whose job was to investigate such incidents—people more qualified. John Steinmeier, for instance, as chief of campus security. Where was he? What was he doing? Callan talked about a presence—someone or something—that watched over him when he was young. Let John Steinmeier be that presence for Marissa and Logan.

Still, however, he couldn't help but think . . .

He glanced to his left at *The Vermillion Post*, one of the papers he'd shuffled off to the side of his desk. He snatched the newspaper, folded like crumpled bedsheets after a restless night. The headline hadn't changed from previous editions. The incident seemed as bizarre and unfathomable to reporters as it was to Callan. He read the lead article again, this time more closely.

Two young men, Conner Whaite and Logan Allister, were found in a tent in the middle of a pasture. A makeshift pyre had been built and used several yards away from it. The tent was heated by stones piled in the center, doused by water to create steam. Both men were overcome by the intense heat despite wearing only boxers and white t-shirts. Conner took the elements extremely hard and succumbed at the scene. If it hadn't been for an anonymous phone call for medical attention, young Logan could and probably would have suffered the same fate.

Callan quickly scanned the rest of the article for any mention of who authorities determined made the anonymous call. Nothing. That seemed odd. It would've been one of the first things he would've tried to discover. Of course, if it was hazing, an anonymous caller who faced possible criminal charges would be difficult to locate if it was determined they had a hand in the men's demise.

But was it hazing? Authorities used the word persistently in the article. There appeared to be no other explanation for what they described as a "ritual", even though they were hard-pressed to find a fraternity or organization that could account for the unusual circumstances. The article also indicated that Logan Allister had been released by the hospital, although he wasn't very cooperative with authorities. His recollection of the event was foggy at best, but closer to dissociative amnesia induced by trauma. They were optimistic the young man would come to and shed additional light on what had happened and why.

Callan frowned. Again, that didn't make sense. Didn't Mitchell Dells tell him that Marissa was with Logan? Marissa denied the fact, but nevertheless, the comment would suggest Logan was cohesive enough to emotionally and mentally reach out to Marissa who, at this point, Callan believed was involved. It would explain the mysterious card with the copyright insignia if he could only tie the card to what happened in the tent.

The tent, or sweat lodge as it were, didn't make much sense to him either. Callan had researched information online about sweat lodges. Other than being a Native American ceremonial rite of cleansing as Leah had mentioned to him earlier, there appeared to be little to no evidence of them being used in college hazing incidents.

Callan read further into the article. No, that wasn't true, he realized.

Callan grabbed his cell and searched under *sweat lodge hazing*. There had been such an incident in North Carolina two years ago. The online article was brief and lacked sufficient information for him to determine whether the situation at

Vermillion was similar, but it was close enough. However, it was the only such incident he could find. Apparently, sweat lodges were not the method of choice for fraternities or sororities to use as a rite of passage for new members.

So that left Marissa Reynolds. Callan set his phone and the newspaper aside to think about the young coed. According to Leah, Marissa knew the men in the sweat lodge—at least, she knew their names. In addition, she was worried about them. He suspected she also knew what they were doing in a tent in the middle of Bal Hinch, a valley known locally as Spooky Hollow for its large trees and steep ravines, conjuring darkness and intrigue. Was she involved? If so, how? He doubted the authorities, if they could find her, would get much information from her. She hadn't been transparent up to this point to her parents or to Leah.

Surely, there had to be a connection somewhere by someone or something.

He drew a sudden breath. His mind drifted away. There he was again. Ten years old, talking of someone or something. A presence not in time for Conner, but for Marissa, perhaps.

Callan shook the cobwebs from his head. No. Not his problem. If he thought about the situation logically, he'd realize Marissa's absence was beyond the scope of his abilities and experience. Besides, he had things to do. He had classes to teach, afternoon and evening classes to consider. Other students who depended on him. There was no time for an investigation that wasn't his to bear. He felt for Greg and Nancy Reynolds and their daughter, and he promised to help, but why? There were others more qualified.

The phone on his desk rang.

He stared at it momentarily, unsure if he wanted to answer it. Early morning phone calls and phone calls fifteen minutes before the end of the day were usually calls that dismantled the rest of his day or evening. He answered the call professionally, however, and added a pinch of enthusiasm into his tone.

"You have a moment, Professor?" the man on the other end asked politely, but urgently. It was Martin Overby, President of Vermillion College.

"Yes, sir, by all means."

"Sheriff Hays just left my office. You know about the death of one of our students, I assume?"

"Yes, of course."

"He had questions. This is a tough situation for the college, Callan. They've traced what happened at the sweat lodge incident to one of our professors. Did you know that?"

"No, sir. This is the first I'm hearing this piece of information."

"Banks," Overby spouted. "Randall Banks, professor of religious studies here on campus. Do you know him?"

An image of the man popped into Callan's head. "I know who he is. We've talked, I'm sure, but only socially."

"Yes, well, he isn't exactly the social kind, and his connection to something that could be illegal and harmful to our students is of utmost concern. I'd appreciate it if you'd take a personal look into it."

"But I . . ."

"I trust you on delicate matters."

"Thank you, sir, but what about . . . ?"

"The authorities are handling it from their end. I need someone on this end," he said.

"Yes, but, what about John Steinmeier? I don't want to step on his toes."

"Oh yes, Steinmeier. I've called him already. He's on alert and doing research on his end. He'll be expecting your call."

Callan hesitated.

"What?" President Overby asked.

"Langrove," Callan said.

"Who?"

"Deborah Langrove."

"Yes, what about her?"

"Is she aware of your concerns?"

President Overby paused. "Why should internal audit be brought into this?"

"Well, sir, I wonder if she's conducted any audits into Professor Banks's department that could be useful to John Steinmeier and me. Has anything been included in past audit reports that have been reported to the Board of Regents?"

"Nothing comes to mind."

"I think, sir, that . . ."

"Yes, yes, by all means," he said. "Give her a call. I doubt if she has much. She's more into operational and financial matters of the college. That's what she reports to the board about anyway."

Silence.

"Anything else, sir?" Callan asked, believing there was.

Martin Overby wasn't known to mince words. Callan sensed pain in the man's shallow breathing.

"No, not at the moment," he said. "As I hear more from authorities, I'll brief you and Steinmeier accordingly. I expect you do the same because . . ." Hesitation followed. "Because it's vital we get to the bottom of this as quickly as possible for the safety of our students. God only knows the extent of what's been happening that we don't know about. No other student must die, Professor. Whatever it takes, please, find out what's going on. These young people may not have a clue to the danger they're in."

President Overby ended the call.

Callan sat back in his chair and contemplated the papers and articles on his desk. So much for staying out of Marissa's business. Martin Overby's words were clear, full of fear and desperation. No other student must die.

CHAPTER EIGHT

Callan didn't know how long he sat at his desk staring at his phone, Apparently, the situation that he'd just convinced himself wasn't his problem was officially now his problem. He took a deep breath and looked up the numbers for John Steinmeier in security and Deborah Langrove in internal audit. He called them individually and requested a meeting as soon as possible. They understood the urgency of the situation, having just received a similar call from President Overby, including Deborah, much to Callan's surprise.

They met in John's office in the administration building. The office appeared just as Callan expected it would—bare, sterile, with beige metal shelving, military-hour wall clock, and a desk stripped of personal identification such as family photos. Pleasantries were short and to the point.

John Steinmeier sat in a chair a size too small for his frame. His figure reminded Callan of pears stacked one on top of the other. His plump face tapered from bottom to top. Broad, floppy jowls met tiny black eyes scrunched in a tight space above his nose. A tuft of short brown hair protruded on top like the fruit's core. His belly protruded in similar fashion, round and bulging above the waistline to a chest abnormally small for his frame. His thighs, however, were just the opposite. Unusually large thighs, tapering to calves that Callan imagined were nothing short of chicken legs. It didn't help that he wore four shades of green: dark socks, olive khakis, a forest button-downed Oxford, and a solid lime tie. Pears stacked on top of each other; the resemblance was uncanny.

Despite his impression of the misshapen security officer, Callan respected John professionally. John's years of experience were highly regarded, coming from a well-known financial institution in Evansville. Callan trusted his judgment, approach, responsiveness and methods without question.

Callan knew very little of Deborah Langrove, however. Dressed in a Ramsey plaid skirt, white blouse, and black blazer, she gave the impression of a conservative auditor of the early 1970s, somewhat introverted, but excellent at detail and follow-through. She wore her long hair bound neatly behind her ears, and she frequently pushed her dark-rimmed glasses back up on her nose. An open notebook rested on her lap, pen in hand. Callan had met her before but not where he had the chance to talk with her in depth about any given topic. He'd read some of the internal audit reports that came from her department and found them to be comprehensive and well written, with relevant and timely recommendations.

John repositioned his frame as if he'd already sat too long. "Dr. Overby was very grave over the phone this morning." He turned his head sharply to relieve a crick in his neck.

"As he should," Callan replied. "What happened has shaken the campus." He turned to Deborah and asked, "You've been updated?"

"Yes, Dr. Overby called," she said, poking at her glasses. "I believe it was right after his phone call with you. Otherwise, I only know what I've heard on the news."

John cleared his throat. "I met with Sheriff Hays this morning. Details are sketchy about what happened, and I can't say I was much help from my end at the time, but we've since done some investigative work in my department."

"Regarding Professor Banks?" Callan asked. "Was a background check run on him?"

"At the time of hire. We don't run annual checks, only if something like this comes up. Another one is being run as we speak. I've got Travis Wellman on it."

Callan glanced to the auditor who wrote furiously on her pad. She appeared compulsive, nervous. He returned his focus to the security director. "What about interviews with Professor Banks and colleagues associated with him?"

"I'm actually meeting with Banks in about ninety minutes," John said, looking down at his watch and tapping upon the case as though the timepiece had stopped. "He sounded concerned when I called to schedule the meeting. He questioned why I needed to talk with him."

"I'd think that should be obvious to him," Callan replied. "What did you tell him?"

"The truth. I told him that his name came up during an inquiry by the sheriff, and I was following up as a matter of protocol."

Callan nodded; his interest piqued. "How did he take it?"

"Indignant but agreeable. Sheriff Hays had already been to see him apparently. He believed my interview was redundant."

"Do you know him very well?"

"I've had a couple of conversations with him before." John frowned. "Not the most sociable educator I've ever met. Kinda dry. No sense of humor. A lot like us."

Callan smiled, taking in John's attempt to crack a joke, then turned to Deborah. "Have you met him before?"

Her eyes widened. She opened her mouth, took in a breath but ended up shaking her head and saying no. She shook her head again. "That's not true," she retorted immediately. "We were introduced, but that was it. He didn't appear interested in carrying on a conversation, but then, many people shy away when I tell them I'm an auditor. I didn't think anything of it."

"I know the feeling," Callan said. "Apparently, we're synonymous with tax collectors and journalists." He turned back to John. "So what were your conversations with Professor Banks about?"

"The odd hours he keeps, for one," he said, shifting in his seat again. "I've had guards notice that he's in his office at all hours. I questioned Professor Banks whether he wanted or needed enhanced security at night while he worked. He said he was fine, didn't want additional manpower assigned just for him. Wellman has had a couple of discussions also. My issue with him is over his general lack of awareness from a security standpoint, especially at night. I lectured him on the safety of our students at late hours and the securing of college assets, that sort of thing, but it went in one ear and out the other."

Deborah's incessant note-taking distracted Callan for a moment. She caught his icy stare and paused momentarily to explain, "In case Dr. Overby asks, I want to be ready to give him an update."

Callan softened his expression and nodded in appreciation. "Yes, we should have notes," he said. "Thank you." He turned back to John. "Did you say that Travis had a couple of run-ins with him as well?"

"Yeah, not exactly run-ins, but unusual circumstances. The

last one was just a few weeks ago. It was after eleven o'clock one evening, just shy of midnight when a guard saw lights from Banks's office. Banks wasn't working alone, however. There were three students, all male, having a theological discussion of some sort. My man said he wasn't sure what they were discussing, but it was intense, and they stopped talking the moment he walked in on them."

"Nothing inappropriate?"

"Only the hour they chose to meet. It was kind of late to have a roundtable discussion with students. Banks said that they'd lost track of time. Nevertheless, like everything that's out of the ordinary, we completed a report on the incident." John glanced toward his desk and scooted a couple of papers around. "Would you like to see it?"

Callan shook his head, believing the paper would take more time to find than it was worth. He said John's account was sufficient. He turned to Deborah. "Would you like a copy though?"

"If you don't mind," she said.

John let out a *hmmph*, as though he considered it one more tedious task he had to do, then he jotted a note.

"Do you remember any audit reports you've issued about Professor Banks or his department, by any chance?" Callan asked while he had Deborah's attention.

Deborah shook her head, pushed up her glasses, and tucked a strand of hair that had fallen from behind her ear. "Not exactly. We do write reports on various departments that appear at the top of our risk assessments, but the closest we have on his department are a couple of management expense reviews. The latest was six months ago."

"Anything of interest come up?"

"No, I'm sorry, I can't say there was," she said, sighing. "I brought the report in case you or John were interested."

Callan said he was very interested.

She opened her pad of paper and pulled out a three-page management report on Professor Banks's departmental expenses. She handed it directly to Callan.

He glanced quickly at the audit objectives and final conclusions but read nothing that was out of the ordinary, just as Deborah had relayed. All expenses appeared to be properly authorized and accounted for.

Deborah lifted a finger to make a point when Callan returned the report. "When you called to set up this meeting, Professor Morrow, I asked one of my staff members, Zola Krivoshia, to conduct another review to cover another six months to see if anything unusual appears."

"I'm glad you did," Callan said. "Line items related to this sweat lodge incident may be in the general ledger if he's brazen enough to run such expenses through the college."

"He's never caused us to consider him an internal control risk in the past. We've had no reason to do a more in-depth review of his department."

A lull in their conversation occurred naturally as the three considered each of their comments. John took the lull to mean the meeting was over. He glanced at his watch. "I'd like to have time to prepare for my interview with the professor if there's nothing more here. I'll have Wellman complete that background check. Deborah, you'll complete your review of Banks's management expenses, and I'll get that security incident report to you. That leaves you, Callan. What are your next steps?"

Callan smirked. "I thought a little interview of the professor on my own wouldn't hurt after you've had yours. I'd like to compare notes. Let me know when you've finished."

"The more the merrier. Between you, Deborah, the authorities, Dr. Overby, and me, Professor Banks should be sufficiently worn down. A person can lie once and keep his story straight. He can lie twice with a little less confidence, but to remember a lie five times in a row becomes a lot more difficult."

Callan shook a finger at him with a warning. "I don't know, John. A good liar revels at perfecting his story. Surely, you know that."

"Oh, I do," he said, pulling himself out of his chair, "but I think we'll enjoy comparing notes just the same."

Chapter Nine

Callan returned to his office to prepare for his next class, and to wait for word from John Steinmeier that his interview with Randall Banks had been completed. Callan's class preparation didn't go well, however. He devoted his anxious energy on what he wanted to ask Professor Banks. Besides, he had two or three hours before class time, and some of his best classes ended up being spontaneous interactive lessons on current events—not textbook recitals.

A wall clock ticked monotonous seconds above him. It did little to hasten John's call. There had to be something Callan could do while he waited. He suddenly remembered Glynis Fordworth. Terese had mentioned that she might've heard scuttlebutt on campus. Glynis answered her phone right away.

"Expecting my call?" he asked, tickled at her responsiveness.

"Like clockwork," she said. "It was a matter of time before I'd hear from you. You're like an ambulance chaser. I'm just disappointed that you didn't call sooner. I must not be your most valued confidant."

"That's not true," he said. "I like to save the best for last."

Glynis chuckled. "Uh-huh, nice save. So how're Terese and the boys?"

"All are doing well. And your husband and son?"

"Boring and awesome, respectively."

Callan could almost see the smirk on her face. Glynis's dry wit was tempered with a tone resembling Ava Gardner, breathy and beguiling. The corners of her mouth rose on certain words, words Callan learned to pay closer attention to, meant to be emphasized. He imagined her lip rose upon using both words to describe the men in her life.

"So I bet you want to know what I know about this *unfortunate circumstance* or however Dr. Overby put it in the bulletin he sent out to the Board of Regents," she said.

"That would be nice for starters."

"I hate to disappoint you."

Callan scoffed. "Come now, Glynis. Don't be coy. You know there's nothing you can't tell me."

"No, seriously, Callan. I don't know anything; I don't know what to tell you. You know I would if I could, but I've never experienced anything as strange and as hushed on campus before. This is so mysteriously under wraps. Such an enigma."

"What about the two guys in the tent? Have you had either one of them in your class before?"

"Conner, yes, that Logan boy, no," she said. "Conner Whaite was in my business class last semester. Good student, handsome as the devil. That shouldn't be allowed, you know. Quiet, very reserved."

"In what way?"

She thought for a second. "Preoccupied, I'd say."

"With your lectures, perhaps?"

Glynis laughed. "Right, because business torts and class

action lawsuits are riveting subjects that ignite the imagination of young students. No, Conner was a good student, like I said. Whatever he was preoccupied with didn't affect his grades or his ability to write an excellent essay, but I had no reason to believe it was something that would eventually get him killed."

"In hindsight, however, that's what you believe," Callan said, reading between the lines.

Glynis hesitated. "I'm sorry. I was out of line to suggest that his preoccupation in class was what got him in trouble. That implies I know more about what I'm talking about than I do. I don't, but I can't help but think of him in retrospect. I keep going over my image of Conner, sitting in class, staring off to the side."

Callan softened his voice. "Tell me then, Glynis, did he have any friends or study partners that you knew about?"

"Oh yeah," she responded enthusiastically. "Conner may have been reserved, but he was very likable. I can't say he had a lot of friends, but he did have some." Glynis paused. "There was one student, though, a young woman, long hair, auburn, I believe. Attractive. I'd see her with him periodically."

"Got a name?"

"Oh, Callan, you're expecting a lot out of me."

"Please try."

"No, I don't have a name," she said without hesitation.

Callan sighed. "I'm asking because I'm trying to find a student of mine. Her name is Marissa Reynolds. Does that ring a bell? She's got hair with a reddish tint, I believe. I don't know. It's hard to tell under the fluorescent lights in the classroom."

"I'm sorry," she said, sounding genuine.

Callan changed the subject. "What about this Logan fellow—Logan Allister? Did you say you didn't know him?"

"Maybe if I saw a picture. There's not been one in the papers."

"Okay then, what about Professor Banks?"

"The religious nut?"

Callan grinned. "Yeah, I suppose."

"Social creep," she blurted. "Callan, you've met him. He was at the endowment dinner three months ago."

Callan tried to recall. Images of attendees popped in and out of his head, Randall Banks wasn't one of them. "Are you sure? Did we sit with him?"

"No, silly, he was at the next table over, but remember? As the evening went along, less and less people remained with him. He scared them off."

"Even his wife? Does he have a wife?"

"He was wearing a ring if that means anything. I looked. I couldn't imagine such a marriage, but then look at mine. If she was at the dinner, she opted for more exciting entertainment and conversation."

Callan paused, assessing what his colleague told him. "Are you jesting with me, Glynis?"

"Callan," she said sharply, "You know I don't jest about uninteresting men."

"But you say we talked to him that night?"

"Oh, you really don't remember, do you?" she asked. "You accidentally made eye contact with him and asked me who he was. Before I could say anything, it was too late. He scooted over to our table, and we became his next victims. Terese and I were furious with you."

"Oh yeah, I remember now," he said, laughing. "When he sat down next to me, you started to leave, but Terese took your handbag and wouldn't let you go. But the conversation didn't last that long if I remember, did it? I don't think I said very much."

Callan could almost feel Glynis leaning in toward the phone. She lowered her voice. "Yes, that's what was so odd. He left, practically in mid-sentence. It was right after you made a lighthearted joke, then he said he was the head of religious studies and found jokes of all kinds offensive. It cracked me up. So hilarious, but he didn't think so. Suddenly, he turned into a bat and flew away."

Callan chuckled. "Boy, I wish I could remember what I said. Something benign, but it had to have been priceless for him to react so."

"It was your garlic cologne, I think," she added. "Or maybe the sun started to come up, I don't know. But tell me what Randall Banks has to do with what happened at that sweat lodge?"

"I didn't say he did."

"Callan, I'm not daft. You ask me about Conner and Logan and this Marissa girl, then you ask me about Count Bank-ula. Am I not to think that's why you're asking?"

"Okay, but I'm not sure how he's involved," Callan replied. "His name came through Overby's office from Vermillion County law enforcement."

Glynis made a guttural noise through the receiver.

"You do know something else," Callan said.

"No," she replied adamantly. "No, but I'm not surprised. He's got a thing for religion."

"You mean like far-right, fundamentalist Christian?"

"No, I mean something altogether different. He's religious but not spiritual. I'm not even sure he's Christian. I'm surprised Dr. Overby didn't explain to you. There's been complaints about him on campus from students and parents. It's about his classes. He teaches his own theology."

Callan took a deep breath. "How do you know this?"

"How do you not?" she responded. "His name has been mentioned in enough circles to associate him as a bit of a crackpot. Perhaps you haven't been on campus as long as I have, but I've heard he's quite unorthodox in his lessons. I hesitate to put my spin on him that might lead you down the wrong path, but it's something for you to follow up on, that's all I'm going to say."

Callan sat back in his chair and thanked Glynis for the information. Another call came through on his phone. He pulled away to glance at the display. "Hey, look, Glen, I gotta go. I believe John Steinmeier is calling, telling me it's okay for me to interview Professor Banks now."

"You're going to talk with him?"

"After what you just told me, how can I not?"

"Okay," she said, "but if you want my advice . . ."

"What's that?"

"Don't look into his eyes this time."

CHAPTER TEN

Don't look into his eyes. It was a lighthearted comment with a dark undertone, something he'd expect from Glynis Fordworth. But Callan had been around the block enough times to know that such comments, while given in jest, had some half-truths in them. Humorously delivered but fraught with wisdom: don't get pulled into Professor Banks's probable excuses and lies.

It was indeed Randall Banks's eyes that Callan noticed first and turned away from. Dark and penetrating, set in a face covered in a five o'clock shadow even though it was just mid-day. He welcomed Callan into his office with the hospitality of a pay-by-the-hour-motel clerk, dubious of his presence and appearing apathetic, hoping Callan would be in and out quickly. He wore dark blue, well-tailored suit pants with a white, button-down shirt, and a silk tie with each of the astrological signs displayed on the front. The professor ushered Callan to his desk where Callan extended his hand and introduced himself more formally. Banks appeared taken aback by the gesture, but he shook Callan's hand before leaning against his desk and crossing his arms at his midsection.

"I believe we've met before," Callan said to break the ice.

"Have we? I don't remember." His voice was bland and weary.

Of course, Callan didn't remember the encounter very well, either, but he replied, "At the endowment dinner three months ago."

Randall lifted his chin in the air to think. "Endowment dinner? Oh yes, I remember the dinner, but I don't remember *you*."

Callan chuckled. "We had a short conversation. It appeared that you were called away, and we didn't get a chance to talk."

"Yes, well, probably wasn't much to talk about then, was there?" He shifted his weight against the desk. "So what do you want with me? I must tell you, Professor Morrow, that I know who you are and what you do, but your credentials and high-profile investigations do not intimidate me in any way. I've already been interrogated many times today. It's becoming tedious, so you'll forgive me if I don't seem very receptive to your questions."

"This won't take long," Callan said.

"I assume Dr. Overby sent you."

"He wanted me to give him my assessment of the incident. I said I'd talk with you."

Randall sighed as he shook his head and dropped his line of sight to the floor. "But I've already talked until I'm blue in the face. In fact, I've talked to the sheriff, his cronies, Dr. Overby, Herr Steinmeier of the Gestapo, that ghastly auditor woman named Langrove and her Russian sidekick, and now you. I'm not up for another grilling. What more can I tell you people?"

"You can start by telling me where Marissa Reynolds is."

Randall's face paled. His shoulders dropped. It was apparent that Marissa was the last person he expected to be asked about. He strummed the edge of his desk as he strode around its side to sit in his high-back leather chair. "Marissa Reynolds, you say?"

"You do know her," Callan replied.

"Oh yes, I know her." He said, hesitating. "But I don't know what I can say about her that has any reference to the sweat lodge incident. The sweat lodge is what you came to talk to me about, wasn't it?"

"In part, yes."

"Well, then, like I told Sheriff Hays and John Steinmeier, my appearance at the sweat lodge was purely coincidental. I got wind from overhearing a conversation during one of my classes that some students were gathering outside of town for a religious cleansing. We'd discussed such practices during one of my classes recently."

"You teach religion?"

"I teach theology."

"Were Conner Whaite and Logan Allister two of your students?"

"Indeed."

A smug expression crossed Randall's face. He seemed to pride himself on telling the truth, even though the questions, in Callan's mind, were easy enough to answer and verify. Hardly anything to be smug about.

"So what did they derive from your lectures," Callan said, equally smug, "that would motivate them to pitch a tent in the middle of a field outside of town, fill the tent with heated rocks from a pyre just yards away, create a sauna-like condition, and suffocate themselves with steam?"

Repulsion replaced Randall's smug expression. "That, I am

sure, Professor, I cannot tell you."

"Because you don't want to tell me?"

"Because I don't know."

Callan stared into his dark eyes. "You were the anonymous caller to the paramedics, weren't you?"

"Yes, I have nothing to hide about that," he said, leaning forward. "As I told the sheriff and Dr. Overby, I arrived in the nick of time to save one man's life. I should be commended for doing so, but instead, I'm being harassed into making a confession about another man's life that I'm not responsible for."

"So what alerted you to the fact that there would be trouble? You said you overheard a conversation in class, but surely you didn't hear enough to know exactly where in a remote field outside of town to send the paramedics. The Bal Hinch is a large area."

"A student called me."

Callan nodded but didn't believe him. "Does this student have a name?"

"The student does, but the student has a right to privacy. I'm grateful the student called when the student did. We all should be grateful."

Callan's eyes narrowed. "Most definitely," he said, "but it's odd that the student called *you* instead of 911 directly."

Randall wasn't moved. "The student wasn't thinking clearly obviously. Surely, you can appreciate the duress the student was under at the time."

"And that's when you went to the scene, after she reached out to you."

Again, he wasn't moved. "I didn't say she."

"My apologies," Callan replied. "So after the call, you went to the scene."

"I did. I found Conner Whaite nearly dead and Logan

Allister very ill. Conner passed away before paramedics could arrive."

There was long pause while the men assessed each other's comments.

Don't look into his eyes.

Glynis's statement was truer than she gave it credit. The longer Callan talked with the professor, the less he liked and believed him.

"You do realize you could be facing second-degree manslaughter charges if the sheriff's office finds your story untruthful and you had a direct involvement with the boys' demise," Callan said.

"It must be proven first."

Callan noticed that he didn't deny being involved.

"Conner Whaite's parents could file a wrongful death suit against you in civil court."

Randall scoffed. "That will be equally hard to prove. My involvement was nothing but to help the young men involved."

"Perhaps, but your life could be miserable for a very long time, entangled in a legal mess for years."

"I should be on to bigger and better things by then," he said. "I'm not worried."

Callan suddenly remembered something Glynis said about him from the endowment dinner. "What does your wife think of all this?"

Randall jerked his head up, surprised. "My wife? Why in the world would she care about such matters? We're estranged. We've been estranged for quite some time. I doubt that she gives a damn."

"Then you wouldn't mind if I talk with her?"

"You can have a candlelight dinner with her for all I care."

"Then I take it you don't believe I'll learn anything from

her that I don't already know," Callan said.

"Why should you?" Randall responded, his voice rising. "She doesn't understand what I've been researching. She doesn't understand the first thing about life beyond this dimension. What's more is that she doesn't care."

Finally, Callan thought, *we're getting somewhere.*

"And what sort of research would that be?"

Randall stood, puffing his chest to exert his knowledge. "A paradigm shift in how we think about the limited time we have on earth." He walked around his desk, and stood in front of Callan, speaking with expert authority. "Oh, I see. You have no idea what I'm talking about, do you? A paradigm shift, Professor Morrow. You do understand paradigm shifts. I'm talking about a fundamental change in our approach to our time in the physical world." His nostrils flared.

Callan didn't waver.

"You're starting to waste my time," Randall said. He turned to walk back behind his desk.

"Be that as it may, Professor, but what you describe sounds more like a virus," Callan said.

Randall sat in his chair and smiled, clasping his fingers together as if Callan's words finally intrigued him. "A virus?"

"I understand paradigm shifts. They're necessary for us to rethink the status quo so that we can learn more from our existence, but it sounds from the little I've heard about this sweat lodge of yours that your research hasn't caused such a shift. In fact, it's done quite the opposite, spreading out of control like a virus, a cancerous mutation of intellectual sciences."

"I can assure you, Professor, that my thoughts are not out of control and certainly not a cancerous mutation. And, please, I must correct you. The sweat lodge wasn't mine; it didn't belong to me."

Callan ignored the assertion. "I remind you that one student is dead, another was released from the hospital. There is no other way to characterize your research or responsibility. We take such matters very seriously at Vermillion College."

Randall leaned forward. Venom spewed from the spittle between his lips. "You forget one thing, sir. I do not know why those boys were in the sweat lodge in the first place. I do not know their motivation for being there. I did not know their state of mind when they entered the tent, and I have no idea why I of all people was called to rescue those boys from their own adventure. I suggest that if you have nothing further to say that is concrete evidence against me, Professor, that you leave my office immediately."

Callan turned toward the door. Before exiting, he spotted two posters on the wall of Randall's office. One was of the various constellations of stars in the sky. The other was a depiction of the signs of the Zodiac, similar to the design on Randall's tie.

"You delve into astrology, Professor?" Callan asked. "Are you infatuated with the stars?"

"I've asked you to leave."

"Are they part of your paradigm shift?"

"I said leave, Professor Morrow," he said. "Leave now."

Callan did so gladly. Before returning to his office, however, he beelined to the administration building where Dr. Overby's administrative assistant produced a photograph of Randall Banks at his request from a faculty directory. Fortunately, the photo appeared to be a recent one. He made a copy, enlarged it, and placed it in an inside pocket of his suit coat.

He walked briskly to his office to retrieve his voice mail messages before his afternoon class. There was only one. It was from Deborah Langrove, requesting that he call her at his earliest convenience.

"May Zola and I see you in your office?" she asked when he did so. "Say, fifteen minutes? It'll take us that long to gather our things and walk from where we are in Nicholson Hall."

Callan glanced at the wall clock. "Yes, I believe that'll be fine."

"We promise not to take much of your time," she said.

"Not to worry," Callan replied. "This sounds important. I'll make the time."

"Thank you. You'll be interested in what transpired during Zola's audit."

CHAPTER ELEVEN

Zola Krivoshia and Deborah Langrove arrived, greeted Callan professionally, and sat stone-faced at a small conference table in the corner of his office. Zola watched patiently as Deborah shifted papers to organize the agenda. She didn't speak. Instead, she lifted her head and, quite by surprise to Zola, turned the meeting abruptly over to her.

Zola accepted the transition with poise, counting it a response to the tremendous pressure Deborah and other members of the administration had been under due to the strange events attached to the campus. The review of Randall Banks's expenses had been nothing but an exercise in humiliation for Zola. Professor Banks accused the young auditor of harassment in a witch hunt to discredit his good name at the college, abusing her surname more than once by implying the review was nothing short of a Russian attempt to strong-arm him into a confession about the sweat lodge incident.

The insult had rolled off her back. She was Russian

in name only, having come to Vermillion from the small Northwest Indiana community of Sumava Resorts, settled by Czech immigrants and named after the Bohemian Forest her maternal grandparents had emigrated from. Zola was more apt to throw a Becherovka than a Molotov cocktail at Randall Banks. His barbs did little to penetrate her.

The young auditor was more concerned about her supervisor. Zola wasn't pleased with Deborah. Her abrupt introduction was a futile attempt to punish her for violating department policy. Zola respected Deborah's professional knowledge and work ethic, but found she favored procedure over common sense sometimes. Protocol over intuition. It was the reason the two of them sat now in Professor Morrow's office, fidgeting often. Deborah was barely able to look Callan in the eyes, all because Zola had deviated from protocol. She exhibited rogue audit methods and placed herself in undue danger that could've backfired miserably and compromised the investigation—or so Deborah had scolded her on the walk to the professor's office.

Zola faced Callan with confidence and humility, however, aware of his experience in high-profile—even dangerous— cases he'd investigated as an auditor before coming to Vermillion. She counted on him to appreciate the information she was about to share despite her unorthodox method of obtaining the information.

Zola explained to Callan that Deborah had assigned her to reevaluate the expenses of the Religious Studies Department to uncover information about Professor Banks that may have been overlooked in her previous audit.

"Although he allowed me an appointment with him face to face, I didn't have a chance to review records he had in his office," Zola said, giving a side glance to her supervisor.

"Oh?" Callan responded. "Did he not have any records for you to review?"

"It's not that. I didn't get that far." Zola turned up her nose and shrugged. "When I called to set up a meeting, he turned me away. He said Mr. Steinmeier was on his way and he didn't have time. I said I didn't need his time; I just wanted some source documents from his office, and I'd be on my way."

"And he still turned you away?"

"Not before insulting me again. Deborah decided that a surprise audit was in order."

"I'm familiar with surprise audits under such circumstances," Callan said, "but what does it entail at the college?"

"I simply requested Zola to appear at his office immediately without advance permission," Deborah said.

"But before I could knock on Professor Banks's door to enter, a student came out," she explained. "Bolted out, more like it." She glanced to Deborah again, seeking approval to go on. "A male student."

"Did you recognize him?" Callan asked.

"No, not at all, but Professor Banks was right behind him when he bolted out the door. He called the student to stop and come back. He yelled, 'Logan, get back here!'"

Callan sat up. "Logan? As in Logan Allister?"

"That's who came to mind immediately. There's only one Logan I know who's been in the news lately."

"Yes, of course, so what happened?"

"Logan didn't stop. He ran down the hall," Zola said. "Professor Banks didn't call out anymore. He just stood there and looked at me. Then he asked who I was. I mentioned my name and told him I was from internal audit, and he said, 'Not now. Go back to Moscow.' I told him what I needed to review would only take a few minutes, but he slammed the door in my face."

"That won't be tolerated," Callan replied.

"That's what I said to her," Deborah added. "That you'd probably have words with Professor Banks."

"I'll do more than that," Callan said. "I'll inform Dr. Overby and John Steinmeier for them to follow up also. Is that what you came to tell me?"

Zola glanced to Deborah again. "No, I did something more."

Callan smiled, seemingly more interested and pleased.

"I followed him," she said. "Logan, that is. I turned around to see where he went. It wasn't difficult. He stormed out of the office and building at a fast clip, but once outside, he stopped on the steps to make a phone call. Then he walked a normal gait across the mall."

"You followed him across the mall? Why?"

Zola shrugged. "Logan was so angry when he left Professor Banks's office that I thought I could talk to him. I thought the information might be useful to us."

"Where did he go?"

"He made a call to have someone meet him at the coffee shop just off campus. Are you familiar with it?"

Callan nodded and prompted Zola to continue.

"He was quite angry," she said. "He was standing on the steps. I was just inside the building. The doors are glass. I stood out of his line of sight, but I could hear him perfectly. He was so loud, screaming that Banks was a fraud, a phony. He said Banks's theories were flawed."

"In connection to what? The sweat lodge?"

"I didn't hear anything about the sweat lodge," Zola said. "He told the person on the other end of the line that Professor Banks promised him something but wasn't delivering on the promise. I figured that was what Logan was angry about. He said Banks led him to believe that he was in line for something, but it never materialized. There were several seconds of silence—like the person was trying to calm him down or something. I don't know. All I know is that Logan said something like, 'Well, meet me at the coffee shop then.'"

Zola stopped talking. Deborah squirmed in her seat. Callan studied their expressions. "There's something you're not telling me," he said.

"Yes, you're probably not going to be very happy with me," Zola said. "Ms. Langrove wasn't, which is why she wants me to confess to you. I followed Logan to the coffee shop. I know it's beyond what I was assigned to do, Professor Morrow, and I apologize for overstepping my boundaries, but the auditor in me just had to find out who he was meeting. I mean, given the recent events with that other student being killed and what I had overheard, I . . ."

Callan raised his hand. "If it makes you feel any better, Ms. Krivoshia, I would've probably done the same thing. I'm glad you did. Please tell me what happened."

"Well, first of all, I think Logan was so concentrated on his confrontation with Professor Banks and who he was going to meet that it didn't cross his mind that someone like me could be following him. I was able to do so without him noticing. I was very discreet. He slipped into a booth across from a female. She had textbooks on the table in front of her as if she'd been studying, so I assumed she was a student also. I slipped into the booth behind them but sitting so that I could see them. Logan didn't turn around, and she didn't look up at me when I did so."

"Describe her to me."

"Very attractive woman. Hair that I'd kill to have, you know?

Full, naturally silky. Olive skin, like of Mediterranean descent."

"Did he call her Dana?"

Zola's eyes lit up. "Yes! How did you know?"

"I've met her," Callan said. "Her name is Dana Weiss. What did they talk about?"

"They didn't have time to talk about much," she replied. "Not long after we sat down, some other guy came into the coffee shop and sat down next to Dana. It was crazy."

"What was?"

"The whole scenario. Get this: I was following Logan to the coffee shop, but it was like this guy had been following *us.*"

Callan couldn't hide his astonishment.

"It's true. The guy that came in after us had this odd look on his face like he wanted to know what Logan was doing. It was so crazy. It felt creepy."

"Did Logan or Dana call him by name?" Callan asked, intrigued.

Zola shook her head. "No, but he was rather tall, lean, solid, sandy hair, self-confident, kind of had an air of cockiness about him when he stepped up to their table."

"Mitchell Dells," Callan said instantly.

"You know him? Did the description sound like him?"

"You had me at sandy hair and cockiness."

Zola sighed. "He wasn't pleased to be there. It's like he didn't want to hear what Logan had to say, he just wanted to know if Logan had talked with some girl they knew."

Callan leaned in. "Marissa Reynolds? Was the woman named Marissa?"

"I don't know. They didn't call her by name," Zola replied. "If they did, I didn't catch it. Logan just said that he called her and that they had a long talk, to which the sandy-haired guy said something like, 'I bet you did.' Logan asked him what he meant by that."

"What *did* he mean by that?"

"I don't know. Dana said she'd had enough and wanted to change the subject. She asked Logan a question, but I couldn't hear what it was. I could hear Logan though. Logan said he was going to prove Professor Banks wrong once and for all. He didn't say how he was going to prove him wrong or what he was going to prove, but he said if Professor Banks didn't pick him, he was going to be sorry."

Zola sat back in her seat as if she had finished her story.

Callan wasn't satisfied. "Pick him for what?"

"Oh, I don't know. They didn't say any more about it. The sandy-haired guy told him to cool it, and this Dana girl agreed. She told Logan it didn't matter anymore. It was over."

"What was over?"

"I don't know, but Logan said it wasn't over for him. He was going to Nero to get the evidence he needed."

Callan frowned. "Nero?" He glanced toward Deborah.

Deborah shrugged.

"That's what he said," Zola reiterated. "He was going to Nero."

"Did he say when he was going?"

"Yes, but I couldn't hear it. All I know is that when Logan told them, the sandy-haired guy got up and said that he'd heard enough. He asked Dana if she was coming with him, but she said no. She had more studying to do."

"Did Logan stay?"

"Yeah. When the guy left, he asked her what was up the sandy-haired guy's craw. Dana said to leave him alone. Everyone's on edge, and Logan's b.s. —she used the actual word—about proving Professor Banks wrong wasn't helping. They started talking, but they kept their voices so low, I couldn't hear them. After a while, I realized I wasn't going to get anything that I could hear, so I left."

Callan took a deep breath and mulled over Zola's account. After a couple of minutes, he thanked the two auditors for their time and said to let him know if they learned anything else related to their discussion. He strummed fingers on top of a knee and tapped his foot.

Zola gathered her things, but Deborah Langrove sat silently, eyeing Callan closely. "What's the matter, Professor Morrow?" she asked. "You seem perturbed or confused. I can't tell which. Is there anything we can clarify for you?"

Callan shook his head and sighed. "Not unless you can tell me where Nero is."

CHAPTER TWELVE

Callan sat in his den at home, nursing a cup of coffee. Too late for coffee, but he wanted something bold to help him think. Cocoa was too sweet, tea too weak. For the moment anyway. He glanced at a mantle clock and debated whether it was also too late to call Glynis. She was the first person he could think of who might know the answer to the question pestering his brain.

"Ever hear of a place called Nero?" he asked as soon as she uttered hello.

Glynis wanted to know why he was asking.

"Because the name came up to one of our in-house auditors. She overheard Logan Allister mention the name as someplace he needs to go to disprove Randall Banks's theories. I searched on my phone for Nero, Indiana, but nothing came up."

Glynis yawned. "I never heard of it, but I'm not good at geography."

Callan glanced again at the clock. He shouldn't have called.

No wonder she yawned. While he had her on the line, he decided to continue. "Is it slang for anything, do you think?"

"I don't know how the word was used, Callan, or the context it was used in. Isn't there a detective series about a guy named Nero?"

Callan thought for a second. "You mean Nero Wolfe?"

"Yes. It could have something to do with one of his mysteries or with the character himself. I don't remember the author."

"Rex Stout, but the word Nero was a person, not a place. The detective series was set in New York City. Not sure what connection there could be."

"Noblesville," she said. "How about Noblesville?"

Callan scratched his head. A connection still eluded him.

"I remember now that you mentioned his name. Rex Stout was born in Noblesville, wasn't he? Maybe that's your *place*. Nero could be a code word. After all, Noblesville's only about forty-five minutes east of here, not that far but far enough."

Glynis yawned again just as Callan's phone buzzed to let him know of an incoming call.

"I need to let you go. You sound tired. That's a good guess." He pulled the phone away from his ear to look at the display. "Looks like my assistant is trying to get through to me."

"You get some sleep too," she said.

Callan said he would but knew he wouldn't. He hung up and took the call.

Leah didn't wait for him to say hello. "Marissa called again," she said. "Called out of the blue. She was upset."

"About what?"

"Logan, but I don't know why."

Callan thought back on his meeting with Deborah Langrove and Zola Krivoshia. "I think I do," he said, and gave Leah a brief synopsis of what Zola had relayed in their meeting. "I take it Marissa's been in contact with Logan again."

"Yes, but I don't know when or what they talked about. She just said she'd been thinking about their conversation and asked if I'd heard anything from him."

Callan exhaled frustration. "I wish she'd call *me*. Next time you talk, have her do that."

"I doubt it's going to happen," Leah said frankly. "She sounded like she's held in some burrow she called a temple."

"A temple?"

"That's what she called it, but she made one reference to it as a house. I caught her on it, but she backed her way out of it faster than a crawdaddy, so I didn't bring it up again."

"Did you get an idea where this house could be?"

"No, but she told me not to worry about her. She's safe and free to meditate and contemplate without distraction. Sounds like she could be someplace out in the country."

Callan agreed, but it wasn't much help. Indiana was almost nothing but country. Rural with miles of open fields and wood lots, meandering roads over babbling creeks. He thought of where Glynis had suggested. Noblesville wasn't exactly in the middle of nowhere, but there was still plenty of open country north of the city.

He thanked Leah for the information and placed the phone on top of his desk. A small tree branch tapped against the side of the house in response to the wind. Callan went to the window to make sure it was secure. There wasn't a storm brewing, just squalls here and there, typical of late summer before the air turned to fall. He glanced up at the moon, hiding behind the wispy streams of long, thin cirrus clouds, reminding him that mid-September was creeping toward the autumn solstice. Soon after the solstice would come

Halloween. He shuddered at the thought. There was enough mystery and wickedness in his life recently without needing a holiday to celebrate it.

He took a deep breath and shuddered again.

Conner Whaite was dead.

Logan Allister had recovered but was now poised for revenge.

Dana Weiss wanted to appear disengaged, but she was more entwined in the circle of young people involved than she let on.

Worse yet, Marissa Reynolds was in a temple, whatever that meant.

Perhaps Randall Banks's interest in the celestials was a clue.

The wind picked up outside. Callan hurried downstairs to secure the seat cushions on the porch's outdoor furniture. One cushion was already on the edge of blowing away. He refastened the straps to the chair's frame and was about to stand when something struck him between his shoulder blades. He jerked to the left then down, relieved to see it was only a broken birch twig, whipped through the air with its dried, brown leaves still attached.

He shivered again, not from the wind but from autumn's sense of emptiness, the warmth of summer replaced by cold, dry, empty air. And there was something else, something impending he didn't or wasn't supposed to understand. A pang grew in his gut. Someone other than Marissa was in danger. He could feel it. A hunch, maybe a professional suspicion. He didn't know which, but he'd come across enough information to justify the angst. But what did he sense? And, more importantly, who was in trouble?

Chapter Thirteen

The flashlight didn't project enough light, not far enough. Logan could barely see but a few steps ahead of his sneakers. He had a more powerful lantern back in Vermillion, but this one was more compact and easier to carry. He thought it would be enough, but it wasn't, and the moon wouldn't peak from the clouds long enough to help him.

His jacket wasn't heavy enough either. He had a heavier one back in Vermillion as well, but this one was lightweight and easier to walk with through the brush and dried goldenrods. Logan thought his undershirt would hold in the warmth, but it didn't. The autumn air found its way around his neck and down his collar.

He stepped into a hole along the path that his flashlight missed. Fortunately, his ankle wasn't sprained. He didn't snap a knee, but he lost valuable time, favoring his ankle and wishing he'd worn boots to protect his feet. He thought his sneakers were enough, but they weren't.

A dog barked in the distance. Logan wondered if the

canine detected his nervous scent and had barked from the nearby farmhouse to keep him at bay. He hoped it was reacting to an opossum intruding the fenced confines of the yard that made the dog yelp with alarm. It didn't matter. The wind carried the sound of a screen door, a man calling for the dog to quiet down, another slam of the screen door, then silence. He sighed with relief when the barking stopped.

The path led farther up the prominence than he expected. Cool air wafted over the hill even though a tree line stifled most of the wind's relentless onslaught. The moon lit the path on-again, off-again as it slithered behind clouds, skimming across the darkening sky, making Logan question what he saw ahead. He increased his pace, not from fear but out of impatience, eager to finish the task he came to complete. His heart pounded faster, approaching the place where he was sure to find the black ammo box he sought. But was it here or over there? He couldn't see well. The flashlight flickered. He stooped in the brush to dig in the soil anyway.

He dug feverishly. The cool breeze suddenly felt more refreshing the harder he worked. He welcomed the wind now. Sweat formed over his brow, his undershirt grew damp. He pitched further into the loose gravel and glacial sediment, grunting when he realized that he'd missed his target. He should've reached the black box by now. Where was it? Logan was sure he knew exactly where the box was buried.

Frustrated, he swung around to reevaluate.

There should be a marker. Find the marker first.

Impatience consumed him. He didn't care if he found the marker at this point. He searched now with brawn and adrenaline over brains, digging wildly into the ground, scattering gravel about his feet and covering the path where he'd come with dirt and uprooted goldenrods.

Finally, his labor unearthed what he'd been searching for—a small, black military ammo box underneath a stone. He shone what light he had from his flashlight inside. Logan didn't care what the contents of the box contained. He was there to add to the box, not take away. He pulled out a white sheet of paper from his coat pocket and scanned what he'd hastily scribbled just a few hours before. Satisfied, Logan placed the piece of paper into the box, clamped the lid tight, then shoved the box and its contents back into the ground. He scratched at the dirt until the hole was completely covered before carefully replacing the stone just as he'd found it.

Logan worked hard, so hard, in fact, that he didn't hear footsteps approaching from behind. He stood from his kneeing position on the path, suddenly realizing a large figure in dark clothing stood before him. Logan didn't have time to react before the first blow was struck. Again and again, the figure attacked, barreling into Logan's gut and upon his skull with precision, knocking him unconscious. Four more blows like the first finished what the figure came to do.

No more digging.

No more hiding from barking dogs.

Logan Allister laid lifeless on clumps of cold dirt and goldenrods.

~

Satisfied that Logan was dead after several nudges from a boot, the figure rolled Logan's body off the path and into undisturbed brush standing stoically over the grotesque scene, then glared unapologetically toward the body.

You knew you weren't the chosen one. Why didn't you leave

it at that?

The figure left as quietly as it came, leaving the Mount Nebo prominence in darkness under the rapidly drifting clouds.

CHAPTER FOURTEEN

The telephone rang on Callan's office landline mid-afternoon the next day. He didn't feel like answering it. He didn't feel like talking. He didn't feel like asking questions, answering questions, or comforting anyone disturbed by what they'd heard on the morning and noontime news reports. Callan was as upset as anyone.

He ignored the call and returned to the morning's *Vermillion Star* he'd been reading. He skimmed the article quickly. Killed in the early hours by an unknown assailant. It had not yet been determined by the Benton County Sheriff's Office or the *Vermillion Star* if the student was killed at the spot where his body was located or killed elsewhere and the body brought to the spot on the prominence. Two geocachers from upstate New York found the body in the brush off the side of a path as they searched for a cache that made the Mount Nebo experience unique. That was all that was written in the article except for the traditional statement that the investigation continued.

Mount Nebo. Callan researched the location but found little online about what appeared to be a mere geological feature in the prairieland of Northwest Indiana. He rubbed a palm down his face. What was Logan Allister doing in the middle of nowhere? More importantly, who knew he was there?

His phone rang again. He glared at it, hoping it would stop, but it didn't. He took the call so that he wouldn't have to listen to its clanging any longer. Glynis Fordworth whispered his name with a sigh of relief.

"I called to see how you're doing," she said.

He didn't answer.

"It's Logan," she added as though he hadn't heard the news.

"I know it is."

"And it was Nebo, not Nero."

"I know it was."

"Mount Nebo."

"I know."

"I've never heard of it," she said.

"Yeah, well, like you said when I asked you in the first place, you don't know your geography very well," he responded snidely.

"I didn't mean . . ."

She paused and Callan sighed.

"I know, Glynis, I'm sorry," he said. "That was undeserved and uncalled for. I apologize. I'm out of sorts. Forgive me. Mount Nebo is a glacial prominence in Benton County."

"What was he doing up there?"

Callan had no idea. "It's one more thing we'll have to find out," he said.

"Professor Banks did it!" she blurted.

He closed his eyes, unwilling to listen to another unsubstantiated opinion. "We don't know that for sure, Glynis."

"We know enough."

His cell buzzed next to him on the desk. Callan glanced at the display—*Leah Carver.*

"Another call, Glynis. I gotta take it. I'll talk to you later, okay?" He hung up to answer his cell. "Leah? I hope you're calling about Marissa."

"I am. She's called again," Leah said. "This morning. She was crying hysterically."

"Then she's heard the news about Logan. What did she say?"

Leah took a deep breath and sighed as if she didn't know. "It didn't make much sense, and she wouldn't elaborate, but she mentioned that Logan brought his death upon himself."

Callan scratched his scalp. "I don't understand. What did she mean by that?"

"She said he wasn't cleansed so he couldn't possibly have received what he wanted from Professor Banks."

"Leah, I still don't understand." Frustration rose in his voice.

"I don't know. She wouldn't say."

Callan cursed under his breath. "Leah, I've just about had it with Marissa, her insinuations, and her refusal to explain her behavior and comments. She never answers any of your questions, yet she continues to call you. Why? I don't get it. This isn't a game of *Clue* we're playing. It's real murder."

"I know, I know, but I think sometimes . . ."

Callan suspected by the way Leah's voice faded that she wasn't sure how he'd react to what she had to tell him. "You might as well go on and say it, Leah," he said. "At this point, there isn't anything that would surprise me about what's going through Marissa's mind."

"Okay, then I think she's afraid," Leah said.

"Understood," he replied, thinking the obvious. "I'm afraid for her," he said out of frustration. "Marissa's in a fearful situation, physically and mentally."

"No, I mean, no, not afraid in that sense."

Callan gave her time to gather her thoughts.

"I meant concerned," she said.

Callan was also concerned, but, again, he figured that's not what Leah meant.

"She doesn't want to give up what she might gain from this situation she's in on campus."

"Oh, shit," he said, frustration turning into alarm. "Then we're never going to get to the bottom of what's happening to her. We may not reach her in time."

"Don't say it like that," Leah pleaded. "Please, Professor."

"How else am I to say it? Marissa is into something that none of us understand completely. I don't believe Marissa even understands it herself, especially if Randall Banks is involved. I don't trust him, Leah. And I don't believe for one second what Marissa says or that Logan's death is about him not being cleansed. That's ridiculous. It's more than that. Logan made some accusations that I believe put him in danger. He said he was going to prove Banks wrong about his theories."

"Then isn't that enough to point the blame directly at Professor Banks?"

"All we have are a couple of overheard conversations by a young auditor."

"At least it's a start," Leah said.

Callan couldn't refute that, but it wasn't evidence. He cautioned Leah that they couldn't accuse Professor Banks or anyone for that matter without material facts and evidence. "Besides," Callan said, "authorities are working diligently. They're going to question him. I'm sure something is bound to turn up."

Leah didn't respond, but Callan could tell by her silence that she had something more on her mind. He prompted her to tell him.

"Marissa did say one thing to me that I thought interesting," she replied. "Marissa said that Logan's death was devastating to Professor Banks's *work*. Not to the professor, but to his work."

Callan placed a finger in his free ear so that he could hear Leah more clearly in the ear pressed against his phone.

"Marissa said the revelations he's working on may never be revealed now."

"What revelations?" he asked.

"Something spiritual."

"You mean paranormal?"

"Marissa said spiritual."

Callan scoffed. He didn't know what that meant exactly, especially coming from Marissa's mouth. "That's fine," he replied, exasperated, "but I'd like to remind her that Conner Whaite and Logan Allister's deaths are more than just spiritual. They're very, very physical, and they're eternal. They're dead, Leah. Let that sink into Marissa's thick skull to see if she gets as hysterical over their reality as much as she does over her fantasy."

CHAPTER FIFTEEN

Callan ended the phone call with his assistant but not before asking if she had Mitchell Dells's or Dana Weiss's phone numbers. Leah soon texted him both numbers. He tried Mitchell's number first but received no response. Dana answered her phone, but her tongue was lethargic, her words slurred.

"Are you all right?" he asked, concerned.

"What do you want?"

"First, I want to know if you're okay," he said. "You don't sound well."

"We've all had a shock, Professor Morrow. Surely, you can understand that."

Callan hoped his silence indicated to her that he was sincere about her health.

Dana softened her tone and said, "Yes, I'm fine. Thank you. Now, what do you want?"

"Have you talked to Marissa since last night?" he asked.

"No."

Callan didn't believe her. He responded, however, with restraint. "She didn't call you about Logan?"

"Yes, she *called,* but I saw it was her and didn't take it."

Callan paused, stunned. "Why not?"

"I didn't want to, Professor," Dana replied, now agitated. "I let it go to voice mail. How dare she call me. Marissa knew how I felt about him."

Felt about him? Her comment took him off guard. "Are you talking about Logan?"

Dana responded with sobs.

"Were you two dating?" he asked, understanding and more sensitive now.

She sniffled. "We had been. Then we stopped, but we still cared for each other."

Callan gave her a moment to recompose. "Did you see him yesterday?" he asked, knowing from Zola Krivoshia that she had.

"Yes," she answered. "At the coffee shop. Mitchell was there too. I just wanted some time to talk to Logan, to ask if we could start seeing each other again, but Logan was irate with Professor Banks. He was talking nonsense. When Mitchell got there, his ramblings only got worse."

"What did he say?"

"Oh, I don't know. Not entirely anyway. I wasn't listening. I was thinking so much about what I wanted to say to Logan when Mitchell left that I didn't listen to what the two of them said to each other. Then when Mitchell did finally leave, Logan and I talked, but we didn't *talk*, not what I wanted to talk about anyway."

Dana sniffled some more.

"Logan just wanted to talk about how angry he was at Professor Banks and how angry Professor Banks was at him," she said, continuing.

"Can you remember anything at all about Logan's conversation with the professor?"

Dana emitted a slight chuckle. "No, he's such a sweetheart," she said, reminiscing. "Logan could tell I was hurting about us. He stopped babbling about Professor Banks. He reached across the table and took my hand. He said he loved me. I couldn't believe it. He said we should get back together."

Callan said he was sorry about what happened to Logan, given their conversation. "No wonder you're so upset today."

Dana burst into uncontrollable sobbing. "No, you don't understand, Professor Morrow. You don't understand anything. I said no. Of all times to turn him down when I wanted him so much. I said no!"

More sobs followed. Callan waited patiently, though his head swam with questions and confusion.

"Oh, Professor, I'm so confused myself," she said. "I told him no because I didn't want a relationship with someone so intent on destroying a person like Professor Banks. I was selfish. I wanted Logan all to myself. I didn't want to share him with his anger. I suppose I'm not making any sense, but every conversation we had lately gravitated toward Professor Banks and his theories. I couldn't stand it. I told Logan he needed to do what he needed to do. Our relationship would have to wait."

"How did he take it?"

"Like how I thought he would. He became even more obsessed with getting to the bottom of Professor Banks's fraudulent practices. He was willing to put his own life on hold until Professor Banks was defeated. He vowed to get it resolved so that we could be together again."

Dana choked on her tears.

Callan waited until she was through. "What did you say to that?" he asked.

"What was I supposed to say?" Anger rose in her voice, directed at Logan. "I liked him. I liked Logan a lot. I'm sorry that he's gone, but there's not much of a future with a guy who believes he must destroy one relationship before he can build another. If not Professor Banks, it would be something else. I feared it would always be something else he's angry at. There are people like that in this world, Professor, but I'm not one who can be with them."

Callan sighed and thanked Dana for her candid and open conversation with him.

"One last question before I let you go, Dana," he said. "Do you know where Mitchell Dells is right now?"

Chapter Sixteen

Callan rushed from behind his desk and hurried to the small café at the edge of the campus where Dana said the dapper young student could be. Mitchell sat solemnly in a booth by himself, his head propped on the palm of his hand as he pecked at his iPad. It wasn't until Callan was close enough to see what was on the screen that he realized Mitchell was seeking online information about the death of Logan Allister.

Callan stood at the head of the booth until the young man looked up, glaring through an anemic expression, seemingly wishing anyone but Callan was standing there. "Please, Professor Morrow, I'm not doing very well this morning."

Callan could see that he wasn't. Drawn, dark eyes drooped into what was a young and vibrant face. His skin was blotched and oily, and his sandy hair—the icon of his youthful body and alluring personality—hung unwashed in listless strands.

He sat down anyway.

"If you're here to ask me more questions, please, I really am begging you—"

"No, I wouldn't do that to you," Callan said, even though it wasn't entirely true. "My purpose for being here is to see how you're doing."

"How did you find me?"

"Dana said you were here. I figured you were taking the news as hard as she is."

"As well I should," he said remorsefully. "I said some pretty awful things to Logan yesterday afternoon, sitting in this very booth. Then afterward, I caught up with him and said some more things. He was angry and upset with Professor Banks, and I blew it off. I misdirected the anger I had for the professor and said some things at Logan I shouldn't have. I can't take them back. They were the last words I ever said to him."

Callan tried some reassurance, but Mitchell wanted to hear nothing of it.

"No, I had no right to say what I said. I've been under pressure with Professor Banks, but not like Logan. He was in the thick of it." He held his breath momentarily before exhaling with frustration. "I never really thought I had a chance, but Logan did. He had a real chance."

"A chance at what?" Callan asked. "What's happening that was so real to Conner and Logan and is now so real to Marissa?"

Mitchell turned away.

"You're not going to tell me?"

"There's not much to tell."

Callan frowned. "I beg to differ. I think there's a lot more that everyone should be telling me—or, perhaps, you'd like to tell the authorities. They'll be asking soon too."

"You know me well enough by now, Professor, that I spout a lot of cool words and hot air to sound important, but I don't know anything. Not really. I wasn't a part of anything important to be cool about."

"Then I assume you tried to be."

"Yeah, sure, I tried but not very hard," Mitchell said. "I talked with Professor Banks once to see if I could join the others in proving his theories. I wanted to be a part of something—anything—on campus that others were involved in. I wanted something new and innovative. I heard that Banks was all that and more, but he wouldn't give me the time of day."

"Why was that?"

Mitchell shrugged. "He didn't like me, I guess. He said I didn't have the right *spirit* to hear the good news. He said I was arrogant and self-centered and that my arrogance was a deep-seated sin that no amount of cleansing could eliminate. He turned his back on me."

For the first time since meeting Mitchell, Callan believed his last comment to be the most truthful. He hoped Mitchell would open up more.

"Why did Logan go to Mount Nebo?"

"I have no idea. I don't know its significance. I don't even know where it's at."

"What about these theories you referred to? What are they about?"

Mitchell's head lowered. "I don't know. I just told you that Professor Banks cut me off from the spiritual awakening that he was offering others because of my arrogance. It's secret. Those provided the cleansing and awakening are sworn to secrecy."

"By Professor Banks?"

"Yes, of course. Who do you think I'm talking about?"

Callan raised his hands in the air in his defense. "I just want to be sure, Mitchell. When I talked to Professor Banks personally, he led me to believe that it was anyone but him involved with these sweat lodges and secret theories."

"That's because he's full of bullshit," Mitchell said, shaking his head. "He ruined Conner and Logan's lives. He practically ruined mine, and now he's after Marissa's. I would've never said the things I said to Logan if it wasn't for Professor Banks's constant pressuring of the issues, dividing us with his awakening theories and creating animosity between us."

Mitchell looked up to see if Callan had a reaction.

Callan stared back without one.

"You can trust me on that, Professor," Mitchell said, burying his face in the palms of his hands. After a few seconds, he looked up. "And you gotta do one thing for me if you don't do anything else . . . you gotta bring Marissa back."

CHAPTER SEVENTEEN

Callan resolved to face Professor Banks one more time based upon the anguish he'd heard in Dana Weiss's voice and the devastation on Mitchell Dells's face. He understood Greg and Nancy Reynolds's torment better now too. Secrecy, doubt, pitting student against student. They were ploys Randall Banks used to further his research, if research was what was actually being conducted.

But why? To publish an academic paper on a scientific theory? What sort of theory required sweat lodges and the cleansing of young, impressionable students before it could be proven? The unanswered questions angered Callan as much as they perplexed him.

Callan found the door to Professor Banks's office unlocked. He entered the small reception area and called the professor's name. No reply, but Callan heard a squeak. An office chair.

"Professor Banks?" Callan called again.

A halfhearted reply came from the back. "What do you want?"

Callan stepped through the office's doorway from the reception area. Banks sat sullenly in his chair, appearing too weary to rise.

"I want to see how you're doing," Callan said, wary of how he'd be received.

Randall Banks called his bluff. "More like you came to see how a murderer lives with himself the day after the murder. Well, get out. Get the hell out of here. I didn't kill Logan Allister any more than I killed Conner Whaite, and I'll not have you stand there, judging me, telling me otherwise."

Callan didn't budge. "I didn't come to talk about the murder," he said honestly. "I don't want to talk about Logan . . . or Conner either."

The professor grimaced and looked away. "I see, then you're still trying to find Marissa Reynolds. Haven't you got it through your thick skull by now that she may not want to be found and that anything we do about it isn't going to bring her back if she doesn't want to come back? And don't tell me about her parents being worried. If she's not reaching out to them, then why would she reach out to you or me? It's more evidence that she doesn't want to be found."

"I didn't come to argue," Callan replied.

"Then why did you come?"

Callan cringed, staring into the professor's dark eyes. "I want to know the significance of being the chosen one."

His eyes narrowed. "The what?" Deep-gutted laughter bellowed out of his throat. "What the hell are you talking about?"

"The chosen one. You know what I'm talking about. I want to know what it is. What must the chosen one do to become the chosen one? Once chosen, what must that person do to remain chosen?"

Randall laughed again. "Have you lost your mind? I'm

not following you, Professor Morrow. Now, if you'll excuse me, I'm sure I'll have additional interrogations by authorities and college personnel that I'll have to answer because of your incessant curiosity over nonsense and your desire to find a student who isn't missing."

"Where were you last night?" Callan countered.

The professor sat back in his chair and smiled. "Ah, so, you did come to talk about the murder."

"Where were you?"

"I was here," he said bluntly.

"At the office? All night?"

"No, at home. If you want to verify, I'm sure you'll find a neighbor or two who can vouch that there were lights shining through the windows as I sat at my dining room table doing work."

Callan frowned. "We all know that a light in a window is a poor alibi."

"It isn't in this case. Now, if you'll excuse me . . ."

"Why Mount Nebo?" Callan asked. "Why did Logan go to Mount Nebo? If you're innocent of any wrongdoing, Professor, I'm sure you won't mind answering that question."

Randall sat in his chair, tapping the ends of his fingers against each other. "I don't know what he was doing there. Contrary to what you may think, I do care about Logan's life being snuffed out as it was. He was a good kid, but it's none of my concern what he was doing at an obscure location like that hill of rocks called Mount Nebo. Furthermore, I have no idea who would want to harm him. It's the truth."

Callan glared at Randall; Randall glared back.

After several seconds, Randall broke eye contact and ended the impasse. "If there's nothing more . . ." he said.

Callan left the office quietly. Nothing more to be gained.

Chapter Eighteen

Callan left quietly but not submissively. As soon as Banks's office door closed securely behind him, an overwhelming resolve welled in his chest. Callan was convinced the man had been to Mount Nebo. He just needed proof.

"You're going where?" Terese asked when he got home. He suspected she'd heard clearly the first time because she followed immediately with, "Mount Nebo? Is that where the student was killed?" She didn't let him answer. "I doubt authorities will let you near the place, Callan. It's a crime scene. You'll drive all the way up there for nothing."

"By the time I get there, it'll be fine," he said. "I'll leave first thing in the morning."

"How long of a trip is it?"

Callan shifted his feet. "Not far."

She scoffed. "I know what *not far* means. You won't be back in time."

Unless Callan had missed part of the conversation, he wasn't sure what she was talking about. "In time for what?"

"A woman called for you," Terese replied. "She said you wanted to speak with her. The message you left sounded urgent."

"I did call Professor Banks's wife. Was it her? Not urgent exactly but important."

Terese wasn't interested in the details. "She's available tomorrow. She asked if you'd be okay meeting at a neutral location, but it sounds like you won't be able to meet with her at all. Perhaps you shouldn't go—to that mount place, that is. I think it'd be better for you to meet with Mrs. Banks instead."

Callan paused to give Terese some breathing room. "I'll be back in time," he said gently.

"How can you be so sure?"

"Because I said I would," he replied, equally irritated.

Terese sighed. "Tell me honestly; are you sure you need to go tomorrow?"

"I *want* to go, Terese," he said, lowering his voice. "I have to see this place for myself to understand its significance to Logan and to see if I can determine whether or not it had a significance to Banks too. Something drew Logan Allister to Mount Nebo, and I'd like to know what it is."

"But I'm pretty sure the authorities are looking into all that."

Callan was sure they were too. She was right. The authorities could gather evidence, facts, take photos, interview witnesses, but that wasn't the point. He wanted to see—needed to see—, feel, sense, and grasp the prominence and all it entailed. No one could do that for him.

There was something else, however. Something Terese wasn't telling him. Silent pleading in her eyes, a soft whimper in her voice.

"Terese . . ." he said, hoping his compassion would help her formulate the words.

She shook her head. She couldn't yet. Terese sucked in and held her breath before exhaling slowly and deliberately. Closing her eyes, she emitted faintly, "Last night." Her eyes opened; a tear glistened in one corner. "There was something. It was in the air. I could feel it." She paused then grasped his forearm excitedly. "You could feel it, too, couldn't you?" When he didn't respond, she added, "Something sinister was going to happen. You could feel it."

Callan's lips parted, not knowing what to say, hoping for the right words to quell her fears, but she cut him off before he could say something glib.

"No, don't," she said, anticipating his answer, her voice cracking. "I don't believe you, Cal; it did happen. That young man was murdered. We could feel it. Last night. It was in the air, but we didn't know what it was . . ."

"Terese."

"It was real, Callan! It happened."

Silence.

Terese drew a deep breath. Courage welled. "And if I let you go tomorrow, it could happen to you too."

A rebuttal came to mind. He opened his mouth.

"No!" she commanded, raising her hand. "If you're going to say that some *presence* is going to protect you, Callan, I swear I'll . . ."

"I wasn't going to say it, Terese."

"But you thought it," she said, lip quivering.

"No, I was just going to say again that I need to go," he said. Finality resonated in his voice. "I just . . . need to go, Terese, to see for myself."

Her throat rattled, but Callan sensed a gradual relenting.

"On one condition," she said. "You talk to John Steinmeier first, and if John says . . ." She hesitated. "If John agrees that a trip to Mount Nebo would be worthwhile, then go. But only during daylight hours. Only in the daylight, Callan. Tomorrow is fine, but, please, promise me this, Cal: you'll be back in time to meet with Mrs. Banks."

He promised.

John Steinmeier answered his phone with his usual impertinence, a short greeting that sounded more like a grunt. A loud thud followed, however, causing Callan to ask if the chief of security was okay. John didn't answer. The receiver had dropped from his hand and crashed onto the desk's surface before falling onto the floor. John grunted again as he stretched his arm underneath his chair to grab the receiver. His large belly pressed against his legs and armrest, making the reach impossible.

"Son of a . . ." he muttered, realizing it was beyond reach. He'd have to get on all fours to grasp it. On top of that, the cord wrapped itself tightly around his plump arm, restricting him further. The long, spiral cord gave unrestricted freedom to move about the office as he talked, but it didn't retrieve very easily from under his desk when he pulled on it.

John could hear Callan's muffled voice from under the chair, calling out to see if he was in trouble. "Just a minute!" John yelled with a few other choice words. "Son of a . . ." he said again, grasping the receiver and situating himself squarely back into his chair. He took a moment to catch his breath. "What the hell do you want? This better be good, Morrow," John said, out of breath, pulling his collar away from his neck. "If it's about that damn background report on . . ."

"Didn't cross my mind," Callan said, "but as long as you

brought it up."

"Yeah, well, getting my skinny ass in and out of this chair is easy compared to getting anything out of the system today."

"You mean you don't have the Banks report yet?"

"*No, I don't have the Banks report yet,*" he mocked. "Maybe tomorrow. Wellman's been working on it, but he's not had any luck."

"Hey, no problem. Then tell me this: Anything new on the Allister boy?"

"Not really. You probably know as much as I do."

"That isn't much," Callan replied. "That's why I'm thinking about heading up to Benton County tomorrow morning."

Hesitation. "You're heading where?"

"Mount Nebo."

John frowned. "Why? What do you hope to find?"

"I'm not sure," Callan said, "and I'm not sure I'll find anything. I just need go and see it for myself."

John paused again. "I don't like it," he finally said. "Benton authorities are doing their job, Cal. Let them do it."

"You sound like my wife. Did she get to you, by any chance?"

"No, I'm telling you from experience. What do you think you're going to uncover that the sheriff's office won't? I mean, let's face it, Cal. Law enforcement here in Vermillion is on Conner Whaite's death like white on rice. I'm pretty sure Benton County has this Allister kid's murder covered too. The only thing up in the air is this missing Reynolds student who doesn't appear to be missing at all, so I'm questioning whether a trip to Mount Nebo will be worth it."

"Wait a minute," Callan said. "What do you mean Marissa Reynolds isn't missing?"

"I'm starting to believe what others have told you. She's not missing, she's just gone away of her own volition for a while. She doesn't want to be where everyone thinks she should be. I remember being like that at her age. You, too, if you'd be honest with yourself. It's not a crime to want to get away from people, and it's not enough to throw valuable manpower at to find her. If you're going to this Mount Nebo because you think that's where she'll be, I think you'll be disappointed. I don't believe Marissa is anywhere near there, and what I don't want, Callan, is for you to go up there to start your own investigation. Benton County has it under control. You're up to your ass in issues here."

"So," Callan said, dejection and frustration in his voice. "You're not going to help me find her?"

"Sure, I'll help when I need to, but I've got plenty to do myself, helping law enforcement here. Let them do their job up north. You concentrate on what needs to be done in Vermillion."

"But that's just it, John," Callan said. "I don't believe the events are confined to Vermillion, or even Benton County for that matter. I think what's going on is far greater than what we know locally. I agree with you. I don't think Marissa is at Mount Nebo either. That's why I need to go, to see what else I can find out that isn't evidence here or there."

John grunted under his breath unconvinced. He switched ears. "Where else are the answers if not in Vermillion or Benton County?" he asked, a mocking tone.

There was a long pause before Callan softened his reply and said, "Somewhere in the stars, I suspect."

Chapter Nineteen

That's exactly why Callan wanted and needed to go to Mount Nebo. *Somewhere in the stars.* He thought back to his conversation with Randall Banks. The professor's necktie and the posters on the walls of his office meant something. Callan was more determined than ever to make the two-hour drive to the prominence to see if there was anything there that could help him make sense of it.

The village of Wadena near the Mount Nebo site was located among flat prairie land in the heart of abundant corn, soybean and mint fields. In its heyday, Wadena boasted of being the smallest town in the nation, sporting the largest number of professional baseball players in history. Doc Crandall, Karl Crandall, Arnold Crandall and Cy Williams had all played ball with professional teams during the years 1906–1918. Now, though, just a few houses, a burned down Baptist church, and a monument where the old Wadena School was once located were all that remained of the village and its memories.

A small creek meandered to the north toward the Iroquois

River, pausing to find its way around rocks along its banks and to provide a cool reprieve for the wildlife that knew the flowing run was there.

Less than two miles east along a straight and lonely stretch of county road, Mount Nebo swelled like a cyst from the fertile ground. The surrounding landscape was flat and treeless, allowing Callan to see far into the distance to his destination. Before he arrived, however, he could see a car pull away from the side of the road up ahead. Callan couldn't make heads or tails of the person or car leaving. He assumed they were curious gawkers of where Logan Allister had lost his life. He scanned the roadside, surprised there weren't more cars filing past the landscape's rise to get a glimpse of what a murder site looked like. Few such events occurred in this isolated part of the state.

Another car was parked alongside the roadway. More curious still was that the old, scuffed-up hatchback was stuffed with sleeping bags and sacks of staples and camping gear. Bumper stickers pleading for peace and a restored climate clustered arbitrarily on the back and side windows. New York license plates were screwed into its rear bumper.

The September sun pierced the back of Callan's neck as he exited the car, but the car he'd seen leaving and the car that remained suddenly gave him chills. He detested morbid curiosity, if that was the reason for their presence. As he trod up the prominence's path, it was clear to him that something sinister had occurred. Tall grasses were bent horizontally to the ground and shorter foliage was stomped into the dirt. Some of it could've been by law enforcement and medical personnel attending to the fallen student, although Callan believed they took extreme care to canvass the area as pristinely as possible.

Callan stopped to peruse the landscape around him. He

saw no one on or off the trail to account for the occupants of the hatchback. Just as well. He only came to see the location and to grasp any apparent reason why Logan Allister would come to such a place in the prairie.

A warm breeze blew across his face, carrying with it the late summer aroma of goldenrods and tiger lilies. Combines and grain dryers hummed in the distance, harvesting and flow-drying hundreds of tons of wheat, corn, soybeans, barley, and oats. He listened for just a moment, contemplating life's continuance despite his reason for standing in the sun on a lonely path.

A large, disturbed area of crushed grasses caught his attention up ahead. Loose dirt was scattered erratically around two shallow holes, and an area of wildflowers had been trampled to the ground. He wondered if that was the spot where Logan was found, or if it was simply the working space authorities needed to retrieve his body. Callan approached slowly, crossing his chest reverently as he did so.

"In the name of Jesus, help us," he said sadly, thinking of the task ahead of solving Logan and Conner's deaths and the mystery shrouding Marissa's absence. His mind expanded to other crimes like it, pathetic events mirroring a broken world. "Please, Lord, we are lost."

"We are, aren't we?" a woman's gentle voice whispered within a warm breeze from behind.

Callan turned quickly. The woman stood behind him, late twenties, wearing ragged jeans, a cut-off, plaid-cotton shirt, a tan sweater tied loosely around her waist, and a bandanna over her head to hide the strands of unwashed hair.

The sun silhouetted a man standing near her. Stubble dotted his tanned face. He, too, wore a similar bandanna and was dressed in jeans covered partially by a lavender t-shirt with a four-letter word expressing his disdain for cancer printed on the front.

"I'm sorry," she added. "We didn't mean to disturb you. We saw you on the path. You looked so sad. We were drawn to you, and your prayer . . ."

Callan nodded, still shaken by their sudden presence.

"Did you know him? The young man, I mean?" she asked.

His brows narrowed. *Who were they?* His eyes darted around the vicinity. *Where did they come from?* Callan finally emitted a "yes," hardly audible.

She smiled.

"Did you?" Callan asked in return.

"No," the man beside her replied. "Only by heart."

Callan frowned. *By what?* "I'm sorry," he said. "I didn't catch that."

The woman continued to smile warmly, but it changed slightly to something more patronizing. "By heart," she said. "We're the ones who found his body yesterday."

Her voice carried a genuine kindness. Callan's shoulders relaxed, but the realization of who they were suddenly caught him alarmed. "Good Heavens," he muttered.

"I know. It was tragic and traumatic for us." She looked at her partner with empathy and took his hand. "It was the last thing we thought we'd find on our adventure to Mount Nebo."

"Why did you come?" Callan asked.

"To see what was in the cache box, but Pete here—oh, I'm sorry—I'm Rhonda. Rhonda Comer. This is Pete Gadsden. We're from upstate New York."

Callan introduced himself. "You came to see what?" he asked, confused. "In the middle of nowhere—from New York?"

Rhonda chuckled. "It's not nowhere to us. It's fascinating here. We're geocachers."

Callan shook his head. "I'm sorry . . ."

"Geocachers. We look for caches that have been buried at significant spots around the country in search of swags planted inside."

"Swags?" Callan's lips gaped even farther.

"Mementos or treasures, however you'd like to think of them as."

"We also leave our own mementos behind in each cache," Pete replied earnestly.

"I see," Callan said in a tone that clearly indicated he didn't. Not entirely. "But that was yesterday, wasn't it? You've come back. Did the authorities have more questions?"

"Oh yes," she replied as if the investigative process wasn't the reason.

"But you came back, I mean, to Mount Nebo. Why?"

"We were uneasy," Pete said. "It wasn't right to leave without closure. We told the sheriff and his investigators all we knew, but it wasn't enough for us. The poor boy. We had to say goodbye again. To his spirit." Pete stared into Callan's eyes to see if he understood then turned away to point to a location in the northeast. "Just like we did at Mount Gilboa."

Callan shook his head to let them know he had no idea what they were referring to.

"Mount Gilboa. It's just a couple of miles from here. Such a powerful place, harmonious and tranquil, so different from here. Death was reconciled to life there. Unlike here, and we couldn't leave Mount Nebo in such turmoil."

Callan nodded his head as if he understood, but he didn't.

"So we came back," Rhonda added. "That poor boy consumed our hearts, Callan. He was embedded in our spirit. We had to come back one more time to see the place before we left with the hope of reconciling his death to his life."

"But it hasn't helped," Pete said. "In fact, the horrible feeling is worse than ever."

"But why?"

Rhonda glanced at Pete and squeezed his hand. "It was that man, Pete. I'm sure of it. Don't you think so? It was that man."

CHAPTER TWENTY

Callan wanted nothing more but to hear about the man Rhonda Comer said they saw. Compassion took precedence, however. "You two must be exhausted," he said. "You're probably hungry too."

Rhonda looked at Pete and smiled. "We are rather tired. That hatchback isn't that comfortable, and you're famished aren't you, sweetheart?" She laughed. "You're always famished."

Callan suggested they get out of the warm sun and drive into town to find a café for coffee and breakfast. The meal would be his treat. Rhonda mentioned she could use a good, hot cup of herbal tea to soothe her aching muscles.

"We'll see what we can do," Callan said, opening the door to a greasy spoon. "Not a lot of herbal-ness in this part of the country, but I'm sure they'll have something for you."

They sat at a corner booth away from other patrons. A waitress in a red checkered dress and white apron produced a pencil from behind her ear and asked if they knew what they wanted. She smirked when Rhonda asked for an avocado spread on sesame seed toast, but politely pointed to the laminated menu and said their sausage gravy and biscuits was the closest they had.

"Sage is our herb of the day," the waitress added.

Rhonda's eyes lit up.

"It's in the sausage." Cynicism loud and clear.

Rhonda lost her enthusiasm and ordered hot tea—whatever they had—and a bran muffin.

Pete shrugged at his partner, said, "When in Rome," and ordered the farmer's breakfast with three eggs, bacon, sausage, ham, fried mush with maple syrup, and three flapjacks on the side.

Callan grinned, grateful that Pete's smorgasbord would give them time to talk. "I assume since you're the ones who found Logan's body, you were the ones who called the authorities?" he asked.

Rhonda shifted in her seat and dunked the tea bag up and down in her cup which the waitress had just placed in front of her. "Oh yes," she said, placing her free hand over her heart. "We were with the sheriff for quite some time. I think they thought for a while that we were the ones that killed him. Here we are, dressed like drifters, with nothing but what we have in our hatchback, driving from cache to cache around the country as part of our hobby. I'm not sure they understood or appreciated what being a geocacher is all about."

"That was obvious," Pete said. "It only heightened their suspicions of us."

"But they must've thought enough of what you told them for them not to detain you," Callan responded.

"We were honest with them. We had nothing to hide and no reason to lie. I think it was evident by our answers that our only concern was for the young man who died. What was his name again? Was it Logan?"

Callan nodded.

"A college student?"

"Yes. I'm a professor at the college he attended."

"Oh!" Rhonda exclaimed. "Then you just missed him!"

The waitress arrived with their order on a tray.

Callan craned his neck around the woman's arms as she set food on the table, trying to get a better look at Rhonda's expression.

"Missed who?" he was finally able to ask when the waitress left.

"The man in the car," she said. "The man I was talking about at Mount Nebo." Rhonda looked down at her food. Her eyes lit up. "Oh, this looks good. Thank you very much for this. You say you're a professor? At Vermillion College?"

"Yes, but how did you know? I don't think I mentioned the college's name."

"When we arrived, that man's car was out front. We didn't see him at first, but his car had a decal on the back window. Printed quite clearly on the decal was *Vermillion College*. It was a wild hunch that's where you taught."

"Did you talk to him?"

"Oh, goodness, no."

"But you saw him?" Callan asked, pouring syrup over his golden slices of mush while he kept one eye on her response.

"Not at first," she said, rescuing a crumb that teetered from her lips. "Now, this muffin is surprisingly good. Here, try some, Pete."

Pete's mouth was full. He shook his head.

"When we came up the path, we stopped to pay our respects close to where we found Logan's body. We searched for the cache once again and then went further up the prominence."

"What for?"

"To look around, to see if there could be another cache somewhere."

Callan set his fork on his plate and swallowed. "Forgive my ignorance here, but what exactly is a cache?"

Pete waved his fork in the air, his mouth too full to answer.

Rhonda admonished her partner. "Slow down. You're going to choke. Goodness." She faced Callan. "It's a box used by geocachers," she said. "We put things in them for others to find. We would've shown it to you back at the mount, but we couldn't find it. The sheriff must've found it and taken it away."

"Was there anything interesting in it when you first found it and looked?"

"Before we found the body, you mean?"

Callan nodded.

Pete swallowed, took a sip of hot, black coffee, and said, "No, not much. There was a logbook that all caches must have. Rhonda and I logged our visit in with our code. There wasn't much else—a few arrowheads, a geocoin, a good luck locket with a picture of the old school, and a small geode." He glanced at Rhonda. "Not a pretty geode, did you think? Nah, whoever put it there must've just wanted to get rid of it without throwing it away."

"Are these contents fairly common for a cache?"

Rhonda and Pete looked at each other. Rhonda opened her mouth to say something, but Pete's eyes compelled her to keep quiet.

"Not really," Pete said.

Callan detected evasiveness.

"The boxes often contain much more," Pete added boldly, glancing at Callan's eyes. "They usually have more local and regional items of historical interest than what we found in the one at Mount Nebo."

"Yes, it was quite uneventful as caches go," Rhonda said. She looked at her partner for his reaction, but Pete maintained a poker face and simply stared at Callan.

Callan paused to give them the once-over. He stuffed some scrambled eggs into his mouth, then asked, "This man you mentioned—if you didn't see him when you first arrived, then when did you see him?"

"Oh," Pete said, wiping his mouth with a napkin, "coming up the path. Not sure how we missed him when we first came up, but there he was."

"I think he was hiding," Rhonda said.

Pete frowned. "Do you think so?"

"How else can you explain it?"

He shrugged. "Dunno, but like I said, there he was."

"Do you think he found this box or cache as you call it?" Callan asked.

"If he did, he didn't register his code into the log. He should've registered it. It's proper etiquette and part of the geocache rules we agreed to follow when we joined the website."

"Website?"

"Yes, there's a website for geocachers like us that list various caches around the country. The world, in fact." Rhonda seemed delighted at Callan's interest.

"We didn't pay much attention to the man though," Pete admitted.

Rhonda lost her enthusiasm. "I didn't like him," she said.

"Were you afraid?" Callan asked.

She looked over his shoulder to think. "No, but he wasn't right, that's all I know, and that's all I cared about. He carried an ill spirit if that makes any sense to you. Are you a spiritual person, Callan?"

Callan nodded, unsure if their belief systems were aligned similarly. He did, however, understand ill will and had a sense of what she was talking about.

"We watched him for a while," Pete said. "He was there for only a short time, about where we found the body. I think he bent down at one point, didn't he, Rhonda?"

"I don't know, Pete. He creeped me out. I didn't look."

"Yeah, I'm pretty sure he did, then he got up and hurried back to his car."

"And you say he was from Vermillion?"

"Oh yes!" Rhonda exclaimed. "The decal on the back window was quite clear."

Callan reached into his pocket and pulled out the photo of Randall Banks he had obtained from administration.

"That's him!" Rhonda exclaimed. She pointed to the photo and turned to her partner. "That's him, isn't it, Pete?"

Pete took another bite but didn't say one way or another. He didn't study the photo long, just long enough for an eyelid to twitch.

Callan reached into his pocket again and pulled out a business card, keeping one eye on Pete's guarded reaction. "I'm going to give you this," he said. "I appreciate the time we had here, if not for Logan's sake. Please take my card. If you're ever back in the area or you can think of anything else, please call me. I'd appreciate hearing from you."

Rhonda smiled and took the card. "We will. Pete and I are firm believers that encounters with others have special meaning. Divine intervention, if you will. Something about that young man brought the three of us together, I'm sure of it."

Callan looked at Pete. The young man nodded as though

it was expected of him to do so.

The trio finished their meal. Callan paid the bill before glancing at his watch. He gasped when he realized how much time had elapsed. An image of Terese immediately came to mind. A burst of adrenaline pulsed him into action as he gathered the professor's photo off the table.

"Gotta go," Callan said to the couple still lingering at the table.

He'd promised Terese he'd be back in town in time to meet with Randall Banks's wife.

CHAPTER

TWENTY-ONE

Callan left the diner with one regret. He appreciated the information Pete and Rhonda had provided, but wished he'd pressed harder for the information they didn't share. It was that moment when talking about the contents of the cache that left him uncomfortable. Was he mistaken? Was there a subliminal reflection in Pete Gadsden's eye, commanding Rhonda not to tell all? Or did Callan only hope there was more?

First things first, however. His next task was to meet with Margot Banks. Terese arranged for her to meet with Callan as soon as he drove into Vermillion. The small coffee shop on the square was convenient for them both. The strong aroma of freshly ground beans lured him toward the counter.

He ordered a large medium roast and perused the patrons for someone who appeared likely enough to marry a person like Randall Banks. He didn't know what sort of person that could be or who to look for. Callan hadn't met her at any college social functions. He pictured an eccentric woman with penetrating eyes, dressed in multicolored layers, white hair frizzled by static electricity under a knitted beanie, clutching a handbag and a hairless cat that spewed hisses at those who passed. No such woman was present, however. Other than students, there were only two other women in the shop, sitting alone. One knitted and one read a paperback, but neither appeared to be waiting for his arrival.

Callan accepted his coffee, doctored it with cream, and sat on a stool so that he'd have a panoramic view of anyone coming into the café. Five minutes turned to ten. Callan glanced at his watch and wondered if his guest had backed out. He gave Terese a quick call to see if his timing was wrong.

"No, she's there already, Cal," Terese replied. "She texted me and said she's waiting."

"Where?" he asked impatiently. "The knitter?" He couldn't believe someone married to Randall Banks had the wherewithal and patience to knit. "Wait. The book reader just lifted her head. She looked at her watch. I think she's the one. Gotta go."

Callan ended the call, grabbed his coffee, and sauntered to the woman, who lifted her head and peered above her reading glasses to give him an icy glare.

"Are you Ms. Banks, by any chance?" he asked politely.

She marked her page with a bookmark tasseled at one end. "Mr. Morrow, I presume," she said with indifference.

"Yes, ma'am, Callan Morrow. I appreciate you taking the time to meet with me. May I have a seat?"

She gestured for him to do so. "You're an investigator with the college?" she asked tepidly. "Or are you with the police? If you're with the police, I've already talked with them.

I detest redundancy."

"No, ma'am, I'm simply a professor at Vermillion College requested by Dr. Overby to look into the events of Conner Whaite's death."

"I see," she said. "Call me Margot, please. I assume you want my perspective of the situation to evaluate whether my husband's behavior and actions at this so-called sweat lodge should be considered unsuitable for the college's reputation."

Callan smiled cordially. "No, I'm actually here in the interest of one of my students who hasn't been seen recently."

Margot appeared genuinely concerned and set her book aside to give him her undivided attention. Despite her arrogance, Callan liked Margot Banks right away. Intelligent, sophisticated, fond of brevity and candidness. He believed he didn't need to hold back any punches with her, as she seemed like a woman who didn't mind throwing a few herself.

"I haven't heard anything on the news about a missing student," Margot replied.

"It's nothing like that."

"Then you'll have to explain. Obviously, you believe my husband has knowledge of this student's disappearance."

"More like information on where she can be located and why she's there in the first place." Callan glanced toward the sales counter and lifted a finger in that direction. "May I get you something to drink? It looks like you've finished your first cup."

"My second cup," she corrected, smiling. "I come here to read often. I find solitude without being alone. No, I'm fine, thank you. But I must say I doubt that I can be of much help. My husband and I are no longer together. We haven't been for some time now."

Callan pulled Marissa's card with the copyright symbol on

the inside and handed it to her. "Have you seen this insignia before? Do you know what it means?"

Margot took the card and glanced at Marissa's name on the front before looking inside and studying the symbol.

"No," she replied, handing the card back.

"But you've seen it before. There was something in your eyes."

"Only by the police. They showed me a similar card, and I told them the same thing that I told you. Before the police, I'd never seen a card like that, and I'd never seen that insignia on anything other than copyrighted material I read."

"Then you've talked to the police," Callan said.

"Yes, as I said already. They asked me a few questions after that boy was found up north. His was a tragic death, but I'm afraid the card means as little to me now as it did when they asked, and I don't see how it could be connected."

Callan started to put the card back into his pocket when Margot lifted her finger for patience.

"How did you come across that card and who is that girl whose name is on the front? Pardon my asking, but I was under the impression that the card and its insignia were information not privy to anyone outside of the sheriff's investigation. I didn't think anyone knew about it, so how did you come across it?"

"This particular card was found on the floor of my classroom," he said. "The woman is a student of mine. I assume she dropped it on her way out of my class."

Margot nodded. "Do you believe it has something to do with these sweat lodges my husband has supposedly conducted?"

"I don't know," Callan confessed. "That's what I want to find out. I haven't tied her specifically to the lodge, no. In fact, I haven't tied her directly to your husband in any way for that matter, but she knew the victims in the lodge. What do you know about sweat lodges?"

"I don't know a damn thing," she replied, disgusted that she was even asked. "I didn't even know what one was before the accident occurred, and I certainly didn't have prior knowledge of my husband's interest in them. When he was gone of an evening, I assumed he was on campus, conducting a night class."

Callan paused to let her collect her thoughts. She turned away from him to do so, turned back to say something, but then had second thoughts. Soon, however, she took another deep breath and said, "I didn't tell the police this, Professor, but I might as well tell you. The accident of the sweat lodge was a complete surprise to me because I had no prior knowledge of his activities with sweat lodges or why he was even conducting them. I don't believe anyone has substantiated the fact that he's even been involved, but I must say that if it's ever found out that he was and is involved in something as unorthodox as a sweat lodge, it wouldn't surprise me."

"Why do you say that, Margot?"

"My husband is eccentric. He has eccentric thoughts, ideals, and actions. He's exhibited such behavior in the past. I'm sorry a young man had to die to indulge his exotic fantasies." She looked down at her book as she flipped the corner of its pages with her thumb. "He's had what I'd call addictive and compulsive behavior patterns in the past. Odd quirks for lack of a better term, if you know what I mean. They were easily overlooked when we were first married, but they've gotten worse and more difficult to ignore."

"Can you give me an example?"

"Classical music for one. He's always favored classical music, but what he'd do is have a composer in his head that he couldn't shake for months at a time. Days upon weeks would be consumed, playing the same pieces by the same composer over and over. Chopin lasted two months at least. A recent spell was Tchaikovsky. Before that, if I heard the 'Water Music Suite' by Handel one more time, I thought I'd go insane. 'Opera 2' has been his latest compulsive passion. It's good for a listen once in a great while, but not over and over ad nauseam."

"Then he likes opera."

"No, he loathes opera," she said. "I didn't say it was opera he played. I said it was 'Opera': '1' and '2.' They're songs, if I had to describe them."

"I'm afraid I'm not familiar."

"Vitas, the Ukrainian singer," she replied. "They're his works."

Callan smiled in a way that indicated his knowledge of Ukrainian singers was very limited.

"Vitas is gifted in being able to reach falsetto notes beyond human ability, especially for a man. Then there's Dimash, Dimash Somebody, his last name will come to me. He's that young singer from Kazakhstan. Ah, yes, Kudaibergenov. Dimash Kudaibergenov. I knew it was on the tip of my tongue."

Callan smiled again. His knowledge of singers from Kazakhstan was even more limited.

"Both men have the falsetto gift," she explained further, "and 'Opera 1' and 'Opera 2' focus on that gift. Take a listen sometime. Randall was captivated by them. It's fascinating music the first time around, but every day, hour after hour, is a bit maddening. And if I heard 'Chum Drum Bedrum' one more time, I hesitate to confess what I was going to do to him."

"I think I get it," Callan said.

"Oh, I don't think you do, Professor," she said. "Listen to it, and when you do, ask yourself if it's something you could be attracted to compulsively without going stark raving mad. I've thought about it, and it's always made me wonder."

He frowned. "What's that?"

Margot glared at Callan gravely. "I've wondered if there were other aspects of his life that controlled him as much as his music did. Whatever is behind these sweat lodges can't be ignored, whether it can be attributed directly to Randall or not."

Callan felt uneasy. Her piercing glare didn't waver.

Margot shifted in her chair and strummed the cover of her paperback with her fingers. "Did you not know that Randall was arrested once?" she asked.

Callan shook his head.

"He should've disclosed it to the university, but by your lack of questions about it, I suspected you didn't know."

"When did this occur?"

"This past June during the summer solstice," Margot said.

"Here in Vermillion?"

Margot shook her head. "Oh, no, not in Vermillion. Up north."

"Benton County?"

"Yes."

Callan leaned forward, suddenly more interested. "What happened? Do you mind telling me?"

"Not at all. He was trespassing on private property near a place called Mount Nebo. Ever hear of it?"

"It's where Logan Allister was killed. It's a topographical prominence on the prairie."

Margot dismissed Callan's statement with a flick of her wrist. "It's more than just a topographical prominence,

Professor," she replied condescendingly. "To Randall, it had religious significance. The original Mount Nebo in Jordan was where Moses was granted a view of the Promised Land."

Callan sat back in his chair and nursed his coffee to process the information. "Is that what he hoped to receive?"

Margot smiled. "Yes, as odd as it sounds. I believe he did. Mount Nebo had great significance to him. Just as Moses was granted a view of the Promised Land, my husband believed that if he stood on Mount Nebo in Benton County, he'd be granted a glimpse of the future."

Callan shook his head. "Whatever would make him believe that standing on an elevated hill left behind by ancient glaciers would give him such insight?"

"He was that way, increasingly so." Margot glanced at her empty coffee cup, appearing to contemplate wanting something more. She quickly dismissed the thought. "He believed Indiana and Ohio held several archaeological wonders that aligned with this Mount Nebo that not only provided such insight but were built by ancient Native Americans as a message for their descendants regarding the future."

"The future of what?"

"That I can't tell you," she replied. "I don't know. What I do know is that his passionate pursuit of discovering an ancient secret to the future sent him to Mount Nebo this past June for the solstice. He was on some farmer's property. The farmer politely asked him to leave. His dogs kept barking, and my husband's presence startled the farmer's family. When Randall refused to leave on the grounds of religious freedom, the farmer called the sheriff. Randall was promptly arrested when he wouldn't budge even after the sheriff ordered him to do so. If that wasn't bad enough, he resisted the arrest, and additional units had to be called to the scene."

Callan smiled, amused by the story. "Interesting," he said.

"Interesting?" Margot replied. "I find it all very strange even for Randall."

"No, I meant that I find it interesting because when I asked your husband if he'd ever been to Mount Nebo before, he not only denied it, but he denied even knowing where it was located."

Margot frowned and shook her head in disgust. "Well, I'm afraid I can't tell you much more," she said. "After he was arrested, I drove to the county seat the next day to arrange for his release, and when we got home, I told him to pack his belongings. I'd had enough. I wanted him out of the house."

Callan nodded and glanced at his watch. "Anything more you can tell me?"

She said no, then reached for a napkin beside her and stuffed it in her cup, ready to go, keeping one eye on Callan. "You don't appear satisfied with what I've told you, Professor."

Callan didn't realize a sour expression had spread across his face. "No, I was just wondering why your husband believed Mount Nebo held the key to such grand visions. The Midwest is hardly a mecca, wouldn't you agree?"

She didn't say anything at first. Instead, she scanned her surroundings for napkins left behind, straightened her blouse, then spoke again. "Do you know your Bible?"

Apparently not well enough, he thought, if Margot Banks was about to give him a lesson.

She smiled, giving him the benefit of the doubt. "As you know, throughout the Bible, God used the meek and most unlikely people to carry out the tasks he wished to have fulfilled. Then consider, for instance, if it's so strange that a small, remote knoll in the middle of an unassuming place such as Indiana would be used in much the same way."

Callan bowed. "I stand corrected, but I hardly consider your husband's theories as God-inspired."

"That's because you're not looking through the eyes of the beholder. Randall's choice of locations has little to do with God, Vermillion, you, me, or any student, Professor. It has everything to do with how his mind has distorted his self-worth and thought process."

Now that was a statement Callan could agree with without argument. "I shouldn't take any more of your time," he said. "I appreciate our conversation. You've been very helpful. I'm not sure what to think at this point."

"Neither do I, Professor. I share your concern, but if you'll take my advice, I wouldn't spend any more time on Randall and his eccentric hobbies than you must."

Callan stood to go. He turned toward the exit but stopped when she called his name.

"I do hope you find that young girl," she said earnestly. "I hope it's sooner than later. All your energy and effort must be focused on finding her."

Callan stared blankly at the door. *Yes,* he thought. *I believe that more than ever now.*

CHAPTER

TWENTY-TWO

Callan no sooner returned to his car when his cell rang. The display illuminated the words: *John Steinmeier.*

"What's the matter now?" he answered in jest, remembering the problems John's department had in getting a background report. "Calling to tell me the hamster running the wheel inside your computer system has died?"

"Go screw yourself."

"Funny. That's exactly what Randall Banks told me to do the last time I saw him."

John didn't hesitate to blurt out, "I need a beer, Morrow. Today was a nightmare. I thought we'd never get this report, but somehow Wellman was able to pull through."

"Where are you?"

"Walking into the Wallace."

"The pub downtown?" Callan asked.

"Yeah, don't act like you don't know where it's at."

Callan chuckled. "I just got to my car. It'll take me five minutes to walk there."

John had already helped himself to a tall, frosty mug of domestic brew by the time Callan arrived. He sat away from the table with one of his large legs crossed over the other. His tie flopped over his belly and extended well below his waistline past his crotch. His suit jacket sat clumsily over his shoulders as if he'd started to take it off when he sat down but gave up. A white piece of paper lay face down on the table before him. John took a sip of beer and belched.

"Cream ale," Callan said to a waitress who hadn't quite approached. She turned immediately for the bar. "You should've brought Wellman along. Sounds like he's the real man of the hour that deserves a drink."

"He's young; drinks like it too. Can't stay that long. Just wanted to stay long enough to give you our report on Banks. I shouldn't kid about him though. Travis did me good today."

Callan looked to the table. "Is that it?"

John slid the white piece of paper toward his colleague but placed his broad hand over the top so that Callan wouldn't read it just yet. He smiled, exposing a gold tooth. "Try to guess what's in it first."

Callan hovered his hands in circles over the report as if he was conjuring a premonition. "Is there free beer if I can guess correctly?"

John laughed. "Yeah, on me. You'll never guess though."

Callan placed his fingertips on his temples and closed his eyes, preparing to astound his audience. "For free beer, Callan the Magnificent can guess anything related to Randall Banks. Wait, I'm getting something. What's this? I see a man, a greasy-haired professor with dark, beady eyes and a warped sense of reality, standing, no, loitering on private property. He's trespassing on farmer's land in Benton County. Wait, there's more. Ah, I see it now, I see this same professor being handcuffed and led to a patrol car. He wrestles with an officer. He resists arrest. I see, yes, I see . . . Randall Banks arrested for trespassing on private property near Mount Nebo."

Callan lowered his hand and smiled at the security director just as the waitress set his ale on the table. He smiled overtly across the table, lifted his glass, and said, "Cheers."

"Smart ass," Steinmeier grunted. "Who told you?"

"His ex. I just came from talking with her at the coffee shop. She said the arrest was the straw that broke the camel's back as far as their relationship was concerned. He lied to me that he'd never been to Benton County before, and here we are, a day or two later, proving that the mad professor is a damn liar."

John reached for the paper and turned it over for Callan to read.

"There's something else," he said. "It's minor but could still have some bearing. He had a similar problem at a place near Cambridge City in the eastern part of the state. Charges were dropped by the person owning the property."

"That's odd," Callan said, wiping suds off his upper lip with the back of his hand. "What's in Cambridge City?"

"Dunno, except there are some ancient Native American mounds outside of town that interest no one except college types. I don't think Banks spent much time in a holding cell if they even held him at all, so I don't think he did anything illegal while there except trespass."

"But still, based upon what his wife told me about his religious compulsions, it may be significant. It may tie into what I learned at Mount Nebo." Callan took a sip and glanced at his colleague.

A frown covered John's face.

"Don't look at me like that," Callan said. "You knew I'd go up there against your advice."

"I didn't have to be John the Magnificent to figure that out."

"I learned something interesting. I talked to the people who found Allister's body."

John started to take a swig of his beer but set it down upon hearing Callan's last comment. "You don't say."

"They didn't say much except that Banks was at the mount right before I arrived. The two hippies that found him described him to a tee."

"I should give the old boy another visit," John said, taking that sip.

"I think you should. It would throw him over the edge. You may get more out of him now. He was pretty stressed the last time I saw him. Tried to disguise it with insults. Looked like he'd been up all night. Either that or else he'd slept with a basset hound pressed against his face."

"Well, Callan, you don't understand," John said snidely, "It's hard work, warping young minds, trespassing on private property, bailing your ass out of jails, and . . . breaking into college dorm rooms."

Callan jerked his head away from his brew. "Say that again?"

"Fixing a broken system wasn't the only thing Wellman did for me today. We got a call from Conner Whaite's roommate that their room had been broken into."

"Really? When?"

"This morning."

Callan paused. "I suppose no one's been caught yet."

"No, we're still trying to see if surveillance will show

anyone coming in or out of the dorm." John shook his head. "It's an antiquated system, nothing like what I was used to at the bank. It'll take us a while to go through the images."

"Wellman go to the dorm?"

"Yeah. The roommate called security when he returned from class. He said that it appeared the lock had been jimmied. When he got inside, he noticed that his top desk drawer was open. He believes the subjects realized the desk belonged to the roommate and not to Conner and were no longer interested. Conner's desk and closet, though, were ransacked."

"So I take it Conner's parents hadn't been by yet to clean out his room."

"Nah, too soon."

Callan nodded. "What was in the desk and closet? Did the roommate have an idea?"

"Yeah, he said there were some clothes, some papers, schoolwork, paper tablets, pens, scissors, that sort of thing. His laptop wasn't there. The subjects looked through everything but didn't seem to have taken anything. We're unsure if they took the laptop, or if Conner had it someplace else. The roommate said Conner was known to take it home on weekends lately."

"Interesting," Callan said. "Makes me wonder what they were after."

"Something tied to that sweat lodge and Banks's involvement, don't you think?"

"I suppose, but I wish there was a way to be sure. The subjects had to be young."

"I don't see how they could've entered and left without being detected otherwise," John said.

"I agree. Still, I'd like to know why they left seemingly empty-handed." Callan looked through the bar's tinted windows to the outside and raised his finger with an idea. "I wonder if Conner took anything of interest home with him. You say he'd been going home on weekends?"

"The roommate said Conner had been doing that more often lately. I haven't tried to contact the parents to confirm. They may have some thoughts on what their son had been doing when he wasn't in class and who he'd been associating with."

"You mind if I do that?" Callan asked. "Where do they live? Carmel? That's not far from where I had a place in SoBro, there in Indianapolis."

Callan nursed his beer while he rambled for several minutes over various hypotheses he had on Randall Banks and how Conner Whaite, Logan Allister, Mitchell Dells, Dana Weiss, and Marissa Reynolds were involved with the professor. "What do you think?" he asked when he was through, hoping for the director's insight.

John guzzled the remaining brew in the bottom of his glass and raised his hand for the waitress. He belched and said, "I think for someone who gets his beer free this afternoon . . . you talk too much."

CHAPTER
TWENTY-THREE

The drive from Vermillion to Carmel took a little over an hour, but it was the longest hour Callan Morrow had ever driven, anticipating the solemn aura in the Whaite household. It'd been just a few excruciating days since Kevin and Beverly Whaite lost their son. He couldn't fathom the unimaginable grief they were experiencing, but the couple was gracious enough to accept Callan's invitation to talk. In fact, they seemed rather relieved and hopeful to discuss the circumstances surrounding Conner's mysterious death, as if, somehow, his visit would provide some comfort in knowing that the incident was not going to be overlooked or, worse yet, swept under the carpet.

The Whaite residence was an expansive ranch-style home in a wooded upscale neighborhood of Carmel. Most of Carmel was upscale, but the Whaite home was older, architecturally outdated, and blended into the environ comfortably without distraction.

"We've been here about twenty-five years," Beverly explained when she welcomed Callan into their home. "Kevin did most of the inside work himself. Our friends in construction did the rest."

Callan gawped. Mon Reale crown molding, Christian Cross oak doors, Turkish travertine tile, and beveled glass windows graced the home with handcrafted precision. He could hardly take it all in.

Kevin led Callan to a comfortable chair in the living room. "The artifacts are Beverly's," he said upon noticing Callan's wandering eye. He patted the delicate hand of his wife that held a small white Kleenex in the fold of her palm. "She's been fortunate to receive many heirlooms from her family that've been passed on to us. Many of the items you see are Pennsylvania Dutch. There are even a couple of Revolutionary War pieces. I've tried to incorporate them into the motif of the house."

Beverly squeezed his hand and nodded slightly toward their guest.

"But you didn't come here for a personal tour of our home, did you?" Kevin asked, taking his wife's cue.

Callan acknowledged that he did not. He said he came to get a closer feel for what their son was like, what his interests were, and whether they knew of the extracurricular activities Conner was involved in at Vermillion College before his death.

Beverly struggled to reach a chair. She mentioned a few things that she thought Callan would want to know, but kept a nervous eye toward a doorway, leading into the kitchen and dining area. After a few more comments were made, she rose suddenly and said, "If you'll excuse me, Mr. Morrow, I believe I hear the dryer going off." She turned to her husband. "Will you excuse me, dear?"

Kevin touched his wife's hand again as she passed him and told her to do what she needed to do. He'd answer Mr. Morrow's questions.

Beverly smiled and thanked Callan for the visit. "You'll see that he gets refreshments, Kevin?"

He nodded. When she'd left the room, Kevin suggested they head out to the workshop he used as a personal sanctuary. He whispered, "I think we'll be able to talk more freely there. Her grief is so great that she wouldn't be much help to you given the circumstances. Besides, I have beer out in the workshop. I can talk you into a cold one, can't I?"

Callan smiled but said he'd prefer pop instead.

"Don't get me wrong," Kevin said when they crossed the drive to the detached workshop. "I'm not in any better shape than Beverly about Conner, and you'll forgive me if I must stop now and then to compose myself, but I want to have our discussion. It's important to me to do so."

Callan stepped inside and marveled at the ultimate man cave Kevin Whaite had built. On the far side of the shop was the garage where two late-model autos and an older F-150 were parked on an epoxy floor coating. The garage blended into a workshop complete with lathes, drills, saws, and other woodworking equipment. A pegboard hung on a wall, tools neatly organized and maintained. A small living area with two recliners and a love seat was off to the side, a custom-built kitchenette sat along one wall, and a large flat screen television hung on another wall, perfect for watching Sunday football and midweek basketball.

Kevin strode to the refrigerator and pulled a cold can of Coke for Callan and a longneck for himself. He tipped his bottle Callan's way and offered cheers. "Have a seat or walk around if you want."

Callan smiled and said, "I better take a seat. If I walk around, I may never leave." He waited to do so, however, until Kevin sat first.

"That boy was an intelligent one," Kevin said, choosing a recliner. "We had high hopes for him. He was naive though, too, as some smart kids are. Gullible, I should say. A father doesn't like to see his kid—especially his son—be so naive and gullible, but that's what gave him his good heart and heightened his curiosity about the world."

"Are you familiar with his interests at Vermillion?"

Kevin arched his back and looked up to think, periodically glancing through a window near the entrance. "Not in detail. I trusted him to be smart about being on his own despite his lack of common sense. I believe his interests at college mirrored the interests he had in high school." Kevin paused to reconsider. "Well, maybe not though. Who knows?"

"Like what sort of things are you talking about?"

"Space and our space missions. He was in a space club, for lack of a better word. He liked astrology, too, although I can't say he followed it much. Oh, and geology too."

"Were any of those his major at VC?" Callan asked.

"Oh, hell, no," Kevin said, chuckling. "That's one thing he had foresight on. How the heck was he going to feed the mouths of his future wife and kids with an interest in astrology?" Kevin laughed some more. "No, he was interested in math but was thinking lately about taking more business classes, maybe even accounting. I hear you're an accounting prof there."

"Not accounting exactly, forensic accounting, subjects dealing with fraud and white-collar crime."

"Ah, he would've liked that. Now I remember. VC has

one of the few auditing and fraud majors that deal specifically with white-collar crimes. Yes, that interested Conner. He even looked into the auditing program at LSU once. It's similar to VC's, I understand. Seriously thought about enrolling down there."

"But his true passion was with space . . . and the stars?"

Kevin put the longneck to his lips but didn't take a sip, instead staring out the window once again. "What?" he asked, suddenly realizing Callan had asked a question. "No, I wouldn't say passion, but it was a hobby of his. I think he found plenty to keep him busy and interested at VC. I was against him going to a private liberal arts college like Vermillion at first. There's little room at a place like that for conservative values that keep a person's feet on the ground and their head on straight. Conner was impressionable. I feared they'd change my son, but Beverly convinced me that VC was a good school and would be good on his résumé, especially if he stayed in the Indianapolis area."

"And?"

"The college was actually good for him. Kept him motivated. His values didn't change, not until this one professor took Conner under his wing and started feeding him a load of crap anyway."

Callan leaned forward. "What professor was this?"

"Oh, you know, that guy whose name keeps popping up on the news associated with the lodge Conner died in. I'd tell you who he is, but Beverly won't allow his name to be mentioned in this house."

"But to be sure we're talking about the same person, can you give me a clue?"

"Professor B."

Callan sat back in his seat. "Ah yes, then we're on the

same page."

Kevin suddenly drifted away in thought. He sat stoically, focusing on an obscure spot on the wall in front of him. "But something was happening, I think," he said, drifting back into his memory.

Callan prompted him to continue.

"Well, I couldn't tell if Conner was pushing toward or pulling away from this guy," Kevin said. "At one point, we heard less and less of Conner as the semester progressed, then suddenly he started coming home more often. On the weekends, that is. He'd bring research home, keeping it in his room rather than taking it back to his dorm in Vermillion. I'm not sure what it was. Beverly could probably tell you. She mentioned to me once that she saw some writings from this professor when she was cleaning his room, something about how the stars and ancient Native American beliefs intertwined to . . . oh, I don't know . . . the future, or something like that."

"The occult?" Callan asked.

"I have no idea. I told her to leave it alone."

"Did she?"

Kevin grinned, a man-to-man smirk, Callan's answer to the question. "Beverly had no intention of leaving it alone. I think she asked Conner about the work, but she didn't get an answer that satisfied her motherly curiosity. I told her it was none of her business. He was an adult, deserving of privacy."

Callan collected his thoughts. "Have you received a phone call from John Steinmeier, VC's Director of Security?" he asked, lowering his voice.

Kevin's expression turned grave. "No, should I have?"

"I'm not sure about that, but I did talk with him. Apparently, there was a break-in in Conner's room. Some of Conner's things were ransacked, but it didn't appear the subjects found what they were looking for."

Kevin glared into Callan's eyes. Seconds passed before he asked, "You think they could've been after what Conner was working on, not realizing Conner was bringing it home?"

"That's what I'm wondering," Callan said, nodding. "Do you still have those papers in his room?"

"Oh, I'm sure they're still there."

"Would you mind if I took a look at them?"

Kevin face brightened. "Take a look, take them with you," he said. "I'll ask Beverly, but I'm sure she'll be as glad as I am if someone like you can make heads or tails out of the scribbles and help us find out what happened to him."

Kevin finished his beer, stood and glanced out the window once again. "I'll go talk with her," he said, continuing to look. "She knows where they are. You don't mind waiting here, do you? Get yourself another Coke."

He left quickly and jogged across the drive to the back of the house.

Callan followed him to the door and watched through the door's window until Kevin was out of sight. He gazed upon a neatly trimmed yard that was lushly green despite it being mid-September. Mums were tucked neatly in their beds, each having their own entitled space surrounding the house. He glanced down the drive and noticed not a spot of oil, grease, or coolant fluid had stained the pavement. Kevin's outside domain was as meticulous as his inside.

Callan suddenly realized he wasn't the only person admiring Kevin's property. A tan car inched past the house. The young driver peered toward the detached workshop. Callan stepped back out of view.

Kevin soon emerged from the house, carrying folders and envelopes of papers, pictures, drawings and newspaper clippings. "Here you go," he said, "This was all that was on his desk and in his closet that Beverly could find. She says, 'Have at it.' We don't want or need them back."

He added that Beverly was grateful for Callan's interest in the research.

Callan thanked him and opened the door to exit the workshop, but Kevin shut it abruptly with the palm of his hand, taking it out of Callan's grip. Kevin craned his neck to peer out the window.

"What's wrong?" Callan asked.

"I don't know. I don't like it. There's a car out there." Kevin turned toward his recliner. "I'm going to get a gun."

"No, wait," Callan urged. "I saw a car drive past the house a moment ago. Is that what you're talking about?"

"A dirty tan one? Two young guys in front?"

"Yeah, tan, not sure how many guys."

Callan sensed Kevin wanted to fetch his gun again.

"They've been driving past every few minutes," Kevin said. "I could see them from where I sat with you as I drank my beer. At first, I noticed they were parked across the street. Did you see them follow you from Vermillion?"

Callan shook his head. He wondered if one of them was the same person who broke into Conner's dorm room. Callan reached for the doorknob.

"You sure you'll be okay?" Kevin asked before Callan could exit. "I have a snub-nosed Colt tucked between the seat cushion and arm of my recliner. You could . . ."

"No," Callan said. "I'll be okay. I know how to take care of myself. If what they're after is the research you gave me, I think I know how to take care of them." He twisted the doorknob and pulled it open slightly but paused to think. A smirk crossed his face. "Yeah, I know exactly what to do."

CHAPTER

TWENTY-FOUR

Callan caught a glimpse of the dirty tan car out of the corner of his eye as he climbed behind the wheel of his vehicle and placed the research papers Kevin Whaite had given him on the passenger seat. His briefcase was perched against the front seat on the floorboard. Callan lifted it onto the seat and emptied its contents, shoving as much as he could under the seat. He pushed Conner's papers as far under the seats as they would go so that they couldn't be seen through the passenger side window.

He then filled the briefcase with an outdated newspaper, then opened the glove box and grabbed all the fast-food napkins he'd stored there because he couldn't bring himself to throw them away. He'd never needed them until now. The napkins—all of them—went into the case too. On the floorboard sat a fast-food sack with part of a greasy sandwich still left in the wrapper. He snatched it up along with coffee and gasoline receipts and loose papers that meant nothing to him anymore and stuffed it all into the briefcase. When he'd cleared his car of all the random, worthless items lying about, he closed the case tightly and locked it.

Callan was sure going to miss that briefcase.

He pulled out of the drive and onto the road and spotted the tan car behind him. Two occupants sat in the front seat, but he couldn't make out their features. Callan smiled when the car pulled from its secluded parking space on the street. He was sure Kevin Whaite saw the car pull out as well.

Now where to go?

Callan knew the city of Carmel well, but on the spur of the moment, as his anxiety welled inside, his mind went completely blank. A coffee shop or restaurant would work, one not too crowded or too noisy. His ruse had to look genuine. He remembered Clay Terrace, an upscale shopping and entertainment district near the heart of Carmel proper. It wasn't too far away. Callan pulled into a parking space near the first bar and grill he came to and exited the car with briefcase in hand.

The hostess at the podium, young and petite with long, blond hair, tight black dress, purple lips, and an orthodontic smile, asked how many was in his party.

"Just me, I'm afraid."

"That's no problem, sir." She grabbed a menu and scanned the dining room. "Would you care to sit at the bar instead?"

Callan said he'd prefer a table if she had one. "I have some work to do."

She smiled. "Will you follow me?"

He did so, looking once behind him to see if he was being followed yet.

The table was conspicuous and in the center of the restaurant, near the bar and within view of the front entrance. It wasn't fancy and the bar's motif was a cross between a fifties' diner and a sixties' supper club, only darker.

"If this isn't suitable, we do have a table toward the back," she said.

"Oh, no," Callan said, setting his briefcase down and nodding his approval. "This is great. Couldn't be better."

The hostess set a menu in front of him. "Lashonda will be with you in a moment."

Lashonda arrived promptly, asking for his drink order. Callan looked over the menu, which listed the local microbrews on tap, but set it down. Two young men he suspected had been in the tan car walked in, one flicking a half-smoked cigarette onto the sidewalk before doing so. His eyes followed them to the bar where they sat a safe distance away from his table.

"Sir? Have you decided on a beer?"

Callan suddenly realized Lashonda was still standing beside him. "Oh, no, I'm sorry. I've changed my mind. A Manhattan. Bulleit Bourbon, please."

When she left, he glanced toward the bar again. The men weren't paying attention to him. They were too busy ordering their own drinks. They chided each other, laughed occasionally, then followed with silence. The man who had flicked his cigarette onto the sidewalk strummed his fingers on the edge of the bar, apparently needing another one. He gestured to his partner that he was going to step outside and set one foot on the floor to do so, but the other man held him back with one hand on his arm while glancing Callan's way.

Callan turned away just in time.

A good time to get my work out, he decided. Callan pulled his briefcase onto his lap and unlocked it just far enough to pull a couple of worthless papers. He set the briefcase beside him and hid the documents behind the bottled condiments on the table just enough for the men to see he was working on something important but not enough to glean that the documents were bogus. He wished Conner Whaite's real documents were in front of him. He was eager to learn what Conner wrote. For the time being, however, the food-stained papers in hand served their purpose.

Lashonda arrived with his drink. Callan took a sip and said it was perfect. She asked if he'd like to order some food.

Callan thought it was a good idea but ordered only an appetizer—a basket of spicy, hand-battered fried pickles. Fast, easy, and filling.

"Thank you," he said. "I'll nibble my way through this research."

She glanced down, made a face, indicating that she thought he had some odd research in his hands, but told him to let her know if he changed his mind and wanted something more.

Callan looked toward the bar. The men had their drinks now too. They appeared content, sitting and talking, periodically turning their heads just enough to catch a peek of him out of the corner of their eyes. Callan pretended to work, making overt expressions as though the information he was reading was quite interesting and informative, if not astonishing. He didn't expect the two to be intelligent enough to interpret his expressions as anything but.

Soon, Lashonda returned and asked Callan if the drink was to his liking. He replied that it was, and could she tell him where the restrooms were located. He pointed in the direction she indicated, hoping the men saw the gesture and realized he'd be leaving his table.

Callan stuffed the worthless papers back into his briefcase, took a sip of his Manhattan, rose, and told a passing busser that he'd only be a minute, he wasn't leaving the establishment. He turned and walked to the back, taking his time, making sure the men saw that he'd left the table with his briefcase behind. When he'd loitered long enough in the restroom, he exited and returned to the dining area.

He glanced toward the bar first then toward his table. Not only were the men gone from the bar, but his briefcase and its contents were gone as well.

Callan's pleased smile was short-lived when a heavyset woman wearing penetrating perfume and gaudy jewelry around her neck tapped him rapidly on the shoulder and exclaimed, "You should never leave valuables behind, sir. That was very foolish. Why, you weren't gone but ten seconds before two men came right over to your table, snatched up your briefcase, and zoomed out the door. I can't believe you'd do such a thing." She craned her neck around Callan toward the front door. "Oh, they're gone by now. You'll never catch them. That, sir, was an irresponsible thing to do."

Callan couldn't agree more and thanked her profusely even though she didn't let up on the scolding. He paid his tab, bid the woman good day, and walked briskly out the door. A short, thin man, weathered by age, limped toward him from the street curb, breathing heavily. He stopped Callan just as Callan exited the restaurant, eager to talk.

"Are you looking for your briefcase?" he asked.

"Yes, did you see the men?" Callan responded, surprised.

"I sure did," he said, grabbing Callan by the shirt sleeve to balance himself, taking a moment to catch his breath. "I figured something wasn't right. I was going in the door, and I saw them. Saw it all. Saw the car they got into too."

"Was it a tan one?" Callan asked.

The man was taken aback. "Why, yes, sir, smudged with dirt too," he said, brushing thin strands of bristly, gray hair from his eyes. "I got close enough to see their plates, but I couldn't make out the numbers because dirt was smeared all over them. Looks like they did it on purpose if you ask me."

"I suspect they did. I thank you very much for trying, however."

Callan turned to walk toward his car, but the old man tugged on his shirt sleeve.

"But I did get their county identification number." The old man's sagging eyes suddenly sparkled with pride.

This time, it was Callan taken aback. "County identification number?"

"Yes, sir, you know, the number in the lower right corner of the license plate that tells what county the car is registered in. I got it. That wasn't smudged. I 'spect they forgot to rub over that number if it makes any difference."

"Yes, yes, the county number would be very helpful," Callan said.

"It was forty-eight, sir."

Callan cocked his head as if he didn't hear correctly. "Forty-eight?" He didn't recognize the county number that forty-eight belonged to. It wasn't Vermillion County, the one he had suspected it to be.

"Yes, sir, forty-eight. Madison County, the county next door to the east." The man paused for Callan to process the information. "That's where the city of Anderson is at. Madison County."

Anderson? Not Vermillion? Anderson was a good hour and a half away from Vermillion. *Why Anderson?*

"Are you sure?" Callan asked.

"Oh yes, sir, yes, sir," he repeated. "I used to live in

Anderson. I'd know forty-eight anywhere. And it was a Chevy Malibu they was a drivin'. They drive Chevys in Anderson, you know, bein' a GM town and all. Oh yeah, it was Anderson all right."

The old man tittered at his good deed, then let go of Callan's sleeve.

CHAPTER

TWENTY-FIVE

Callan jogged to his car. There was no place he had to be, but adrenaline spurted through his veins. Jogging released the energy. When he reached for the door handle, his cell rang from his pants pocket. He pulled it out and stared at the display. The number meant nothing to him. He declined the call, lobbed his phone into the passenger seat, and hopped in. The phone rang again.

This time, Callan waited until the caller had a chance to leave a voice message. When the message was received, the voice was unmistakable. Not urgent but unmistakable. The voice was that of Pete Gadsden, one of the geocachers at Mount Nebo, needing to speak with him.

"Where are you?" Callan asked when he called back.

Fortunately, Pete and his partner, Rhonda, were within driving distance of where he was. He met them halfway at a restaurant Callan was familiar with, which he thought the couple from New York could also find easily.

They arrived shortly after he did, friendly as he remembered but more reserved, even nervous. They had on the same clothes, but they appeared dustier and even more worn, as if they'd been hiking to find more caches or sleeping uncomfortably in their car.

A waitress guided them to a cozy table in the corner of a room dominated by a large stone hearth. Dim lighting and rich mahogany paneling subdued the couple even more.

"Two Sun King Crème Ales, please," he told the waitress. "Sweet tea for me; no, make it half and half." Callan glanced at Pete and said, "My treat. If you're hungry, let's also eat."

Pete quickly grabbed a menu off the table while Rhonda touched his hand to stop him.

"Oh, we couldn't," she said.

"But I was hoping you would," Callan replied to make her feel more comfortable. "I'm kind of hungry myself. Perhaps you'd like a Beef Manhattan."

"Manhattan?"

"Kind of like an open face, but it's not. Totally not. It's an Indiana thing. Or maybe a breaded tenderloin? You can't return to New York without having one."

Pete said he'd like to try both. Rhonda gave him a look but agreed to a tenderloin, reminding him that they didn't come to eat. She engaged in small talk until the waitress returned with their beers and tea.

"Cheers," Callan said, lifting his glass.

The men drank heartily. Rhonda sipped. She sat her mug gently on the tabletop, licked her top lip, and stared at Callan intently.

"We have a confession to make," she said, turning to Pete

for his reaction. "We're rather embarrassed to have to tell you this, but what we did wasn't right. We hope you'll forgive us and tell us what to do."

Callan set his glass down as well, alternating his sight between the two.

"We may have obstructed the sheriff's investigation at Mount Nebo. That's why we called you."

Callan remembered their last conversation when he didn't believe the two were being transparent. "You'll have to explain," he said. "I'm afraid I'm not following you." Although, clearly, he believed he was.

Rhonda looked at Pete for motivation.

"We talked about geocaching with you briefly in Benton County," Pete said, "but are you very familiar with it?"

Callan admitted that he wasn't, only what they'd told him.

"People like us are called geocachers. We find caches that other people bury, all over the world. We use our GPS to locate these caches based upon coordinates provided by the geocacher who buried the box. Usually the swag, I mean the treasure in each cache, is nominal in value and in a waterproof container of some kind. You find all types of caches, but most are placed in ammo boxes. On our website, each cache is required to have a paper log for each person who visits to record their personal code and the date they visited. A pen or pencil is usually provided."

Rhonda interjected. "Before we found that young man's body at Mount Nebo, we were at Mount Gilboa, just a few miles to the east. There's a geocache there too."

"Is it similar to what you found at Mount Nebo?"

"No," she said reservedly. "It's very different. At Mount Gilboa, the cache is a memorial to a young child who died. It's a traditional cache and very easy to find. Mount Gilboa is peaceful, one of the more peaceful locations we've been to. There's a church amid the countryside. Cattle grazed in a pasture. Birds sang in the trees. The sounds harmonized. We couldn't help but feel as if we were as one in spirit with them."

"There's a cemetery too," Pete said. "The cache directed us to the gravesite of this couple's little girl named Lila. We found her grave in the Mount Gilboa Cemetery. It's a granite stone, pinkish in color, with the inscription *Precious in His Sight.* It touched us very deeply."

"I'm sure it did." Callan listened closely but felt he was missing something. "But why are you telling me this?"

"Because it was in stark contrast to the experience that we had at Mount Nebo," Rhonda replied sternly. "The little girl's stone was a wonderful but solemn reminder that all life is precious. Mount Nebo was a grim reminder that it can also be evil and terrifying."

"You see," Pete said, taking a sip of beer as he collected his thoughts, "we'd just come from Mounds State Park in Anderson the day before. There's a geocache near the Great Mound at the park there. With it being an ancient Native American burial ground, we just knew the experience would be fascinating."

Pete and Rhonda exchanged glances.

"But we were wrong," Rhonda said. "We couldn't find the cache. The website warned us that it would be difficult to find because of the steep terrain. And the foliage was thick. There were too many obstacles to face, so we turned back."

"I see."

"I'm not sure you do. I didn't explain myself very well. When I said there were obstacles, they weren't physical obstacles. We've been in steep terrain before. It wasn't that. There were many unseen spiritual obstacles that prevented us from moving forward. We were very much alone in the park as we looked for the cache, but . . . we didn't feel alone. Am I making sense?"

Callan studied Rhonda Comer's eyes. She didn't make sense, yet her pupils had a compelling attraction, gravitating toward an inner soul, genuine and thoughtful.

"It felt as if something was in the ferns and foliage where the cache was supposed to be," she added.

"Like what?" Callan asked. "Is there even a cache near the Great Mound? Was it a hoax?"

"No, it's not a hoax," Pete said adamantly. "There have been too many valid accounts of finding the cache exactly as the website indicates at the coordinates specified. No, we knew we were very, very close. We just chose not to pursue it any further."

Callan turned his attention to Rhonda for an explanation.

"The park has an astonishing ancient connection to the stars and sun, Mr. Morrow," Rhonda said. "We'd have loved to have stayed, but it was unsettling. It wasn't worth staying."

"And so, you left the park?"

Rhonda nodded. "There's a meadery nearby. I'm quite fond of braggot, so we stopped to refresh ourselves and reconnect spiritually to determine what we should do next. That's when we decided to go to Mount Gilboa and Mount Nebo."

"But why there?" Callan asked. "I mean, it's so out of the way from Anderson and other parts of the state."

"I know, but there seemed to be a tie between Mounds Park and Mount Nebo. Mount Gilboa was just a stop for us because it was near. It was Mount Nebo we really wanted to see."

"What's the connection?"

"Astronomical," Rhonda said. "We read somewhere that Mounds Park was tied to other ancient mounds in Indiana as a way of reading stars and predicting the future."

Callan grabbed his tea but shook his head before taking a swig. "And that was attractive to you?"

"Oh yes," Rhonda responded excitedly, leaning forward. "Isn't it to you?"

He shook his head again in a way not to insult their beliefs but to let them know that he was not a follower of astronomy, astrology, or the occult. His attraction was limited to solving Conner and Logan's murders and finding Marissa. "Then I take it you were disappointed in what you found at Mount Nebo," he said.

"We realized immediately something wasn't right about the place. You see, it was the same feeling that we had at Mounds Park, the exact opposite of the peacefulness at Mount Gilboa. That's when we found the young man's body. It was horrifying. It really was. We've been shaken by the experience ever since."

Rhonda started to say more but stopped.

"There's a reason we contacted you," Pete said. "We have a confession to make about the cache."

"First of all," Rhonda said, lifting her index finger to make a point, "I want you to know it's perfectly legal and within the etiquette rules of geocaching to take things from a cache when you find something of interest to you."

"As long as you replace the item you take with something of equal or greater value," Pete added. "That's what we did. We left three arrowheads and a geocoin of our own that directed other geocachers to a spiritual astrological website where they could locate other geocache sites of a similar nature."

"Okay," Callan said apprehensively. "Not sure I understand completely, but okay. So what are you confessing to?"

"What we didn't tell you was that we took something from

the cache. We concealed that information from you . . . and from the sheriff who was investigating."

Callan's eyes narrowed. "What did you take?"

"Information that disproved the reason why we came to Mount Nebo in the first place. We'd read that it was a site tied astronomically to Mounds Park, but inside the cache was a crudely written documentary about how the connection was all a hoax."

"I'm sorry, but I'm still not connecting why you feel you must apologize to me for taking this piece of paper."

"Perhaps we don't need to," Pete said. "Perhaps it's the authorities we need to speak to."

"I'd say so, especially if this piece of paper explains a motive for the murder."

"But we came to you first because you seemed to be an intelligent man who had a particular interest in the young man's death and would know what to do with the information."

Callan shrugged. "Sounds like you've already told me what you need to do: go to the authorities in Benton County."

"No, let me explain," Pete said. He looked at Rhonda who'd buried her face in the palms of her hands. "Before we found Logan's body, we found the cache and the piece of paper disproving Mount Nebo as a significant astronomical site. We took the paper because we didn't want others who came to the site to be as disappointed as we were. That was wrong. We shouldn't have taken the document. We decided we needed to return to Mount Nebo to replace the piece of paper into the cache."

"Did you?" Callan asked.

Pete sighed. "No. That's what we're trying to confess. Before we could do that, we saw that man there."

Callan shook his head. "What man?"

"You know," Rhonda said. "The man that creeped me out."

"He's the one who left right before you arrived, with the decal of your college on the back window of his car," Pete said. "And . . . we didn't tell you something that could be helpful to the investigation."

"Something we saw," Rhonda said.

The two hesitated. Callan grew impatient. "What was it?" he asked sharply.

"We saw him, that man, trying to find the cache, but, of course, the sheriff had already taken it away as evidence."

"Where's the paper now?"

Pete reached into a side pocket and pulled out a worn, crumpled piece of white college-ruled paper. He unfolded the creases and handed it to Callan.

"We want to give it to you," he said.

Callan raised his hands to stop him. "I don't want anything to do with it. No, what the two of you must do is return to Benton County immediately and turn this over to the authorities. If you suspect the man in the car with the Vermillion decal was there for this piece of paper or had anything to do with Logan Allister's death, then you have an obligation to go straight to the sheriff. After all, Logan may have been the one who placed the paper in the box before you found it, hoping to be the one to disprove the significance of Mount Nebo. The murder and this paper may be linked."

Both Pete and Rhonda took a deep breath.

"What's the matter?" Callan asked.

The two turned to each other with solemn expressions of hopelessness.

"What's the matter?" he asked again more boldly.

"We can't," Pete said. "Somehow, we have to return to New York from here."

"That's fine. Head back as soon as you return to Benton County."

"No, you don't understand. We're not even sure we can make it back to New York."

Callan studied the glum faces of the young couple. Their eyes took on a sudden and embarrassed look of sadness. He lowered his voice with compassion. "You need money, right?"

Pete nodded. "We don't know how we're going to make it back home let alone back track to Benton County before we head there. We didn't budget very well."

Callan saw the waitress coming from the kitchen toward the table with a steaming tray of food. He reached into his billfold and pulled out all the cash he had, three twenties and a ten. "Here. Take this for now. I'll go to the ATM in the restaurant's entry and get you more cash after we finish our meal."

"We couldn't do that," Pete said.

"You have no choice. You must go to Benton County, and you must get home. What choice do you have?"

The waitress placed the breaded tenderloins under their noses. The smell of the hot, spicy sandwiches tantalized them. They appeared to remember suddenly what it was like to have a hot meal. Their eyes reflected a desire for more.

Pete reached for the cash and thanked Callan humbly. "Okay," he said, "we'll head back as soon as we're done eating. I promise. Thanks. I mean it."

He folded the ragged piece of paper in his hands and started to replace it in his pocket, but Callan grasped the letter before Pete could do so. The young man stared at him confused.

"I said I didn't want to take it," Callan replied, unfolding the edges. "I didn't say anything about not wanting to read it first."

Chapter

Twenty-Six

"New briefcase?" Terese asked the next day.

She sat on the couch, flipping through pages of a magazine, as Callan prepared to leave for the college. She took notice of most everything about her husband recently, including his uptight demeanor, lack of attention to neatness, what clothes he wore, how he wore them, and, more importantly, his increasing lack of transparency about the details of Marissa Reynolds's absence and the death of the two young men.

He didn't respond.

"What happened to the other one?" she asked.

"I wish I knew," he said, continuing to get ready without looking up.

"You don't know . . . or don't want to tell me?"

He turned abruptly. "It was stolen," he said as if it should satisfy her.

Terese set the magazine on her lap. "Stolen?" She tried not to sound alarmed. "Whoever would want to steal a briefcase of yours?"

"My thoughts exactly."

She sensed irritation, not toward her necessarily. "I hope you didn't have anything you needed in it. Did you lose anything valuable?"

"An old cheeseburger I was starting to get attached to," he said flippantly.

Terese wrinkled her nose, no longer caring to sound compassionate. "Where did this happen?"

"At a restaurant yesterday. I left it carelessly behind when I went to the restroom."

"Oh, Callan, how many times . . ."

He lifted a finger. "If you must know, two men were eyeing my case because they wanted the information that was in it."

Terese rose from the couch, this time not willing to hide her alarm.

Callan told her about the events in greater detail in between bursts of his wife's objections to him continuing with the case.

"I don't like this," she said. "I don't like this whole mess at all."

He stopped giving details and walked toward her, arms outstretched. "Please, don't worry," he said, kissing her forehead.

"How can I not, Callan?" she asked. Sadness reflected from her eyes as he left the house.

~

Callan's walk across campus to his office was unremarkable except for meeting Glynis Fordworth who greeted him as he entered his building and remarked that he didn't look at all happy.

"I'm afraid you'll be even less pleased," she said. "Your early appointment didn't stick around."

"Appointment?" he asked confused.

"Didn't you have an appointment with a student this morning?"

"Not to my knowledge."

"Well, then, a student must've stopped by, hoping to catch you."

Callan glanced at his watch, then turned away to think. "He or she?"

"He."

"Did you recognize him?" he asked.

"I've seen him around, but I'm not sure of his name," she said.

"What did he look like?"

"Tall, nice looking, sandy hair . . ."

Callan frowned and continued his trek into the building.

"You know him?" she asked, turning as he held the door open.

"Yeah, I'll give him a call later. Thanks for telling me."

Callan gave Mitchell Dells a call when he reached his office, but it went immediately to voice mail. Just as well, he thought. He had more important things on his mind, such as reading the research papers Conner Whaite had collected and kept in his bedroom.

Most of Conner's documents were handwritten. He leafed through them quickly, dismayed that there didn't seem to be anything substantive from a reliable source. There were no documents from Professor Banks, no published material, just handwritten notes in Conner's handwriting. To make matters worse, Conner's penmanship was nearly illegible. Callan surmised he must've used his own brand of shorthand to either mask his findings or to write down as much as he could as fast as he could.

The more Callan read, the more he suspected the latter. Dates at the top of the notes indicated that they were written recently, but that was the extent of what seemed to make sense.

Solar alignment was a recurring theme. There were scribbles and rough sketches of what Callan thought to be earthworks and other ancient Native American mounds with arrows pointing to the sun and star constellations.

The word *Pleiades* appeared more than once. The only thing he knew of Pleiades was that it was a constellation. Where in the sky it was located, he couldn't remember. Conner's illustrations were not specific. Callan couldn't even recall what the constellation depicted.

Place names also repeated in the notes, even though they were abbreviated and never fully defined. He realized eventually that AND stood for Anderson and NC was not North Carolina but the east central city of New Castle. He never did figure out CC, B, or CHIL. He searched on the map feature of his phone for clues, but nothing made sense. What Callan did decide, however, was that Conner had tried to tie locations together for a specific, but unidentifiable, objective, including the abbreviation MtN for Mount Nebo.

Callan sat back in his seat and tapped a pencil rapidly on the surface of his desk. Perhaps he didn't need to rely entirely on Conner's notes to determine what Professor Banks's theories were all about. If he could identify the class the notes were taken from, other students who attended the lectures could clarify the theories for him. An idea came to mind. He grabbed his phone and dialed security.

"John?" Callan asked when the director answered.

"Where are you?" John replied, a tone of sarcasm in his voice. "Mount Arafat? Marrakesh? Oz, even?"

"My office."

"That's a novel place for you to be."

"Yeah, yeah, I get it. Hey, is Travis around?"

John cleared his throat. "Yes, he just came back from a round. Need to see him?"

"Phone conversation is fine if he's available," Callan said.

He waited patiently for John to transfer the call.

"Wellman here."

"Travis? Callan Morrow. You work late some nights, right?" Callan asked. "Were you the guy that found Professor Banks in his office late at night with students in a class discussion?"

"Yes, sir, twice. Both times were similar, really. It was during normal rounds at night. I noticed lights coming from Professor Banks's office suite. The door was locked, with no response to my knocks. So I used my master key to enter."

"What time was this approximately?"

"I'd say one time was around eleven o'clock, the other around eleven thirty or so."

"Who was gathered with the professor?"

Travis paused to think. "Well, the first time I'd say four to five students, all male. The second meeting had less, maybe only three."

"Did you recognize any of the students?"

"Can't say that I did at the time," Travis said. "I wish I could go back and see their faces again, knowing what I know now. I'm sure I'd recognize at least some of them."

Callan continued to tap his pencil on the desk with his

free hand. "Tell me something, were you able to hear anything of what they were talking about?"

"No. As soon as they knew I was at the door, their discussion stopped. I did see some writing on the professor's whiteboard. He held a marker in his hand, and he was standing, so I'm pretty sure he'd been configuring something on the board when I walked in."

Callan set the pencil down, suddenly interested. "What were you able to make out?"

"I didn't look all that hard," he replied candidly. "I was there to make sure the situation was safe, and everyone was in the office of their own free will. I didn't pay that much attention to the whiteboard. If I had to guess, however, I'd say the drawings were celestial in nature. I saw a drawing of the sun. There were also circles and rectangles with arrows and dotted lines from one drawing to another." Travis paused. "What I noticed most, however, were the expressions of the students in the office at the time. They looked like they'd just come out of a trance when I walked in. I thought they'd been hypnotized at first, but that wasn't the case. I think they were just engrossed in what the professor had to say."

Callan thanked Travis for the information. It didn't give him the insight he wanted, but Travis's observations were interesting just the same.

"May I make a suggestion, sir?" Travis said before the call ended. "Someone who might know more about Professor Banks's group discussions and teachings might be Professor Leonard."

"Warren Leonard?"

"Yes, sir. He teaches astronomy. Do you know him?"

Callan knew Professor Leonard quite well. An excellent

suggestion. He wondered why he hadn't thought of the man himself.

"He might be able to help you," Travis said. "I hope so anyway."

Callan hoped so too.

CHAPTER

TWENTY-SEVEN

To Callan's surprise, Professor Warren Leonard was equally eager to meet and speak with Callan. They greeted each other briefly, mentioned the weather, and questioned whether VC would finish with a winning football season.

Callan found Professor Leonard personable and lighthearted as he'd been in previous encounters. Papers and books were scattered in neat little piles on his desk, stratified by a system he was sure only Professor Leonard understood. He wore a smart blue pin-striped Oxford shirt and dress pants, neatly pressed, and presentable. Not a hair on his graying head was out of place, all trimmed to fit the contour of his scalp. He was fit and tanned, with a solid handshake. Callan wasn't sure why the man's appearance and demeanor astonished him so much. He assumed it was because he always thought of astronomer educators as being somewhat out there in space . . . physically and mentally appearing more like a mad professor in a white lab coat. That wasn't the case with Professor Leonard. He was grounded, alert and extroverted.

When their football conversation had run its course, the professor leaned back in his chair and touched his fingertips together. Callan presumed his glowering demeanor reflected what he thought of Randall Banks and how best to preface their discussion without sounding overly critical or biased.

"Theories?" he asked Callan. "You called and said you'd like to speak with me about Banks's theories." His sarcastic tone was thick and biting. "I'll certainly be happy to talk with you on any matter you'd like to discuss, but I must tell you that I don't like the man, much less care for his theories."

Callan smiled, hoping he didn't appear amused.

"Oh, not that I have anything against him, mind you," Professor Leonard continued. "But his research protocols are, how should I put it, unorthodox. And if you're wondering what I'm talking about, I'm referring to those damn sweat lodges he conducts."

Callan's eyes widened with curiosity.

The professor saw the interest on Callan's face and backtracked immediately. "Forgive me. I shouldn't have made that comment. I have nothing to back up my statement, only what I've read in the papers, but it'd be something I'd believe that man to be behind. Yes, I'm sure of it, but I'm also sure you didn't come here to listen to my unfounded opinions. How can I help you?"

Callan pulled Conner Whaite's notes from a briefcase and handed them to Professor Leonard. He explained what they were, how he got them, and what he was trying to decipher from them. What he'd concluded from them wasn't much. Callan asked if the scholar could shed some light on the student's notes.

Professor Leonard took out a pair of reading glasses and scoured through the pages, taking time to look for familiar words, phrases, and themes that he knew to belong to Randall Banks's teachings. He scratched and shook his head numerous times, tsking often, and chuckling periodically. As he leafed through the pages, he placed them methodically in neat columns on his desk, referring to specific stacks as he read something further.

"Mr. Whaite took copious notes, didn't he?" the professor asked, peering above his glasses, breaking the silence. "Much of it gibberish, of course."

"That's what I made of it," Callan replied. "Do you believe the parts that don't make sense are the lessons themselves or how Conner interpreted the lessons?"

"Oh, undoubtedly the lessons, but even more gibberish than what usually comes out of Banks's mouth." Contempt spewed from his lips. Professor Leonard sighed and leaned back in his chair to stretch. He rubbed his eyes and shook his head. "Lord, what a mess we've made," he said.

Callan didn't understand. "*We?*"

"The college, administration, educators, colleagues, all of us. If this is the type of unabashed bull-hocky we're teaching our young men and women, we've lost our way, Professor. Is no one looking over Banks's shoulders to see what he's teaching? Where are his lesson plans coming from? It appears Mr. Whaite has captured what he's heard quite thoroughly, but I have to say it's nonsense. Pure and simple nonsense."

Callan exhaled a plume of frustration into the stale air. "So where do I go from here? I mean, Dr. Overby has charged me with getting to the bottom of what's been going on—alongside the authorities and John Steinmeier in security, of course."

Hope glimmered from the professor's eyes. He leaned forward and pointed with two fingers at Callan. "Then let me do this," he said. "Instead of telling you what I believe Conner Whaite is trying to document in his notes, let me give you what other researchers more credible than Banks have written."

Professor Leonard rose and strode to a tall bookshelf on the opposite wall. Much like his desk, reference books, some on top of others, hiding other books behind them, were organized by a method only Professor Leonard seemed to understand. He pulled several books and returned to his chair, smiling warmly at them as though meeting good friends after a long absence.

Callan readied his pen and notebook.

Professor Leonard raised his hand for patience. "I have several white papers and books very much related to what our Professor Banks is theorizing, and I could overwhelm you with data, but no information, so please, give me a moment while I look." He opened one book, a bland, dark brown, hardbound reference worn from age. "You probably gathered from Mr. Whaite's notes—one of the few things that could be gathered—that the mounds and earthworks at Mounds State Park near Anderson, Indiana, are very significant to Professor Banks's teachings."

Callan said that he understood that but hadn't gleaned much more.

"Well, there are two experts, Donald Cochran and Beth McCord, who wrote a book entitled *The Archaeology of Anderson Mounds*. It relates so closely to your investigation, Professor. I'm almost positive that you'll find the information useful. No, not just useful, but invaluable. Do you know what I mean?"

"I will, once you explain it to me and can tie it into Banks's theories."

Professor Leonard flicked the mention of the word theories away with his wrist. "Oh, those damn theories. They're not new and not even original."

"Wait, what do you mean? Are you saying that he's a part of a larger, more organized society that he's promoting?"

"No, not at all. No, Banks is too narcissistic to use someone else's ideas. What I meant to say is that geologists have come to their own conclusions about the mounds at Anderson and their relationship to other earthworks in the region. Professor Banks has taken these new developments and created his own interpretations."

"Interpretations of what?"

"Astronomical alignments." Professor Leonard smiled proudly, glowing as he thought of the information he was about to reveal. "You see, the mounds at Mounds Park are made up of several earthworks," he explained. "These earthworks vary in size, shape, and location. In addition to the Great Mound, there are the Circle Mound, Dalman Mound, Fiddleback Mound, and Mounds Bluff where human remains have been located. There are smaller, less significant mounds throughout the park as well, but less is known about them."

His eyes widened with excitement as he took a breath and wet his lips. "The Great Mound is the largest and most impressive, Professor Morrow, measuring over 350 feet across in a circle. A ditch about sixty feet wide and ten feet deep is on the inside of the outer circle of the Great Mound. Then, on the inside, is a platform that looks like a mound itself."

"What's significant about them?"

"In 1988, archaeological teams determined that there was a specific purpose and order to the Great Mound and the other smaller mounds in the vicinity. They believed they were astronomical in nature, relating to the solstices and equinoxes. On December twenty-first of that year, the scientists returned to test their theories. They learned that the platform of the Great Mound served as a horizon. They were able to document solar and lunar alignments with the mound and believed these alignments were in sync with other mounds."

"You mean, other mounds within the park."

"No!" he exclaimed, his voice rising. "With other mounds within Indiana."

Professor Leonard set the books aside and hurried to a whiteboard near his desk. He began drawing circles at various areas on the board. "They aligned with mounds at New Castle and the Bertsch farms near Cambridge City. Look here! If you draw a straight line from Anderson to Bertsch through New Castle, you'll see they align perfectly. I'd go out on a limb and say that the mounds near Chillicothe, Ohio, also fit into this alignment."

Callan remembered a CHIL abbreviation in Conner's notes, but he shook his head, still unconvinced. "How controversial is what you've told me with other researchers, Professor?"

Professor Leonard took a deep breath and stared at the carpet as he made his way back to his chair. "Well, you'll always have controversy and researchers who dispute the solar alignments that I just showed you. There's no getting away from naysayers."

"Who do *you* believe?" Callan asked.

The professor smiled and lifted his index finger in the air. "I believe it can't be denied that the Adena and Hopewell people who built these mounds knew more about our Mother Earth and the celestial heavens than we ever hope to attain even with our sophisticated technology and pompous intelligence."

Callan nodded. "But there's one thing that bothers me," he said.

"And what's that?"

"Why weren't these alignments discovered before 1988, and why is Professor Banks taking the alignments one step further than what you explained to me, to Mount Nebo in Benton County?"

Professor Leonard laughed heartily. Callan didn't mean to be funny, but his questions amused the senior professor deeply.

"First of all, in answer to your first question, we didn't have accurate and appropriate maps and documentation of relationships of all the mounds before 1988. As unbelievable as it sounds, researchers had to develop accurate maps at each site in Indiana, precise in every way, before they could make these final conclusions. That was a huge undertaking, requiring a precise method in protocol, which couldn't be shortened."

"Okay, that makes sense, but what about Professor Banks's fascination with Mount Nebo? How does Mount Nebo fit in with this alignment research?"

Professor Leonard shrugged. "It doesn't, as far as I can see."

"What?" Callan asked, surprised. "Then what's he thinking?"

"Let's look at it from Randall Banks's perspective," he said. "If Banks took the solar and celestial alignments to heart, as I believe he did from a spiritual and religious standpoint, then Mount Nebo could also have spiritual and religious significance to him. If you find a map of Indiana, Callan, and draw a line from where the mounds are from Cambridge City to New Castle to Anderson and beyond . . ."

"We'd find that the Mount Nebo prominence aligned right along with them," Callan said, suddenly understanding.

"Exactly, but forget about Mount Nebo for a moment.

Look at the religious significance of the original Mount Nebo in Jordan."

"Where God gave Moses a view of the Promised Land," Callan said.

"Yes, and even though Moses wasn't allowed to enter, before he died there God did grant him a look, a precious glimpse of that land and His promise."

Callan took a deep breath and exhaled slowly.

Professor Leonard allowed the information to sink in for several seconds.

"You don't think," Callan said eventually, "I mean, you don't think that Banks believes that God is going to give him a similar view of something precious at this Mount Nebo in Indiana, do you?"

Professor Leonard leaned in. "Why not? I'm not sure the candle is lit all that brightly in his pumpkin. You must admit that he's not dealing with coherent thoughts regarding the sweat lodges."

Callan raised his hand in objection. "Banks hasn't been officially linked to the sweat lodge incident yet," he warned.

"But that doesn't make it not true."

"I understand, but the sheriff . . ."

"The sheriff," Professor Leonard scoffed. "Forget the sheriff. Think for yourself, Professor. Think about the facts you've gathered."

Callan nodded and thought back to the facts he did have. Although not tied directly to Conner's death yet, Randall Banks had been seen at Mount Nebo where Logan died.

"Okay," Callan said, relenting. "I'll agree on one thing. Banks is on a self-centered quest involving our students. I know he was at Mount Nebo on the day of Logan Allister's death. I have witnesses to that effect."

"Ah!" Professor Leonard said. "He has a vision, Professor. I'd bet Randall Banks is working on a vision and wants to see it come to fruition. I'm sure of it." He returned suddenly to Conner's notes, shuffling a certain pile he'd set aside earlier. When he found the piece of paper he was looking for, he raised it in the air to make his point. "I was concerned the moment I saw this one page, but I didn't know at the time what I was looking at."

"I'm almost afraid to ask," Callan said.

"As well you should. It's in reference to the Pleiades constellation."

Callan remembered the name. "Yes, what is that?"

"Stars of the Seven Sisters. It's the most visible and nearest star cluster to Earth. In mythology, the name not only has to do with seven sisters, but with seven *divine* sisters."

Callan couldn't think fast enough to know where Professor Leonard was going with his line of reasoning, but hearing the word *divine* caused him to pause. "You mean heavenly?" He remembered his conversation with Margot. "Banks expects a vision from heaven, according to his wife. He hopes to receive this vision very soon—I suspect during the equinox."

"You must act quickly then."

"But why? About what?"

Professor Leonard rifled through the papers he'd been reviewing until he apparently found what he was looking for. He lifted a single sheet in the air. "Conner Whaite and Logan Allister were both men," he said.

Callan shook his head, not understanding the relevance.

The professor shook the piece of paper wildly. "Pleiades. Seven sisters. Don't you see? I suspect in the back of Banks's mind he believed using men for his theory wouldn't work. He may have had a revelation of some kind from somewhere or found additional information from research that made him feel that way. Their deaths by accident or murder only confirmed his suspicion. It meant he wasn't going to accomplish the heavenly objectives he'd established."

"So you're saying that the Pleiades or using seven divine sisters may be the key."

Professor Leonard sat back and smiled, seemingly content that Callan had finally followed his train of thought.

"But that means Banks may put Marissa through the same ceremonies that killed Conner and injured Logan."

"That's exactly what I'm saying."

Callan looked away, unable to think or fathom anything more. "I had hoped it wasn't going to be like that," he said. "I had hoped, as others did, that Marissa was just wanting to find herself somewhere."

"Oh, I believe it's much more serious than that," Professor Leonard said. "I believe she's in grave danger, Professor. Marissa Reynolds is in very grave danger."

CHAPTER

TWENTY-EIGHT

Callan practically stumbled back to his office. The warning Professor Leonard professed as he left his office chilled him to the core, leaving him emotionally and almost physically paralyzed. He sat on a park bench in the campus mall, rested his elbows on his knees, and buried his face within the palms of his hands. Callan could hardly breathe as fear for Marissa crept slowly up his spine. Perspiration formed at his brow. Sticky. Uncomfortable. He wiped it away. The beads returned, heavier than before. He took several deep breaths.

"Oh God, what am I to do?" he prayed. "Where do I go from here?"

He tried again to rationalize that Marissa's disappearance and Conner and Logan's deaths were not his problems to solve. There were authorities in Vermillion and Benton counties capable and responsible for solving the crimes. But not him.

The situation was beyond his scope of expertise.

Callan took several deep breaths. He closed his eyes and remembered the night his parents died. A glowing bronze aura in his room. Close, still, warming. Taking him in his arms, telling him it was going to be okay when he didn't know how it could be. Holding him in arms, a distorted resemblance of wings. Physical but spiritual. Strength with gentleness. Male and female. Surrounded by infinite love.

He looked up into the sycamores on the mall, remembering the comfort that remained when the presence left. Suddenly, a thought crossed his mind. Crazy at first. Or perhaps divinely planted. Either way, he grinned, his perspective changed. What if *he* was the presence Marissa needed? An angel, of sorts. A pang struck him in the gut . . . of guilt, remorse, conviction . . . realizing he'd been blessed with such a guardian but was unwilling to pay it forward. Callan stood, facing a cool breeze that blew into his face.

"But nothing's going to get done sitting on my butt," he said.

Callan arrived back at his office and scanned through Conner's notes once more, using insight Professor Leonard had provided about the mounds near Anderson and their possible connection to Mount Nebo. Perhaps he could now read Conner's notes with more clarity and understanding. He didn't have a chance to read for very long. Three timid knocks at his door broke his train of thought.

"Yes?" he asked, gathering the notes and stuffing them into one of his larger, lower desk drawers.

The door inched open. Callan saw strands of Mitchell

Dell's sandy hair first peep around the edge. "Professor?"

Callan acknowledged him.

Mitchell entered, head held low, his gaze on the floor. When he finally made eye contact, his sparkling blue eyes were dull, distant, void of clarity and interest.

Callan asked him what was wrong.

"I haven't seen Marissa," he said, keeping his distance. "I haven't heard from her, either—not since Logan's death anyway. It's not like her."

Callan urged him to come closer and to take a seat, but he refused. "Has she contacted anyone that you know of?" Callan asked.

"That's just it. No one. No one's heard from her. I don't get it."

Callan remembered a visitor that Glynis said had come earlier. "Did you try to see me this morning?"

Mitchell nodded.

"How can I help?"

Mitchell clenched his jaw and peered off to one side. "I don't know," he said after he'd given it some thought. "I don't know what more can be done."

"Then why did you come?"

He shifted his feet and admitted, "I didn't come to talk about Marissa even though she's on my mind. I don't think there's anything that can be done until Marissa wants it to happen. That's the way it is. I came to talk about Logan."

Callan hoped his surprise didn't show on his face. He extended his hand toward a chair. "Please, Mitchell, won't you take a seat?"

The young man stood his ground. "I can't stay long."

"You don't have to stay long. Tell me what's bothering you, and you can be on your way. It can be as easy as that."

Mitchell stepped forward but didn't sit. "Did you know that Logan and Professor Banks had words right before he was killed?"

Callan nodded. He didn't want to reveal that he'd first heard about it through Zola Krivoshia, the internal auditor.

"Yeah, well, he said that he'd had it after the sweat lodge thing. Logan said that everything Banks was doing was a fraud and that he was going to expose the professor for what he was. He said Banks just laughed it off and said he was a fool and a sore loser, or something like that."

"Do you know what the professor meant by that?"

"No."

"Were there any other threatening remarks?"

"What?"

Callan eyed Mitchell more closely. "I asked if Professor Banks made any threatening remarks to Logan."

"Oh," Mitchell said, eyes darting around him. "I don't know, but don't you see? It doesn't matter. Logan had an argument with Professor Banks and then a few hours later, he's dead. Isn't that enough?"

"I have no reason to doubt your sincerity in telling me this, Mitchell, but, quite frankly, no, it isn't enough. It's circumstantial. It's enough to investigate, but if you're looking for an arrest . . ."

"That's exactly what should happen, Professor," Mitchell said, agitated. Out of anger, he forced a combination body punch at stomach height to an imaginary figure in front of him. He started to hyperventilate, stumbled, then stopped, taking deep breaths to compose himself.

Callan didn't flinch. Alarmed, of course, but he watched Mitchell's anger grow and subside within seconds, realizing he could have easily become a misdirected target. When Mitchell had calmed, he asked, "What just happened, Mitchell?"

Mitchell brushed it off like it was nothing, and said martial arts was how he dispelled his frustration.

"No," Callan said sternly. "I won't accept that. I want to know what just happened there."

"I can't help it, Professor!" he said, rubbing his face, then brushing his fingers over his scalp. "The whole thing pisses me off. Doesn't it you? I mean, Conner's dead, Logan's dead, and Marissa's out there somewhere. Banks is behind it, and I don't know what to do because no one else seems to be doing anything."

Callan stood, walked around his desk and approached Mitchell, touching him on the shoulder to ground him. "We'll get there," he said. "Right now, though, we have to be patient. You must be strong enough to be patient through this, Mitchell, or it'll break you."

The young man nodded and said he'd try. "But you gotta do one thing for me, Professor. You gotta let me help. You gotta keep me in the loop . . . about Marissa, I mean. You'll keep me in the loop? It's the only way I'll keep my sanity through all this. Will you do that for me?"

Callan stepped back and paused, studying his face. "Sure," he said calmly.

Mitchell stumbled out of the office with his head hung lower than when he arrived.

Callan closed the door behind him and locked it.

CHAPTER

TWENTY-NINE

Steam shrouded the darkness. Macabre visions danced. Tears of sweat blocked the eyes. Blinking made them sting. Gasping for breath didn't help. No air to grasp. There was no help. No one was coming. Just the visions.

Logan, is that you?

The stillness grew timeless.

When are they coming? I can't take much more. Why aren't they coming? Why aren't they coming?

~

Callan woke with a start, drenched in perspiration. He stared into the darkness, unsure of his surroundings, but surprisingly calm. He was comfortable. His pillow was familiar. He reached out and felt Terese beside him. Warm, soft, cocooned in flannel nightwear. He turned his head to peer out the window. The morning sun peeked bashfully above the horizon.

He pulled off his covers and sat on the edge of the bed, massaging his face and temples to rid himself of the cobwebs that clouded his senses.

Terese stirred. She turned and reached out, too, but he was too far away.

"Were you dreaming?" she asked.

He lifted his head. "No." He could say that with confidence. He hadn't been dreaming. At least, he didn't think so, but something had happened. He could sense it. That's why he woke.

"I'll make you some coffee," she said, lifting the heavy comforter off her.

"No, don't," he insisted. "I'm fine. I can make it on my own."

"Are you sure?" She didn't sound convinced.

He leaned across the bed to give her a kiss. "Yes, I'm positive."

The phone beside their bed rang. Louder than usual. All phones seemed to ring louder in the early morning while it was still dark.

"Get ready," the voice said, gruff and impertinent. "I'll be there in thirty minutes."

The phone disconnected.

"Who was it?" Terese asked, concerned.

"John, apparently." Callan rose to find his footwear. "Something must've happened this morning. Do you mind making that coffee after all? I'll take a quick shower. No, no breakfast. Coffee'll be fine."

Callan readied quickly and was sitting on the front porch of his Victorian home when John Steinmeier pulled into the drive.

"We have trouble," John said as Callan climbed into the passenger seat. "Some woman called, a young woman." He backed the car out, put it into drive but didn't move forward. "She identified herself as a VC student." John accelerated. They sped down the street. "She said Mitchell Dells didn't call her this morning like he said he would."

"This early?"

"I didn't ask."

"Did she give a name?"

"No."

"Well then," Callan said, unable to fathom why he had hurried out of the house with no more information than John was offering, "how do you know it's not a hoax? Guys don't always call women the next morning. So what if Mitchell didn't call?"

John gave Callan a dirty look. "She didn't sound like a hoax," he said, "and I'm in no position right now to be the judge of when someone is playing a trick on me. Given what's happened to the other two young men, I don't want a third tragedy on my hands, and you don't either."

"Why didn't she call 911 then? Why don't we?"

"Not sure it's that kind of help Mitchell needs," John replied, softening his tone. "Hey, let's just go and assess the situation. We'll call the authorities when we know for sure we have something on our hands worth calling about."

Callan kept still. He'd have called 911 if it was him, but he didn't know enough of the situation to second guess his colleague. He wanted, at least, to know where they were going.

John focused on the road. He looked once into the rearview mirror but otherwise kept driving silently.

"I'd like to know, John. Where are we going?"

John glanced out the side window. "To the field where Conner Whaite and Logan Allister were found."

Callan released an expletive under his breath. His muscles tightened and his jaw clenched. He lifted his rear off the seat to reach his cell tucked deeply inside his pants pocket.

"What are you doing?" John asked. "No, you're not calling the sheriff. Not yet. Keep your phone in your pants."

"Give me one good reason why I should," Callan said, unconvinced.

"What this gal said was that Professor Banks called Mitchell Dells and asked to meet him at the place of the sweat lodge. Dells told her that Banks wanted to show him how he couldn't have possibly been involved in what happened to Whaite and Allister. Mitchell told this girl he wanted to hear what Banks had to say, so he left and said that if he didn't call her by the break of dawn, she was to call me immediately. Morning broke, but Dells hadn't called. She got worried and rang me up."

Callan frowned. "Does that make sense to you?"

"Like I said, I'm in no position right now to make a judgment of that."

"I know, but think about it for a sec."

"I have, but what makes sense anymore, Callan? Tell me that," he said.

"No, I'm serious. Do you believe her story?"

John sighed, glancing out his side window at the passing landscape. "I have no reason not to believe it until I talk to the Dells kid," he muttered. "Then I'll make up my mind, and I suggest you do the same."

John sped into the Bal Hinch to where the original sweat lodge was conducted, where Conner Whaite lost his life and Logan Allister was transported to the hospital. Brown, dry leaves blew across the road to a pasture past a small woodlot on the edge of a stream. He and Callan spotted a tent almost immediately.

"I'll be a son of a gun," John said under his breath, opening the car door.

"What's the matter?"

"That tent," he replied. "It shouldn't be here. After law enforcement was done investigating the lodge where the boys were found, they dismantled it. The damn thing shouldn't be here."

The tent was at the edge of the field close to the woodlot, but far enough from the trees that shadows from the morning sun had yet to reach it. Upon nearing the tent's entrance, they spotted a VC sweatshirt, a pair of jeans, and two boots in the grass, all what would be reasonable for a young man of Mitchell's age to have been wearing. A firepit smoldered a few yards away.

"Mitchell," John called from outside. "It's John Steinmeier and Callan Morrow."

A groan came from inside the tent.

Without hesitation, John whipped back the tent's flap and entered. A groggy Mitchell Dells, clad only in a white t-shirt, briefs, and a pair of dark socks sprawled on a blanket aside a circle of once burning, hot stones. The young man rubbed the back of his head as he tried to sit up.

"Hold on, hold on," John urged. "Not so fast. Lie back down."

"Wha . . . wha . . . oh, man," he moaned but did as he was told.

"Take it easy. Lie still. Just tell me when you're feeling better."

Mitchell continued to grasp his head and moan. "Yeah, but what happened?"

"Do you feel like sitting up?" John asked. "Cal, get his clothes. Can you put your pants on, son?"

Mitchell nodded. "Yeah, but what just . . . ? How did . . . ? How did you find me?"

John told him about the anonymous phone call from a female.

"Oh my God, I forgot I told her to call you." Mitchell's eyes widened. Relief exhaled with each breath.

"Who was she?" John asked.

"What?"

"Who was the girl who called me?"

"Oh, it was Dana." Mitchell rubbed his head some more.

John glanced at Callan who'd just come in with Mitchell's clothes.

"Dana Weiss," Callan said. "She's a friend."

"Here. Take your clothes. They're a little damp from the dew. They'll be uncomfortable. You gonna be all right? Need help getting them on? If not, we'll step outside and wait for you. You sure you're doing okay?"

Mitchell assured them that he was fine.

John and Callan stepped out. Callan turned in a circle, scanning the area for clues that might help them validate Mitchell's story. John stepped casually around the tent, studying its crude construction.

"I'm not finding much," Callan said when John made a full circle around the lodge.

John grunted, never taking his eye off the tent, speaking in one- or two-word sentences only he could hear.

Mitchell poked his head out between the covers that overlapped the entrance. The tent's flimsy frame of slim branches and twine wobbled.

John pointed to his car. "Let's get you into the back seat.

Is that your car over there along the road?"

Mitchell said that it was. He stumbled but caught his balance.

"Callan'll drive it back. You shouldn't drive," John said. "You sure you're okay? I'll take you to a doctor. You're fine? All right then. Do you feel like talking?"

"Yeah, but I gotta sit down," Mitchell said, holding his head once again. "I can't make it to the car."

The three took a few more steps toward the path lined by trees and small hedges. Mitchell sat on a log as John and Callan stood over him.

"What was this about, Mitchell?" John asked. "What were you doing in there and for how long?"

Mitchell looked up, eyes glazed and groggy. "How long? Oh, man, I don't know. What time is it anyhow? I don't know how long I've been here. I mean, I got here about eleven o'clock last night, maybe eleven thirty."

"You've been here all night?"

"Yeah, I guess so. Yeah, if it's morning," Mitchell said, focusing on the sun.

"Why so late last night?" John asked.

"What? Oh, that's when he called. Some guy on behalf of Professor Banks."

John paused, staring at Mitchell.

Mitchell must've felt the scrutiny by the silence. He lifted his head. "What? I'm telling the truth, man."

"What did this guy want?"

"Oh, wow, it's hard to remember. I'm still a little . . . I'm still a little out of it. Yeah, well, he said Professor Banks wanted to talk to me privately. I asked if it could wait until tomorrow—today, I mean—and the guy said . . ."

"Guy who? Did he identify himself?"

"No. If he did, I don't remember what he said," Mitchell responded. "But he did say that Professor Banks wanted to prove to me that he couldn't possibly have been responsible for Conner's death—Conner Whaite, that is. This guy said Professor Banks wasn't responsible, and he needed to show me."

John paused again, giving him the once-over. "Why you?"

"I don't know."

Silence.

"I don't know, I said," Mitchell repeated, glancing at John's doubting glare. "I think I asked that question, and the guy told me something to the effect that I was Conner and Logan's friend, and I was the best and closest person who cared about the truth."

Callan frowned.

John saw the expression. He turned back to the young man. "Didn't that strike you odd?"

"Odd?" Mitchell asked. "Like hell odd, sure. Yeah, like, I mean, I care about all my friends and such, and I've been curious to know what happened to them, but it's not like I needed to be convinced or anything."

"Did you tell him that?"

"What? No. I just said that it sounded like something they needed to tell the police rather than me. I think I said something like that."

"So what happened?"

Mitchell shrugged. "So I called Dana, then drove out this way. I could see the tent from the road. They had it lit, not brightly, but enough for me to make my way."

"Was Professor Banks there to meet you?" Callan asked.

Mitchell looked up. "No, that's just it. He wasn't there at all."

"Who was there then?"

"Some guys, a couple of guys. Never saw them before. They weren't students. Didn't act like it, didn't look like it. I don't know, it was dark. I couldn't see all that well."

"What did they say?" John asked.

Mitchell drew a breath. Fatigue reflected from his eyes. He tried to sit back, but there was no place to do so on the log, so he arched his back and stretched. "They said they recreated this sweat lodge just as it was the night of the accident and wanted to show me what happened, just the way it happened to Conner and Logan. I said no. I said I wasn't ready to die. I tried to leave, but they wouldn't let me go. They said I wasn't going to die. It was all an accident, what happened to Conner and Logan. I still said no. I tried to get away."

"Why couldn't you?"

"One of them hit me on the head," Mitchell said, rubbing his scalp.

Callan stepped toward the young man and rubbed his hand over his scalp but felt nothing.

"I think I blacked out. I don't remember anything after that until I heard you two outside. They must've taken off my clothes. Looks like they wanted to make it look like I was trying to have my own sweat lodge ceremony but got overcome by the heat. Isn't that what it looks like to you? I mean, if I constructed my own sweat lodge, then maybe it would look like to the police that Conner and Logan constructed theirs too. That would remove suspicion from Professor Banks." Mitchell rubbed his head some more. "I think that's why this happened to me."

Chapter Thirty

Margot Banks pulled into the short cul-de-sac where her home aligned with others, admiring the powder dip on her nails. Much better this time. Last time, some of the nails weren't properly prepped. That's why they popped off. The technician denied it, of course, but Margot knew nails, and the salon owner agreed the process had been improperly applied above the technician's objections. She smiled, pleased with herself. The powder dip looked fabulous.

Her pleasantness changed as she approached her home, which she used to share with her husband. Randall's hatchback, a small, dull, little car with a trashy-looking Vermillion College decal on the back window sat squarely in the drive. *What the hell? What is he doing here?* He wasn't sitting in the driver's seat, waiting. That could only mean he must've gone inside.

"Oh, the bastard," she spewed under her breath. He knew she went to the salon on this day of the week. It was like clockwork. "How dare the son of a bitch; how dare him!"

Margot blocked his car from behind and set hers in park.

On second thought, maybe she'd surprise him inside. Yes, a surprise would be much more satisfying to her. She pulled the car out of the drive and drove two or three houses toward the end of the cul-de-sac. Randall would never see her car parked in front of others on the street. Only one way led out of the court.

She hurried as fast she could down the walk. Her mid-heel pumps weren't made for jogging, but she tiptoed quite skillfully to their porch, careful not to cause alarm. Strange. The door was partially ajar. Margot inched the door open and peeked into the foyer. The living room was off to the right. She was relieved he wasn't sitting in a chair, rubbing his hands, waiting in ambush. But what the hell was he doing? Anger welled.

Margot crept inside and listened. Nothing came from downstairs toward the kitchen and nook. She glanced up the staircase. At first, nothing came from the upstairs bedrooms, but soon she heard some rattling and what sounded like repairs being done in the bathroom. *Repairs?* Randall Banks hadn't repaired a damn thing in the house the entire time they were married. What was he doing? Suddenly, it sounded as though he'd finished what he was doing and was cleaning up.

Her eyes darted around the room, looking for a place to hide. In her own home, yet she didn't know where to hide. *The coat closet under the stairs.* Margot tiptoed to the closet constructed under the stairwell into usable space, closing the door behind her but leaving a gap wide enough to hear when her husband had left.

Randall soon descended, clomping his way down, sounding as if he missed a step along the way.

Margot leaned forward to look through the small opening. She couldn't see anything, but she sensed when he stopped.

Her heart pounded, relieved when she heard the faint beeps of his phone being used.

"Banks," he said. "Listen, I put everything in a lockbox. If something happens to me, it's all there. Yeah, yeah, exactly where I said I'd put them." Silence. "No, you're not to do anything unless something happens to me, y'hear? They're fine where they are. I'll take care of them later if I need to." More silence. "What? No. I'm heading back right now. I said no. You just do as you're told."

The front door slammed shut. Footsteps faded down the walk. A car started, then sputtered down the cul-de-sac toward the main road. Deafening silence.

Margot placed her fingers to her lips, relieved. She sighed, then inhaled broken breaths but remained in the dark closet for several seconds. She wiped small beads of perspiration from her forehead and thought about what to do. She had to do something. For the first time in her marriage, Margot Banks feared her husband.

~

Callan returned to the college for his morning classes—one being an advanced class on white-collar crime, the other on auditing. Under the circumstances, the classes should've been spellbinding for the students. Callan often started his lectures with a current event to elicit their thoughts. Doing so kept the students engaged and provided an interactive learning experience. Recent events on campus not only provided an excellent topic but also they were pertinent.

The students asked curious questions about what he knew. He turned the tables and asked what they'd heard. Apparently, what was once a taboo topic was now ripe for criticism and speculation. They'd heard plenty, but from what Callan gathered when he divided the class into discussion groups, the facts were fraught with inaccuracies, sensationalism, misinformation and embellishments.

Callan arrived home for lunch, tired and disheveled, finding the Victorian house unusually quiet. No creaking from footsteps on the second story. No muffled yowling of a door being opened or closed. No rumblings from the air ducts. He strode into the kitchen. Terese was nowhere. He stepped to the stairwell and called upward.

"Are you home already?" Terese replied from their bedroom.

"Yes, I need a break," he said.

She peered down the stairwell and offered an empathetic pout. "I can't be with you. I'm doing my hair. Thought about doing some antiquing. Care to come along?"

"No," he said, turning away. He walked into the front room and sat in a pin-striped wingback chair with raised armrests that he usually found uncomfortable.

Terese hurried down the stairs, minutes later. "Then do you want something to eat? Would you care for some lunch?"

He glanced at her and smiled. "Yes, I think that's exactly what I'd like and need. A good lunch, but I'd rather go out." Then, in an effort to engage her, said, "I've been neglecting you."

She bent down and kissed the top of his head. "You've had much on your mind. I can make something here."

"Black Forest Cake."

She gasped slightly. "What?" she asked, confused.

"Moist chocolate cake . . . tart cherry brandy filling." He licked his lips. "Luscious, whipped cream . . ."

Terese stepped back. "Are you seducing me?"

Callan smiled.

"Where?" she asked.

"Younts Inn, outside of town."

A smile crept across her face, coy, provocative, compelling. "Just the two of us?"

He winked and blew her a kiss. His stomach growled.

She laughed. "I knew it was too good to be true," she said as his belly continued to echo. "You can seduce me all you want with cake and brandied cherries, Callan Morrow, but that stomach of yours gives you away every time."

~

The Younts Inn sat off a winding country road in the Bal Hinch valley, just a few miles outside of Vermillion. Sunlight filtered through faded green maple leaves, showing its summer's age, preparing for autumn. Warm air blew across the golden fields, soft and dry.

Terese pulled her sweater off her shoulders. "I doubt I'll be needing this."

"You may," Callan warned. "I don't know why restaurants keep their dining rooms so cold, but you may need it."

They entered the foyer, facing a stone wall under massive wood beams with the aroma of sweet baked goods blended with savory entrées. A middle-aged man, attired neatly in a maroon button-down shirt and black dress pants, welcomed them. Callan and Terese followed him into a secluded room with expansive windows overlooking a garden of prairie wildflowers and a glowing fireplace in the corner. Terese clutched Callan's hand, squeezing it gently, a gesture of gratitude for the time together. The decorated walls, romantic ambiance and reserved presentation almost caused the two of them to miss the only other couple in the room, also taking in an afternoon in the country.

"Are you kidding?" the man at the other table said. Across from him a woman just as plump held a glass of chardonnay and stared at Callan and Terese perplexed.

Callan turned and grimaced. He introduced the man to Terese. "John Steinmeier."

"Oh!" Terese uttered, suddenly realizing their intimate lunch was no longer going to be intimate.

"You might as well join us," John said.

The woman across from him frowned.

Callan turned to Terese who returned a wide-eyed expression of doubt. She glanced down at her chair. He pulled it out for her. "Oh, I'm . . . I'm sure the two of you would like some . . . time together, John. Looks like the two of us had the same idea. This is my wife, Terese, by the way."

"Nina Steinmeier," the woman said coolly, not waiting for John to swallow the bread roll he'd stuffed in his mouth.

Callan sat down, catching the disappointment in Terese's eyes.

"Black Forest cake," he whispered, smirking.

She couldn't help but smile.

The two couples ate quietly, neither saying a word to each other until the cake, oozing with cherry cordial filling, arrived at Callan and Terese's table for them to share. Callan poured two cups of hot, freshly brewed coffee from a carafe the waitress had set on the table beside them.

"You must be the other woman," Nina finally said across the aisle to Callan as her husband chomped on the last of his meal.

Callan glanced at John and wiped a dollop of whipped cream off his upper lip to give him some time before answering.

John shrugged, belched, and said, "You do look mighty handsome after a couple of beers."

This time, Callan laughed, and apologized to both Nina and Terese for the time the investigation had consumed without tangible results.

A server freshened Nina's glass of chardonnay. "Case sounds fairly cut and dry to me," she said. Nina raised her wine glass as though toasting to an accurate opinion. "The two of you should be home on a regular basis very soon, shouldn't you?"

John reached over the table and flicked a crumb off the side of his wife's face but didn't respond to her comment.

Callan returned to his coffee, avoiding eye contact. The lunch was meant to be a diversion from the frustrating case he and John were involved in, not a discussion of it.

"Why are you two being so tight-lipped?" Nina asked, unwilling to be ignored. "Do you or do you not think Professor Banks killed those two boys?"

Callan gestured for her to keep her voice down.

"Well then, please join us at our table like John asked you to in the first place," she said. "Come on. I promise not to eat your cake."

Callan said they were fine where they were. "*May have* is a better way of characterizing Professor Banks's involvement, Nina," he said to appease her.

She looked at her husband for an explanation.

"Banks has denied being at the sweat lodge where Conner was killed and at Mount Nebo where Logan was killed," John said.

"Of course he has." Nina shrugged and smirked, stating the obvious.

"He'd have us believe the boys were acting upon their own free will in those tents, including what happened to Mitchell Dells this morning."

"You don't believe it, though, do you?" Nina asked, alternating glances between the two men.

Callan waited for John to answer. John had been mum on divulging his opinions about the case to date. Apparently, he'd been mum at home as well. Nina's eyes focused on Callan, pleading for information her husband hadn't shared.

John grabbed another dinner roll from the basket on the table, buttered it, and gnawed, his pear-shaped cheeks flapping with each bite. He chewed without blinking, staring blankly at his wife, irritated that she couldn't read his demeanor directing constraint.

"Well, regarding Conner's death," Callan said, contemplating words to use. "I believe Professor Banks was not only at the sweat lodge the night Conner died, but he was there until Conner started having problems. Do you agree, John?"

Nina jerked her head toward her husband. He shrugged and said he agreed.

"What about that Logan boy?" she asked.

John swallowed. "It's hard to tell if he was there at the time of the murder. He was there after the fact, I'll grant that, but nothing ties him to Mount Nebo yet."

Callan started to respond but changed his mind.

Nina caught his apprehension. "Go on," she said.

He hesitated.

Terese noticed the apprehension too. "Perhaps we shouldn't talk about this in public," she said. "It's a sensitive matter and not wise for others to overhear."

"She's right," John said.

"What others?" Nina objected. She twisted her head in each direction. "There's no one else in the room."

"But one never knows who's right outside the doorway,"

Terese countered.

Nina Steinmeier scooted her chair away from the table and lifted her heavy frame. She raised a finger. "We'll see about that." In so doing, her water glass toppled, spilling its contents, soaking the tablecloth underneath.

Terese frowned and glared at Callan as she waddled toward the doorway. John sopped up the mess.

Nina poked her head in the small hallway and glanced in both directions. "No one's there!" she exclaimed. She turned abruptly and said, "Besides, it's in the papers and on the radio. I even saw it on the Terre Haute television station. I doubt you'll be saying anything the public doesn't already know." Nina eyed Callan closely for his reaction.

"It's just that I haven't discussed it thoroughly with John yet," Callan replied. He relented to Nina's impertinence by drawing his chair closer to the Steinmeier's table. Nina took her seat, leaning forward farther than she intended, the wine appearing to take effect.

"I met the two geocachers again. They'd taken a letter from the cache that Logan had presumably written," Callan said to John. His voice lowered. "They've probably returned to Benton County already to hand it over to the authorities there. I couldn't make out much in the letter. It was hastily written with scribbles intended to be drawings. Sentences seemed to run together in no cohesive sequence. It was very clear to me that Logan simply wanted to get as much down on paper as fast as he could to disprove Professor Banks's teachings, and he didn't care if it didn't make much sense to outsiders."

"Then it may not make sense to the sheriff in Benton County," John said.

"That's my theory," Callan replied. "The only thing that stood out for me in the letter was Logan's description of the earthworks' solar alignment in relation to the earth's solstices and equinoxes."

"The autumn equinox is rapidly approaching," Nina said. "What I don't understand is what these kids find so fascinating about all this."

"I believe," Callan continued cautiously, "that for whatever reason, Professor Banks provides these intelligent young people a fulfillment they aren't receiving elsewhere, whether it be spiritually or emotionally. They yearn to be a part of something important, creative and new. Ancient Native American ingenuity and tradition intrigues them. Right or wrong, Banks is providing the intellectual stimulus they long for."

"But why the deaths?" Terese asked.

"I'm not sure they were intentional, at least not Conner's death anyway. I do believe something went wrong, so wrong that Banks couldn't reverse what was happening, but not wrong enough for him to stop the ritual. Would you agree, John?"

John, who'd been conspicuously quiet throughout the meal, stopped chewing. He swallowed slowly and reached for his beverage but didn't pick it up.

"What is it?" Callan asked.

He shook his head. "Nothing is adding up yet," he replied, lifting his glass to wash down the bread.

Nina turned to her husband. "What do you mean, John?"

"I saw the lodge that Conner died in," he said thoughtfully. "It was meticulously constructed, with equal length vertical branches and precisely cut horizontal branches, all of similar quality and density. The branches were chopped and carved into shape from willow trees in the woods. Primitive but genuine, tied together with cordage from the bark stripped from the willow. The covering of the lodge was made of blankets—quality blankets, sturdy and full to contain the heat from the hot stones used for cleansing. The firepit used to heat the stones was also constructed with care. A depression was dug, meticulously carved out of the earth for maximum fire and heat generation. But the lodge Mitchell was found in this morning—and I use the term lodge very loosely—was built much more crudely."

A hush fell across the two tables.

"What are you saying?" Callan asked.

"I'm saying that it didn't look like the person or persons who built the first lodge that Conner and Logan were found in were the same people who built the lodge Mitchell was found in today. I scoured every inch of Mitchell's tent this morning. The first lodge was constructed by someone who knew exactly what they were doing and took painstaking measures to ensure it was built as Native Americans would have built it—to be effective. If Banks built the first lodge and those two men that Mitchell talked about built the one I saw today, that would account for the difference."

Callan studied the expression of his colleague. "But you're not so sure, are you?"

A buzz from Callan's phone interrupted John's response. Callan glanced at the display, then side-glanced at John and said, "Let me get this. Hello? This is Callan Morrow."

"Professor Morrow?" Silence. "Margot Banks." More hesitation. "I have something at my home you should see."

Callan turned to Terese. "I need to go," he said earnestly. Turning to the Steinmeiers, he excused himself from their conversation and said he'd call John later. Callan paid the bill while Terese gathered her belongings.

"Sorry about the lunch," he whispered to her as they scurried out the door.

"The least of my worries," she replied. "I'm more concerned about you and who called you. Unexpected phone calls haven't been good news lately."

Callan nodded as he opened the car door for his wife. He understood her apprehension, but with reserved optimism he hoped this phone call was just the break he'd been waiting for.

CHAPTER

THIRTY-ONE

Callan hurried up the stamped cement walk to Margot Banks's home. Well-kept and smart-looking, the two-story structure of white brick with a partial stone facade appeared cold and unwelcoming, even though the afternoon sun bore warmly on the back of his neck. Mums bloomed in hues of oranges, yellows and burnt reds, while the burning bush blazed with glory beside golden privets, but still there was something chilling about their presentation, a facade themselves.

Margot led him to a large living room off to the right of the foyer. She was drinking chamomile tea to settle her stomach and calm her anxiety, or so she said. She offered Callan something stronger, but he politely refused, choosing to sit in an overstuffed chair he doubted he'd be able to rise from with any grace.

She fought back a tear. "He was in *my* home," she said.

"Did he have a key?"

"I didn't think so. I changed the locks. The front door wasn't broken into, but, oh, I don't know, I'm sure he found a way to tamper with it."

Before Margot could look away, lost to anger and doubt, Callan spoke to bring her back. "You said you had something important you wanted to tell me."

"No," she replied emphatically, alive again. "It's something I want to show you. You might find it useful in your investigation."

Margot rose, setting her tea on a marble-top end table, and stepped to the corner of the room. She opened the center drawer of a small writing table and removed a white envelope. She extended it to Callan then returned to her place by her tea.

"I have no idea if it can help in any way, but it looks promising. Randall was quite mysterious this morning when I caught him upstairs. I suspect the contents have to do with a place where he's been conducting his private business. I'll let you read it for yourself."

Callan extracted the contents which were nothing more than a cover letter written to a Thomas Bradford from a Mr. A. D. Wainstetter. Attached was a standard lease agreement between the two men.

Mr. Bradford,
Please find enclosed your copy of the signed lease agreement for the cottage and property on Kikthawenund Lane. Per your inquiry, the property is located within Union Township of Madison County, Indiana, and is not located within the corporation limits of the city of Anderson or the town of Chesterfield.

Kind regards,
A.D. Wainstetter

"Curious," Callan said to his hostess. "Who is this Thomas Bradford the letter is addressed to and the lease agreement that accompanies it?"

"I have no idea," she said. "I thought you might know. If this Mr. Bradford was an associate of Randall's at the college who helped him with his experiments, I thought you might've run across the name before."

Callan shook his head. "The cover letter by this Mr. Wainstetter was obviously written for the sole purpose of putting this Mr. Bradford and, possibly, your husband's mind at ease about the location of a certain piece of property."

"As if they wanted to make sure they wouldn't be violating any city ordinances with it."

"Exactly, like operating a sweat lodge, perhaps."

Margot sighed. The thought seemed to disgust her.

"The lease is over three months old," Callan said. "Did you know about it?"

"No, according to its date, it was signed while we were still together, but I only knew about it this morning."

"How did you come across it?"

Margot told Callan about finding Randall's car in the drive when she returned from the nail salon. "The front door was unlocked. I pushed it open but couldn't hear anything," she said, looking away to recall. "Suddenly, I heard noises upstairs. I hid in that closet in the foyer and waited for him to leave, then I went upstairs to find out what he was up to. I started with our bedroom, but everything was intact."

"By intact, you mean . . ."

"None of my belongings were rifled through. My jewelry

was exactly how I left it. Forty dollars still on the dresser. He wasn't after money. I looked through the remaining bedrooms but found nothing out of line there as well. It wasn't until I looked through the bathroom door that I noticed something unusual."

"What was that?" Callan asked, intrigued.

"Drywall dust." Margot picked up her tea, sat back and took a sip. "You know how a bumblebee leaves wood shavings on the ground after it's burrowed into a porch railing? It was like that. A pile of undisturbed drywall dust on the floor of my bathroom."

"Where did it come from?"

"From a panel on the wall. You see, we had a leak from the pipes in that bathroom shower not long ago. A plumber came in and tore out the wall to get to the pipes. I remember Randall asking the man if he made a permanent fix, but the guy said that the type of fixtures used were known to cause problems. Unless Randall wanted to replace all the fixtures, there could be more issues in the future. I remember Randall told the plumber to put a panel door on the wall so that the pipes could be reached if future repairs were needed."

"Sounds reasonable."

"Yes," Margot replied, "but not today. I didn't call Randall about any leaks. I've had no problems with the shower since it'd been fixed. So why today? Why get behind the panel when I wasn't here?"

"I see what you mean."

Margot waved her fingers in the air. "At risk of damaging these nails after I'd given my technician the what-for for ruining my last nails, I found a screwdriver and got behind the panel. I don't believe my husband wanted easy access to the shower pipes at all. He wanted a safe hideaway to store confidential documents in between the studs."

"What else was in the wall besides this lease?" Callan asked.

"His employment contract with the college, some news clippings of him accepting service awards in town, and his last will, revised shortly before we split up."

Callan's brows rose but she dismissed any thoughts about his will being significant.

"A meaningless piece of paper, Professor. What assets? He's squandered what was his on his celestial theories. More curious than that is what wasn't there. He always kept an advanced directive with his will. Always. It was missing." She smirked, fighting back the urge to laugh. "I suppose he believes he'll leave this earth by means that won't require an advanced directive. Only the stars know, I'm afraid, Professor, only the stars."

Callan looked over the lease agreement carefully, interested in the terms of the lease and an address of the place being leased. He asked her about it.

"Don't expect this cottage to be on a major thoroughfare or parkway, if you have any intention of finding the place," Margot said.

"Yes, I plan to."

"I thought you would."

"Are you curious about it too?"

She laughed. "Oh, good heavens, no. No, but I did call a realtor friend this morning after I found the agreement. I thought I should, to keep one step ahead of Randall and this Bradford fellow in case he has an accomplice. My friend described the property as being mostly land, heavily wooded, with a small clearing and a modest home. Apparently, the road leading back to the property isn't maintained by the county. He said it was more like a lane, coming off a larger road out in the country near the state park."

Callan lifted the cover letter and the agreement so that she could see what he wanted to take with him. "May I?"

Margot nodded and flicked her wrist again to indicate that he could do whatever he wanted with the documents. She didn't care.

"Knowing that your husband and this Bradford man rented a place at this location is a promising clue," Callan said.

"How so?"

"Are you familiar with Mounds State Park?" he asked.

She shook her head. "You've probably gathered by now that I'm not one who trots on muddy park trails."

He ignored the jest. "The park has significance from a solar standpoint, Ms. Banks. The mounds are accurately aligned to the seasons and multitudes of stars and planets. Apparently, that has some appeal to your husband, but I'm still grappling to what extent."

"He's a solstice worshipper," she said.

"Yes, but it seems to be something even grander than that," Callan replied. "I'm concerned because I believe Marissa Reynolds could be with him."

"If it's any consolation, Professor, I doubt very seriously if it's sexual. He's not wired that way. I provide this insight to you so that you don't waste your time on a motive that isn't there. He's not a predator."

"But is he capable of harm?"

"That seems to be a silly question given the recent deaths, doesn't it?" she asked. "Directly or indirectly, something he's involved with isn't right."

Callan wrestled out of the chair and thanked Margot Banks for the documents.

Margot stood up with him and took a deep breath. "I

don't want to hear from him again," she said decisively. She folded her arms at her midsection as if she'd just felt a sudden chill. "I don't want to see his face or hear his voice. I shudder at the thought of opening the morning paper some day to find his photo plastered on the front page, attached to an article about something terrible he's done. I can hardly bear it."

Callan nodded and tried to reassure her. "Hopefully, it won't come to that," he said, turning to leave.

Margot Banks accompanied him to the door. "Of course," she said gravely, "you and I both know that isn't true, don't we?"

CHAPTER

THIRTY-TWO

Before now, Callan had been hard-pressed to find a solid reason for investigating Mounds Park. He was curious about the place, but that wasn't reason enough to waste time or energy on what could be a dead-end lead. John Steinmeier was lukewarm on the idea that a trip to the park would be productive. It was potentially more dangerous than his rogue jaunt to Mount Nebo, he said. With new evidence from Margot Banks related to a rented cottage near the park, Callan argued that it was now worth a visit. John didn't say Callan was crazy for going, but he didn't sanction the trip either. He just told him to be careful and to call him if he needed help.

Terese said he was crazy.

"I can't believe you're thinking about going," she said. "I can't believe you think it'll make a difference."

Callan put a change of clothes and some toiletries in a

duffle bag.

She grabbed him by the shoulders and turned him around. "Oh, I see. You're not thinking about going. You *are* going. You've already made up your mind."

Callan recited a dozen reasons why it made sense. "And it *will* make a difference," he said. "Margot Banks's discovery of the lease agreement changes everything."

"How?" she asked, unconvinced.

Callan replaced her hands on his shoulders with his on top. "Because it's a location, Terese, a location where Marissa Reynolds could be. I have to find out."

"Call the sheriff in Anderson," Terese pleaded.

"And say what? Please check on a young woman who's someplace she wants to be but no one else does? They'll think I'm a lunatic. I can't do that. I have to see for myself. Honey, I promise I won't be long." He finished packing, zipped the duffle bag and walked into the hallway. "You're welcome to come too if you'd like."

Terese gave him a sad look at the patronizing invitation and told him to go. "A kiss first, though, please."

~

Callan drove east over rolling farmland to the city of Anderson in east central Indiana. He arrived early evening, just as the sun hung precariously over the horizon, and grabbed a sandwich at an eatery along Scatterfield Road. He took a chance that a sign reading *Mounds Road* was one that would lead him on a path to the state park. The road wasn't a straight shot, but it curved along a tree-lined setting until it wound toward an entrance.

He passed the old Bronnenberg home near the park's

entrance. Built in the 1840s, the house was the home of Frederick Bronnenberg's family, who built the house from surrounding resources, including limestone along the White River quarried for the foundation. Callan also learned later that it was the Bronnenberg family who understood the historical and spiritual value of the Adena mounds. They first protected the mounds' existence.

Callan parked near the pavilion and studied a map given to him at the gatehouse. Given the hour, he didn't have much daylight left. He had to make the most of what he could find out about the park's layout while he had the chance. Finding the Great Mound was his top priority.

He hurried along the boardwalk on Trail 2. A light fog manifested in the clearings between the woodlots, chilling the air as he made his way through. Damp, slimy moss covered the railings and the posts that lifted the walk two to three feet above the stony forest floor. A small run meandered over rocks underneath, rippling purposefully toward the river. Deep ravines cut into the eroded hillsides lavished with hardwoods and ferns. The boardwalk followed the contours of the ravines with precision, shrouded now with haze that slithered between trees and ruddy rock formations.

Callan soon reached an open area, free of mist and fog. The Great Mound loomed before him, larger than he envisioned, nearly a quarter of a mile in circumference and surrounded by a log-strewn fence. Callan believed there had to be an opening to the mound's platform in the middle. He walked to the left and followed the circular mound. Before long, he spotted a path across the outer mound and over a large ditch to the flat, raised platform ahead. Hundreds of years of tree growth made it impossible for Callan to see the evening horizon. He had difficulty envisioning the dips that made the mound significant to the Adena people. Still, even with the forested background, the Great Mound was massive and incredibly impressive.

He turned from his observation point and walked around the Great Mound to another clearing and a sign introducing Fiddleback Mound, named for its configuration in the shape of a violin. Callan deviated from the path and crossed the outer wall, through the inner ditch, to stand on Fiddleback's large platform. Here, Callan could see more clearly the horizon that the Adena people might have seen.

Callan stood stoically on the mound, taking in its surroundings, understanding what the mounds might have meant to the Adena, and realizing he was standing on top of a sacred burial and ceremonial ground. The daylight sounds of birds began to wane, replaced by nighttime cicadas. A wisp of fog passed in front of him. Shrouded by macabre shadows from the setting sun, he felt a sudden chill as he stared across the expansive platform into the crowns of trees in search of answers to a journey that only had questions. Darkness blocked his senses, and he grasped for a semblance of place and time. His body seemed weightless and immortal even though his feet were grounded. A breeze blew lightly across his face, suddenly letting him know that he was very much in control of his senses.

A little girl no more than eight or nine years old startled him when she walked past him on the right and stood just a foot or two ahead of him. She wore a handmade gray jumper suit, faded and plain, with white leggings. Two ponytails, one on each side, adorned a face sweetened by innocence, smooth as porcelain.

"This place is creepy," she said.

Callan didn't respond, too stunned to do so. Instead, he

turned in search of the little girl's parents. He spotted them on a nearby trail—mother and father, talking casually, the father holding the hand of a boy no older than three. He was astonished that they walked without a sense of where their little girl had wandered. They didn't seem concerned, and they certainly hadn't noticed her absence. Still, Callan was troubled by what it looked like for him, standing alone on an earthwork platform with a small girl he didn't know far from her parents' side.

"You need to go back to your parents," he said to her.

She glanced back to the couple and the little boy. "They aren't my parents."

"Where are your parents?"

She didn't answer. "What were you looking at?" she asked instead. She looked up. "There's nothing in the trees."

Callan ignored her. Instead, he turned to the couple, who was drifting farther away, and raised his voice to get their attention. They didn't hear him.

"If you're searching for pukwudgies tonight, you're wasting your time," she said. "I told them not to come out."

"Young lady," he said adamantly, "I think it's about time you tell me where your parents are."

She frowned. "I have to go now." She looked back into the trees. "It's too creepy here."

The young girl turned around. Callan watched her walk unafraid toward the Great Mound until she was out of sight. He didn't stop her, and he didn't try to follow. There was no assistance to offer. Somehow, Callan believed she didn't need his help.

He stood alone in the eerie silence for only a few seconds before a chill shot up his spine. Time to leave Fiddleback Mound. The place creeped him out too.

CHAPTER

THIRTY-THREE

The sun's low-lying rays filtered through the trees. Spooked or not, it was too early for Callan not to make the most of his visit to the park and gather as much information he could about its surroundings. Rather than turn toward his car, he followed Trail 1 to the river. The edge of a steep ridge gave him a panoramic view of White River—*Wapahani* to the Delawares, meaning great white sands.

Fog engulfed the path ahead. He heard dogs barking in the distance and drawing closer. He stopped upon seeing a dark figure manifest through the mist, calling for the pups to obey her commands. Her sights were on her dogs. Callan's presence startled her.

"My apologies," he said.

"Oh, none needed," she replied, hand over her heart. She carried a soft, compelling Hoosier twang, one from the

217

countryside. The woman turned to look back into the thick foliage of the woodlot. "I should apologize to *you* for the dogs. They should be leashed." She lifted two leashes for Callan to see. "Lotta good these do in my hands," she added.

"Sounds like they've found a critter to chase," Callan replied.

"They're chasing their own scent, I'm afraid. Not too bright."

"I don't know," Callan said unconvinced. "Looks to me like they're tailing something worth catching."

"Yes," she said, her voice fading, "unless, of course, they find them to be real, then they'll wish they'd come when I called."

Callan didn't grasp her last comment. He looked back into the darkness. Did he miss something she saw? "Find out what to be real?" he asked.

The woman called for the dogs. "Let's go, Plaid! Come on, White!"

"Find out what?" he asked again.

Her eyes narrowed, suddenly realizing he was a stranger. "You're not from around here, are you?"

"No, ma'am. Why? Does it make a difference?"

She shrugged, smiled, then shook her head. "Not if you don't believe in them. Plaid! White! Let's go!"

Two young beagles, full of life, emerged from the foliage onto the path, panting and shaking what burrs they could from their long ears. They beelined toward their master, stopping first at Callan's feet to give him the once-over.

"Stop that! Stop that now!" the woman called. "Oh, I'm sorry. Again, my apologies. Meet Plaid and White."

Callan laughed as he repeated the dog's names, more to clarify that he heard correctly rather than to greet them.

"Yes, names given to them by my husband," she said as

she leashed them. "Old school colors from the high school he attended—Highland—now closed. I forgot you're not from around here. Come, pups, time to get home."

"Don't go. Not yet," Callan said.

She stopped, but the dogs tugged on her arm.

"Them what?"

"I'm sorry?" she asked.

"You said what the dogs were chasing didn't make a difference if I didn't believe in them. Them what?"

"Oh, pukwudgies, of course." The dogs pulled harder. She resisted to slow their pace but was thrust forward. The woman looked back and said, "I wouldn't stick around to find out who they are."

"No, but, you . . ." He followed quickly behind her, not knowing what to ask. "You're the second person in less than twenty minutes who's mentioned the pudwucks-geez to me, or whatever they are."

"Pukwudgies. Oh, really?" she asked, quite surprised.

"Yes, a little girl . . . on Fiddleback Mound . . . she came up to me and . . ."

"Arla May?"

Callan hesitated. "Who?"

The woman pulled on the leash to drag the pups back toward her and Callan. What was left of the sun's rays barely illuminated her face, but excitement reflected from her eyes. "Did you see Arla May?"

"She didn't give me a name."

"Who was she with?"

"I'm not sure she was with anyone," he said. "There was a couple with a small boy, walking on the path toward the Great Mound, but they didn't seem to be concerned for her."

"But you talked with her?"

"Why, yes, briefly."

The woman glanced into the woods, smiling contentedly. "Interesting."

Callan thought the encounter was more than interesting, almost paranormal. "She just walked up to me out of nowhere. Stood right in front of me. Scared me half to death. Said this place was creepy, referring to Fiddleback Mound. Then she said the Pudwuk . . . or whatever they are, weren't here if that's who I was waiting for."

The woman stepped forward. "What did you say to that?"

"I didn't say anything," Callan said candidly. "I didn't know what a puk . . ."

"Pukwudgie."

"Pukwudgie was, and I didn't even want her around."

"You didn't want Arla May around?" she asked, disappointed.

"Well, no, a small girl talking to a strange man in a park on a burial mound around dusk, talking about imaginary creatures. It's not exactly a good scenario to tell a judge should I be hauled off to court for an explanation."

"Yes, yes, I understand, but unfortunate just the same."

"Unfortunate?" Callan asked. "I'm sorry, ma'am, but I'm not sure I know what you mean."

A wisp of fog glided past. The woman shivered. She tucked her jacket closer and said, "We hardly know anything about her, we, the neighbors and I, that is. We believe she lives with a family near here behind our property, somewhere in one of those rented cottages, but we haven't been able to talk with her. Not really anyway. She's rather odd. You've probably sensed that, and you've probably gotten the most out of her of anyone."

"I didn't get much," Callan said.

"You got enough. She knows about the pukwudgies.

That's good enough for me."

The woman wrapped her windbreaker even tighter around her abdomen and called for the dogs to lead.

Callan followed. "But you still didn't answer my question."

She eyed him and frowned. "Why are you asking anyhow? You obviously didn't come just to roam the park at this hour. You don't appear to be a weirdo or anything, but you're intriguing just the same. What are you doing here?"

"My name is Callan Morrow," he said, quickening his steps to keep up with the tugging dogs. "I'm a professor at Vermillion College. I have a student that's been absent from class of late. Several of us at the college have been concerned, including her parents. I've reason to believe she could be in the Mounds Park area."

"Vermillion College? I've read something recently about Vermillion College. Didn't a young man or two pass away from a mysterious hazing incident there?"

"Yes, but it wasn't hazing."

"It wasn't?" she asked. "The papers here made it sound that way. So you think this absent person you're looking for is involved in some way?"

"Not as a suspect, but perhaps as another potential victim, an unsuspecting victim."

The dogs suddenly darted back into the foliage, stopping their forward progress. She called for them, gazing into the forest's darkness.

Callan spoke softly. "I'm looking for a specific piece of property in the vicinity."

"Where at?" she asked, interested but concerned.

"A lane with an Indian name. Kik something."

She took a small step back.

Callan thought he noticed her cheek flinch. "You've heard

of it?" he asked.

"Kikthawenund."

"Yes, that's it! How did you pronounce it again?"

"Kik-tha-when-nun," she said slowly. The woman started down the path again, pulling the leash. "It's a lane, as you say, a one-horse lane, no wider than a car width. It leads to a few small cottages and a clearing in the woods."

"Will you tell me how to get there? It doesn't appear on my GPS. It's very important."

The woman called for the dogs to keep up. "I'll do you one better. Follow me," she said. "The lane is in back of our property. What's there may interest you, but I can't talk about it here. Not here."

"Why not?"

Her expression hardened. "Not here."

Callan chuckled. "Why? Will you anger the pukwudgies?"

She gave him a disapproving glare.

Callan knew immediately he shouldn't have teased about the creatures out loud. He didn't understand why, he just knew he shouldn't have.

CHAPTER

THIRTY-FOUR

Callan followed the woman and dogs to their modest-framed home that sat across from the state park, back from the road under mature trees. She ushered him in and gestured toward a chair at the kitchen table. He removed his boots first.

"I'm Penny Donnelly, by the way," she said.

Penny hung her windbreaker on a hook near the door as the dogs scampered to their bowls for fresh water. She called to her husband to let him know she was back from the park and they had a guest. Her husband, Harold, sat reclined in the living room, watching a television program. The volume blared even though Harold sat half asleep in his chair.

"Did you hear me?" Penny called.

She sighed and hurried to the TV, turning the volume down and telling Harold again that they had a visitor.

"Who is he?" Callan could hear him ask.

"A professor from Vermillion College."

"What does he want? If he wants a donation, we didn't go to no college. Tell him so."

"He wants to talk about something that happened at Vermillion."

"We don't know anything," he said. "Tell him we keep to ourselves. We don't put our noses in things that don't concern us."

Penny lowered her voice so that she couldn't be overheard by Callan in the kitchen. She made a few comments that seemed to calm the old man. Callan heard him say "okay" more than once as she talked. Soon, Penny emerged from the living room, shaking her head, and asking Callan if he'd like some coffee. He said he'd love to have a cup.

"Hope Folger's okay because that's all we've ever had in fifty years." She filled the coffee pot before sitting down with Callan at the kitchen table, lowering her voice once again. "I don't mind talking here at the house. I'm sorry for my reluctance to say anything at the park."

"That's all right. I shouldn't have joked about the pukwudgies."

Penny scoffed. "It wasn't about the pukwudgies," she said, chuckling. "You never can be too sure who's listening in, even on a desolate path in the park."

Odd, Callan thought. Who'd want to listen? However, he said he understood but was curious about the cottage behind her property.

"Yes," Penny said, approaching a chair to sit near him. She wrapped her arms around her midsection. "An old man named Wainstetter owns all the cottages along Kik Lane. The lane was named after a Delaware Indian chief, William Anderson, whose Native American name was Kikthawenund. Wainstetter was very good about renting the cottages to credible people. He had a vetting process, requiring the renters to be of good character. I don't blame him. I wouldn't want my properties torn up like so many are nowadays. They didn't have to be rich or from what we call around here good families, but they had to be of good character. Rumor has it among us neighbors that some out-of-towner with no business of his own around here offered the old man plenty of cash to rent this one specific cottage."

"What was so special about it?"

"Nothing that I know of except that it's at the end of the lane. In the back of the cottage is a clearing, surrounded by trees—a nice, open clearing, but very secluded. The property was hard to rent as I understand, so I don't know why this renter would've offered old man Wainstetter so much money for it."

"What was wrong with it? Why wouldn't it rent?" Callan asked.

"We have our suspicions around here, but they wouldn't make sense to an outsider," she said, looking back to see how the coffee was brewing, as its aroma filled the room. "Do you like cream or sugar?"

"Cream, please. I'm very curious, Penny."

Penny rose and chuckled under her breath as she reached for two cups out of a cupboard. She turned to look at him and smiled. "You'll think us silly, being a college professor and all, educated and lacking nonsense as you are."

Callan laughed. "I can assure you there is plenty of nonsense being taught in colleges nowadays, most of which would top whatever it is you have to tell me."

"Well then," she said, returning to stand by her chair,

"the property has, or at least had, a fairy circle in the clearing. There you go."

That wasn't at all what Callan expected to hear. "A fairy circle?"

"Well, yes, you know, a barren patch of ground in the yard in the shape of a circle or grass of a different color, forming a circle. A pixie circle, that sort of thing."

Callan shrugged. "Okay, so what does that have to do with anything?"

"My, you do have a limited knowledge of folklore," she said, putting their hot coffees on the table. "They're attributed to danger or misfortune, sometimes the other way around, wealth and good luck. Either way, some people don't like having them in their yard."

"I've never heard of that," he said. "I must've led a sheltered life. So do the pukwudgies have a similar history?"

"Much grander," she said. "They were a part of Native American legend, especially the Delawares. The Delawares proliferated in the area at the time a Moravian mission was established. I don't believe in the creatures myself. Just find them interesting, but legend has it that they are the source of all trickery that goes on around here."

"Toward whom?" Callan asked.

"Humans. Pukwudgies hate humans. They once liked us, but not anymore. If they're not deceiving you, they're doing something harmful to you, even enticing you to your own death."

"Are they human?"

"Oh heavens, no," Penny said. "They're like trolls if I can use that word. Human-like, but only two to three feet tall. They have large noses, eyes, and skin that glows on and off under the foliage where they hide to surprise and snatch their victims."

Callan shook his head, unable to comprehend how such creatures continued to have such a strong presence in the community.

"They're all over the world," she said, "but they have a very prominent presence at Mounds Park. I'm surprised you haven't heard about them. They've been used in numerous stories and tales, poems and books, but they're very real to some people."

She pointed to her husband in the living room.

"A while ago, Penny," Callan said cautiously, "I got the idea from you that this little girl, Arla May, had something to do with these creatures."

"Don't listen to me," she said. "What people think is circumstantial. Some say she isn't a little girl at all."

Callan arched his back. "What do they say she is?"

"An apparition." She raised her hand. "Look, I don't know what to believe about her, so I'm not the best one to talk."

"But I saw her, Penny," Callan implored. "I talked with her. She was no apparition."

"So you did, and that I believe," she responded reverently. "But you must understand, her story is also based on local folklore. You see, one hundred years ago on the south side of the Great Mound was an amusement park. There were rides, a roller coaster, a roller-skating rink, a carousel, a shooting gallery, and river boat rides. The pavilion had a dance hall where marvelous Roaring Twenties dance marathons were held. People came from miles to the park for the entertainment until, one day, a little girl wandered away from the amusements. She took one of the paths toward the river."

"Arla May?"

"I don't know her name," Penny said, testing her coffee

and finding it too hot to drink. "I don't believe anyone else knows either. Not really anyway. There's a lone unmarked grave of a little girl in Bronnenberg Cemetery. They say her name was Arla May, but I don't think people really know. They believe what they want to make sense of it all."

"So what happened to her?"

"She wandered toward the river. At the time, there were six caves in the limestone cliffs along the river's edge. This little girl climbed into one of the caves and was lost for over eighteen hours. Men searched throughout the night for her. When they found her alive and safe, they vowed to dynamite the caves' openings to prevent the tragedy from ever happening again."

"Did they?"

"Yes," Penny said, touching the side of her cup with her finger to test the coffee again, "and to this day no one knows exactly where these caves in the cliffs are located, except for the pukwudgies, who have holes under the foliage that lead down to the caves where they live."

Callan frowned. "Even though Arla May was saved on that occasion, she must have died young. Why else would she roam the park as a child?"

Penny nodded sadly. "Yes, she survived the cave, but developed pneumonia soon after, having been in the cold, dark dampness for over eighteen hours."

"I suppose she knows where these caves are, doesn't she?"

Penny shrugged, finally taking a sip of her coffee. "Who's to know? Many believe she still walks the paths down by the river and climbs into the caves where she got lost to relive the terrifying hours of her captivity. They believe she's a troubled soul, Professor."

Callan shook his head. "I find this story fascinating but

unbelievable, personally, but if some people around here are as superstitious as you claim, I'm surprised clairvoyant individuals haven't tried to reach her. It would be something such people would be attracted to, it would seem."

"Oh, they have," Penny said. "Long ago, several mediums at the camp tried to reach her through séances but were unsuccessful."

"Camp?"

"Chesterfield."

Callan shook his head. "I've not heard of that place."

Penny pointed north. "It's right in town along the river's edge."

Her brief description still meant nothing to Callan.

"Surely, you've heard of it," Penny said, surprised. "It's one of the largest and most well-known spiritualist camps in the nation. It's yet another addition to the folklore complexities of the area. The town of Chesterfield is quite unique."

Penny stopped talking when she heard the shuffling feet of her husband coming from the living room. He stumbled toward the refrigerator.

"Milk is on the top shelf," Penny said to him.

"No, I don't want that," Harold replied. "I want milk."

"Top shelf."

"Oh."

Harold carefully pulled the carton out of the refrigerator. "I can't drink all this," he said.

"Get a glass."

"Oh."

Penny gestured that her husband wasn't doing very well. Callan figured she meant with dementia.

"Harry is from Chesterfield," she said to Callan loud enough for her husband to hear. "He can tell you a lot about the town, can't you, dear?"

"I can't tell you nothin'," he replied curtly. "Don't know nothin'. We don't put our noses in places where it don't belong."

"We're talking about Chesterfield, dear."

"What?"

"Chesterfield. We're talking about Chesterfield."

"Oh."

"You were raised there, you know."

Harold shuffled to the counter with the milk carton and held his glass as he looked away to remember. "Yes, but it was a long time ago. It's all changed now. It's all changed. Use'ta be a cute li'l place, Chesterfield was, back in the day. Ever'thing a kid wanted. Not no more." He sighed and returned to his milk. "Not no more."

Penny urged him to walk back into the living room and relax. He turned, glass in hand, to do so. When Harold was out of sight, Penny rose to put the milk carton back in the refrigerator. "I suppose all of what I'm telling you is what drew this renter to Mr. Wainstetter's cottage and why it was worth so much for him to pay what he did for it."

"This renter," Callan asked, "have you ever met him?"

"Yes, once, at Frisch's in North Anderson. I walked into the restaurant and was led to a booth where Mr. Wainstetter, who I know well, sat adjacent to me with another man. Wainstetter introduced him to me as the new renter to the cottage behind us. I introduced myself, welcomed him to our neighborhood, and that was that. Nice-looking fellow, professional man, he was."

"Would you recognize him if you saw him again?"

"Of course," Penny said with confidence.

Callan removed the picture of Randall Banks that he'd obtained from administration at the college from his pocket.

He slid the photo across the kitchen table to Penny. She looked at it carefully and slid it back.

"Yes, that's him," she said. "That's the renter. That's Tom Bradford, for sure."

CHAPTER
THIRTY-FIVE

"Tom Bradford?" Callan asked.

"Yes, I caught his name quite clearly," Penny said. "Is something wrong?"

"Something could be very wrong, or it could be the piece that fits the puzzle together. May I ask a favor?"

"Anything. What is it?"

"Will you take me to the clearing?" Callan asked. "I'd like to see it for myself."

"Tonight?"

"If we can." His eyes pleaded to her.

"You aren't afraid of the woods at night, are you? Our property is heavily wooded out back."

"I'm sure I'll manage," he replied, offended she'd even say such a thing to him, "but without the dogs. I'd prefer going without the dogs. They yap and carry on. I don't want anyone to be alarmed by our approach."

"Very well," she said, scrutinizing her windbreaker, hanging by the door. "Let me get a heavier jacket, and we'll be on our way. I'll grab some flashlights for the first part of our trek. We can turn them off the closer we get to the clearing."

Callan met her at the door, eager to see the property Thomas Bradford or Randall Banks had rented. He and Penny stepped carefully across the backyard. The ground was uneven. Clumps of grass humped in lines where moles had dug across the yard in search of grubs. Penny's beagles whimpered behind them. Callan turned to see Plaid and White pressing their noses against the glass patio door, tails wagging profusely, howling pitifully, pleading their cases to come along.

As soon as Callan and Penny entered the woods, the sounds of nightfall intensified. A coolness shrouded them. Callan wished that he'd brought a heavier coat, as Penny had done.

Their flashlights cast a dim glow on the path, restricted by ferns and trees on both sides. The path bore signs that it'd been traveled often.

"Do you take walks back here frequently?" he asked.

Penny said that she did, usually in pursuit of the pups. A son had cleared the way at her request to make the jaunts easier. "But we'll have to veer off to the right up ahead to see the clearing," she said.

Callan glanced behind him once again. Lights from the house were mere flickers. An uneasiness shivered up his back. His intellect reassured him that they weren't being followed—there was no way they could've been followed—but the small of his back tightened with each step.

"What's the matter?" Penny asked.

"Nothing," he said, barely audible.

"Then why do you keep looking back?"

He didn't know. He couldn't answer her. Was it paranoia? Was it a culmination of recent events with Conner and Logan's deaths, Mitchell's lodge incident, Marissa's disappearance, the men in the tan car that followed him to the restaurant, and the sensations of danger that he'd been feeling? Callan looked up into the trees, hoping to see his angel, the bronze presence of his youth, the one that comforted and protected him so long ago, hovering above in a haze to reassure him once again.

"I've walked these woods hundreds of times at night, Professor," Penny said, inching forward. "Nothing is ever out of the ordinary."

Callan sensed a reticence in her voice. "But tonight?" he asked.

"Tonight," she said, pausing before she answered, "tonight I have you on my tail. That's the difference. I hardly know you. I can't believe I'm traipsing out into the woods with you." She laughed. "Am I a lunatic?"

He chuckled. "No, it's highly unusual, I'll agree, but I have no interest in harming you."

"But still," she said, "I don't know what to make of all this. What are you trying to find?"

"I'd like to confirm that this place is what I think it is—a hiding spot for the man who I fear has my student."

"This Tom Bradford?"

"Or this Randall Banks. I believe he's using the Bradford name as an alias, but I don't know why."

"Oh, dear, this is becoming more ominous, isn't it?" Penny slowed on the path. "Here, we'll want to veer at this point and walk to the fence line."

The two diverted to the right, hiking further into the trees and brush, pushing low-lying branches out of their way and stepping over fallen logs and small piles of rocks. They reached a barbed-wire fence with posts made from the trunks of trees cut by property owners long ago. More trees on the other side of the fence blocked their view to the rented land.

Music whined from the clearing, faint and forbidding. Callan couldn't make out the words. High-pitched falsetto voices, difficult to understand. Periodically, he'd hear a note that lingered for several seconds.

"What's that sound?" Callan asked.

Penny stopped to listen. "I'm not sure. We often hear it at the house in the evenings."

"I can't make out the words, can you?"

"You won't be able to," she said, batting a small branch out of her face. "It's Russian. That's what some of the neighbors say anyway."

He wondered if it was the "Opera 1" and "Opera 2" songs by the Ukrainian Vitas that Margot Banks had told him about.

"We need to go down further if we want to see the clearing better," Penny said. "The brush is too thick here."

They followed the fence to a place where the trees on the other side had thinned enough to see lights from cottages along a dark lane.

"You can't see it very well, but that's Kik Lane," she said, pointing in the dark. "Those lights that are yellow and barely visible through the shrubs are coming from the cottage Mr. Wainstetter rented to your suspect. Those lights beyond belong to other renters of other cottages."

She turned slightly and pointed in another direction. "And I don't know what that is. I've not seen it before. Looks like a tent of some kind."

Callan studied the crude structure in the shape of a dome. It wasn't large or impressive.

Lights from a car rolling down Kik Lane diverted his attention. Callan recognized the model of the car immediately and surmised it would be a dirty tan in the daylight. He wasn't surprised when he also recognized the two men who emerged from the car and hurried to the front of the cottage.

"You seem to know them," Penny said, squinting to see his face.

"No, I just know who they are."

"They don't look good," she replied, tightening her jacket around her. "Nothing here looks good."

Callan remained still. He watched the house carefully for signs of activity within the cottage. Overgrown shrubs around the perimeter impeded his view. A cold chill ran up his back. Uneasiness. A feeling of being watched. Suddenly, he realized he'd been negligent at not taking their safety more seriously. Staking out the premises could be dangerous, especially to Penny. "If you need or want to get back to the house, Penny, I understand."

"No," she replied emphatically. "I want to know what's going on behind my house. If it's illegal, I have a right to know. If it's just weird and creepy, I want to know that too."

Just then, the cottage door opened. Out came the two men who'd come from the car, dressed in black. They stepped toward the tent, slow and methodical. Next came Randall Banks, adorned in a ceremonial robe, holding a lighted candle. He followed the two men to the tent's entrance.

The scene was quiet for several minutes. No one else emerged. Randall Banks went into the domed tent momentarily before coming back out to stand in front of the entrance. He lifted a handbell and rang it three times. The clanging wasn't loud and hardly alarming enough for someone within the cottage to take notice, but a door soon opened, and two young women came out, carrying lighted candles, followed by two more young women behind the first couple.

Randall rang the bell again and the cottage door opened on cue. This time, two small girls, each around eight years of age, came out dressed in white vintage dresses, carrying candles.

"Oh, no," Penny whispered.

Callan grasped Penny's hand to keep her from crying out any louder.

"But one of them is Arla May," she said. "I know it is. The girl closest to us is Arla May. Can't you see her?"

He did. A pang of sadness hit his stomach. He wondered aloud who the other girl was.

"I don't know," Penny confessed. "I only know of Arla May. Oh, what should we do?"

"Nothing," Callan whispered. "We don't do anything."

"But there she is."

"I know, but we have no evidence of wrongdoing," Callan warned. "Not yet anyway."

The handbell rang again as the young girls approached the tent. Callan and Penny's attention were drawn back toward the cottage. The door opened. A young woman exited, dressed in white, holding a lighted candle, inching across the lawn with her head held proudly, her gaze fixed upon Randall Banks.

Callan squeezed Penny's hand tighter. The young woman was Marissa Reynolds.

"Oh, now you must act for sure," Penny said.

"And do what?" he asked, releasing her hand to rub his face. "Create a scene because a grown woman is walking across a lawn in a flowing gown with a candle?"

"You know what I mean."

"No, I'll not do anything now, but at least I have proof where Marissa is and that Randall Banks, or Thomas Bradford, whoever he claims to be, is involved."

Marissa entered the tent. Callan expected Randall to follow her inside, but he didn't. He stood stoically outside the entrance, staring straight ahead in a trance.

"Is that it?" Penny asked.

"No, look," Callan said, pointing to the cottage. "One more person is coming out."

No handbell clanged to announce the new individual, but an older woman dressed in a black gown, holding a book and a lighted candle, walked ceremoniously toward the tent. This time, it was Penny who recognized the person coming from the cottage. She gasped.

"Who is she?" Callan asked.

"Oh my God, she's a friend of mine," Penny said. "Her name is Rita McGarry. She's a medium at the camp in Chesterfield. I can't believe what I'm seeing here."

They watched for several more minutes. Penny's friend and Randall Banks entered the tent, but nothing else happened. The music stopped. No voices. The only sound came from cicadas, the only movement from the heavy breathing in their chests. Callan's leg cramped from his awkward positioning. He told Penny he was ready to leave.

Penny didn't want to move.

"We should go," he said, taking her by the arm. "It's getting late."

"But what does it mean?" she asked. "What were we seeing?"

"I don't know, but tomorrow we'll know more. Will you do something else for me?"

"Certainly," Penny said, shivering from the cool air and experience. "Whatever I can."

"Will you give your friend, this Rita woman, a call and

tell her that I'd like to meet her?"

Penny sighed. "I don't want to get her in trouble."

"Who said anything about trouble?" Callan asked. "I want to get her take on what's going on if she'll talk to me."

"I'll give her a call. I don't know what she'll say. She keeps her professional medium activity confidential." Penny led the way down the fence line toward the path, leading them back to the house. "But if she'll talk, if she'll be transparent about anything we've seen, I'm sure you'll find what she has to say very interesting."

The comment was an understatement. "I'm sure I'll find the entire day tomorrow interesting," Callan replied.

Chapter

Thirty-Six

Penny Donnelly arranged for Callan to meet Rita McGarry midmorning the next day. He lodged overnight in a small roadside motel near the interstate and arrived early in Chesterfield, wanting to get a feel for the town and a semblance of what had drawn Randall Banks to the area. Remnants of a vibrant past were evident throughout the small town. He could imagine a child such as Penny's husband, Harold, having everything he wanted within a few spins of his bicycle. Spiced with Federal-style buildings built and preserved from the mid-1800s, Callan wished he could meander inside the old Makepeace House on the corner of Water and Main Street and the Dilts House on the east side of town.

Chesterfield was indescribably quiet and peaceful, not necessarily from inactivity, but from solitude and the relaxed lifestyle the residents chose to live. And for a town of only twenty-five hundred people, Callan found it astonishing that it boasted several well-maintained parks with traditional playgrounds, and two sports and recreation areas with a skate park in one and a ball park in another. Their love for little league baseball had been forever recorded proudly on signs when their 1987 baseball team shared third place in the Little League World Series in Williamsport, Pennsylvania.

Callan turned at the stop light on Washington Street and headed north. The modest gatehouse leading into Camp Chesterfield welcomed him at the end of the street. He entered slowly, choosing to walk rather than drive through the tree-shaded camp as sun filtered through the hardwoods. He parked in front of the old Sunflower Hotel and made his way past Founders Rock, a huge glacial boulder quarried from the banks of the White River, made into a memorial of the camp's 1890s' founders.

He stopped and gazed under the trees into the parkland. Stillness and peace consumed him. Everywhere he looked, places had been created to express beauty, a love for a divine creator, and spiritual balance with nature. A cool breeze mixed with the warm rays of sunshine added to Callan's awareness of well-being.

He strolled deeper into the camp's living memorial. Even the historic buildings that dotted the camp exuded a sense of peace. The Chapel in the Woods, the cathedral at the top of the bluff overlooking the river, and the Hett Art Gallery nestled in the trees. Tree of Life Book Store and Maxon Fellowship Center were grouped conveniently along Lincoln Drive to avoid blocking the serene views of the shaded mall.

Callan stopped to admire the Buddha Gardens, the Garden of Prayer, the Chesterfield Sentinel Angel, and the Quan Yin Goddess of Mercy statue before finding the Trail of Religion that paid homage to each of the great religions of the world. Special homage, however, was made to the spirit of the Native American on Inspiration Hill with the American Indian Memorial and Totem Pole.

Cottages along Grandview and Parkview Drives intrigued him. He paused momentarily in front of several of them, where residents of the camp had permanent and seasonal homes. Most maintained their quaint architecture. Modest signs posted over the door or near the walk revealed the resident's spiritual specialty.

As he finished his circular walk around the camp, Callan noticed a woman sitting contentedly at one of the toadstools under a grove of trees. Callan later learned that mediums used the small tables with two seats for readings. The woman didn't sit as if she was anticipating a reading. She sat in waiting. Callan wondered if she was Rita McGarry and, having noticed his mindless wandering, she had chosen to meet him outside in the pleasant breeze.

The woman appeared to be midthirties. Her skin was naturally smooth with a creamy hue, her nose softly rounded, lips rosy and thin, and her blond hair was full and styled neatly in a crescent pattern to the back of her head. Sunflower-studded earrings glistened in the sun as he approached. He called out, asking if she was Ms. McGarry.

"You must be Professor Morrow," she said, extending her hand. "Please, call me Rita. I hope you don't mind, but I took the liberty of sitting at one of our stools. It's rather nice today, isn't it?"

"Very much so, Rita, and please call me Callan. I hope you weren't waiting long. I arrived early and decided to see the camp for myself before we met. I may have taken more time than I should've. For that, I apologize."

"Oh, please, don't. The time was well spent. It gave you an opportunity to feel the serenity of this place and to gain an understanding of the inner peace we strive to exhibit and achieve."

Callan said it did.

"Good," she said, smiling gently. "It's important to have a sense of peace and tranquility before we talk."

"Did Penny tell you why I wanted to have this meeting?"

"She wasn't totally transparent."

Callan sensed restraint in the tone of her voice. He turned away to focus on something that he hoped would take her mind off any concern for their meeting. "I noticed the sunflower has a subtle presence throughout the camp," he said.

"Yes, you're very observant. It's a hearty, beautiful plant for one. Mostly, though, we like how it faces the morning sun and embraces its rays throughout the day. Our camp's motto is '*As the sunflower turns its face toward the light of the sun, so spiritualism turns the face of humanity toward the light of truth.*'"

"Is that why I see the history of various religions here?" he asked.

"Yes," she said, admiring the grounds. "Spiritualists believe that all religions carry some truth. That's why you'll see representations of all the great religions of the world. We respect all religions and draw upon their teachings."

"I can see the importance of that," he said.

She smiled, somewhat patronizingly. "But you stop short in saying that you believe they *are* the truth."

Callan's pleasant demeanor dissipated but he meant no disrespect. "I want to be upfront and tell you that I believe Jesus Christ is the true Son of God."

"As do I, Callan," she said adamantly in her defense. "I'm

a Christian first. Many here are not, but they respect my beliefs as I do theirs. We're all different in our beliefs at Camp Chesterfield. That's what makes us human, and our spiritual lives balanced."

"I'm not judging you or anyone else at the camp, Rita. I leave all judgment to the One who knows each of our hearts best. I must, however, get to the truth about Randall Banks. You know him as Thomas Bradford. His real name is Randall Banks, a professor at Vermillion College."

Rita sighed. Callan suspected the news didn't surprise her much. "So how may I help you?" she asked.

"Did Penny tell you that we saw you last night at the cottage Professor Banks rents?"

"No, she didn't mention it, but I suspected as much when she divulged tidbits of knowledge that she could've only gained if she'd seen what happened."

"May we speak candidly?" he asked. "The motive for my being here is to get to the bottom of why a young woman, a student of mine at Vermillion, has consciously stopped attending classes to spend her time with Professor Banks."

"Then, yes, please, be candid as long as I may be candid with you also."

"Agreed," he replied, "and thank you. I'll start off by saying that last night appeared to be some sort of a ceremony. Is that correct?"

"Let's say it was ceremonial, at least in Mr. Bradford's mind. I'll leave it at that. I was led to believe that I was there to conduct a séance, but it turned out to be more like what you said—a ceremony."

"Penny and I didn't stay to the end," Callan said. "Did he conduct a sweat lodge along with a séance last night?"

"No, or else I wouldn't have agreed to be there. I'm

familiar with what happened near Vermillion, and it's my understanding that he's conducted such cleansing experiences at the property on Kik Lane, but I didn't put two and two together. I didn't realize the Vermillion incident was related."

Callan pulled from his pocket the card with Marissa Reynolds's name on the front and the copyright symbol on the inside. He'd carried the card with him since he found it on the floor of his classroom. The edges were worn, the card creased somewhat, but it was still legible. He handed it to Rita, anticipating that he was handing it to someone for the last time.

Rita took the card, read Marissa's name, and opened the card. She frowned immediately upon seeing the insignia. "It's the Circle of Chesterfield," she said, returning the card.

"Nothing to do with a copyright?"

"The Circle of Chesterfield. That's exactly what it stands for."

"But what is . . ."

"I can't give you a simple explanation, Professor," she said, squirming on the stool.

Callan paused to let the medium collect her thoughts. "Any explanation you can provide would be helpful. It'd be more than I have currently."

Rita nodded. "You'll have to be patient, though, because I must first tell you what's behind the circle and how I came to know Randall Banks as Thomas Bradford."

Callan replaced the card in his pocket, folded his hands, and rested them reverently in his lap.

Rita glanced to where the Garden of Prayer grotto and Sentinel Angel watched over the camp. "If you've never heard of Thomas Bradford of Detroit and the story associated with his name, then my explanation will make no sense," she said.

"I have no idea what you're talking about," he admitted.

She sighed. "Very well, then Randall Banks's delusional twists will sound even more extraordinary to you. The Circle of Chesterfield and activities along with it, such as cleansings, ceremonies and séances, all have to do with the professor's obsession with the second coming of Christ."

"The second coming?"

"Not so fast," she said, raising her hand. "Professor Banks's idea of the second coming isn't quite accurate. I believe he has the second coming confused with the rapture. They both deal with the end of time, but they're two totally different events. The professor mixes and combines the events either because he's confused or because he needs attributes from both events to achieve his self-serving objectives."

"I wouldn't be surprised if it's the latter," Callan said.

"I'm with you," Rita replied, "but it gets odder. The bottom line is that he's interested in learning the timing of the second coming. As you know, the Bible is very clear. The time and place is unknown to everyone, even to Jesus."

"Only the Father knows," Callan added. "So why is he so adamant that he's the one that God is going to reveal this information to?"

"One can only guess, but I'm sure a little narcissism is involved and his self-serving need for attention, not just within the Circle of Chesterfield, but to the world. He has a compulsive need to be recognized for something extraordinary."

Callan shook his head. He still didn't understand completely. "But what does he hope to achieve?"

Rita sighed. "He wants to pinpoint its exact timing."

"That's beyond extraordinary, Rita," Callan said. "It's impossible!"

"And dangerous," she added. "I feared for myself last

night. I feared for those in the tent. The circle has taken an evil twist. It's more than just a curiosity of the sun, stars and ancient earthworks built by the Adena people who understood their relationship. His plans reach beyond them."

"To include what?" Callan asked.

Rita McGarry stared gravely into his eyes. "Death."

CHAPTER

THIRTY-SEVEN

"That's a serious accusation," Callan said. "What happened last night for you to say that?"

Rita glanced again across the camp's shaded park. "About three weeks ago," she said, "this man named Thomas Bradford called and asked for me specifically. I didn't know him, and he didn't know me. I believe he saw my profile on the internet and said he was interested in a psychic reading, maybe a séance in the future."

"You were agreeable to that?"

"Of course. I had no reason at that point not to be. I asked if he'd received such a reading before, but he said no. I told him it didn't matter but asked what he expected from it or what he hoped to achieve. He was quite sincere when he said he wanted to reach peace with recent decisions he'd made and to find out if he had reason to believe these decisions would be successful."

"Sounds fairly benign," Callan replied. "Did you give him one?"

"No, he met me here by the toad stools and discussed a desire to have a series of séances. The Circle of Chesterfield was mentioned, but he raised the subject more as an idea than an organization or group, meant to achieve knowledge and wisdom as no human had ever received before."

"Was he talking about the second coming?"

"Not at first, but eventually I realized that was exactly what he was talking about."

"What did you say?" Callan asked.

"I recited passages from the Bible. He listened intently. Not sure he comprehended or understood, but he smiled and nodded at all the right times. In hindsight, I believe Mr. Bradford—or your Mr. Banks, whoever you want to believe he was at the time—wanted me to object to the circle's mission and to his theories."

"Really?" Callan asked. Rita's statement astonished him. It contradicted his own experience with the man. "Why would he want that?"

Rita smirked. "I believe he wanted an objective opinion of what he'd be up against when he faced the outside world."

Callan held his breath and thought for a second.

"He wanted to use me as a sounding board to develop defenses to those who'd object or refute what he wanted to do. He didn't realize he was talking to the biggest naysayer of all. I recited *Matthew 24:36* to him."

"Not much one can say to that. Isn't that the verse that says no one knows the day or hour of Christ's coming, not even angels or the Son, only the Father?"

A pallor blanketed her cheeks. "Yes, and you're right, he

didn't say anything; he just laughed." She reached out to touch Callan's arm. "He believes, truly believes, Professor, that he can outsmart God."

Callan couldn't help but chuckle. "How in the world is Randall Banks planning to do that?"

"He believes quite seriously there are clues in heaven that we wouldn't know about on earth. Clues that a saint may have picked up somehow. Spiritualists communicate with the saints. He was counting on that."

"But God is God, Rita. He doesn't slip up like you or me."

"I know, but that's how arrogant and delusional this man is."

Callan scratched his head and thought for a second. "Okay, so Banks called upon you to be a conduit between him on earth and a saint in heaven, is that it?"

"Precisely, but I told him that our connection with the saints doesn't work that way."

Callan laughed again. "I don't see how he thinks it could work in *any* way. I mean, out of all the saints in heaven—everyone who has died before us—how does he expect to find that one special saint who has overheard or picked up on one of God's clues?"

Rita sat back on the stool and said solemnly, "That's where the Circle of Chesterfield comes in. Professor Banks needs his own alternative way of getting the information he needs. He can't expect to find the one or two saints in heaven that might have received some information."

"So what does he need?"

"His own saint."

"I don't understand," Callan said.

"He needs his own dedicated saint in heaven to communicate back to him what he or she has learned. If

Professor Banks has his own saint to call upon specifically—a saint who can be called upon by name—he believes he can obtain the information he's seeking."

"That's why he needs you."

"Yes, to be the medium during the séance to communicate with the saint he's chosen."

"But," Callan responded, pausing, "that means someone has to die."

"Yes, exactly," Rita said. "Someone must die. Professor Banks must know in advance who he'll be talking to in the spirit world for his scheme to work. So someone must die, Callan. That's why they're called the chosen one."

CHAPTER

THIRTY-EIGHT

Callan sat back and looked off into the distance. "Forgive me," he said gravely, "but I'm still not following you all the way."

"I didn't understand it at first until I sought the counsel of one of my friends here at the camp," Rita replied. "I asked her if a Thomas Bradford had ever sought counsel at Camp Chesterfield before. She looked at me oddly and asked, 'Did you say Thomas Bradford?' I said yes. Then she repeated his name, *Thomas Lynn Bradford,* as though the name had special significance."

"I take it his middle name was very relevant," Callan said. "Who was this guy?"

"Someone from Michigan. Apparently, about a hundred years ago, there was a Thomas Lynn Bradford in Detroit. He dabbled in spiritualism. He considered himself a spiritualist anyway. He was obsessed with proving that the human body contained a soul and that there was life after death."

Callan shrugged. "Both you and I believe in such a thing without having to prove it, don't we?"

"Yes, but what we have is faith and believing before seeing. This Thomas Lynn Bradford wanted more than faith. He wanted evidence of life after death for himself."

"How was he planning to prove it?"

"He committed suicide."

Callan's mouth gaped.

"Yes, exactly," Rita replied. "Oh, I researched this man from Detroit after my friend mentioned him. I'm sure he's who your Randall Banks took his alias from."

"What did you find out?" Callan asked.

"On the sixth day of February in 1921, Thomas Lynn Bradford rented a room in Detroit, sealed it completely shut, blew out the pilot light on a gas heater, turned up the gas jets, and allowed the noxious fumes to take his life—all to prove his point."

"The only point I'm seeing is that he didn't take many other lives in the building with him."

Rita scoffed. "Self-centered individuals like Thomas Lynn Bradford and Randall Banks aren't concerned about other people's lives, Professor."

"But, still, I can't see how his suicide proves anything, especially not life after death."

Rita leaned closer. "It doesn't, but a curious thing happened before he died. Thomas Lynn Bradford solicited the help of a woman named Rita Doran, also of Detroit."

"Was she a friend of his? How did he come across this Rita?"

"He put an ad in the newspaper, seeking someone interested in spiritualism as he was."

Callan nodded. "And this Rita Doran answered his ad."

"Much like the young students Randall Banks solicited at Vermillion."

"You're not suggesting . . ."

"I am, Professor," Rita said adamantly. "That's exactly what I'm doing. I believe Randall Banks knew about Thomas Lynn Bradford in Detroit, became obsessed with his plan for the afterlife, and determined that it was an excellent way to prove his own theories about the second coming."

"I take it you believe Randall Banks came to you, portraying himself as Thomas Bradford to hide his real identity," Callan said thoughtfully.

"That and to be in character for his charade. Wouldn't it seem that way?" she asked. "I don't believe him calling me a few weeks ago out of the blue was a coincidence. My name is Rita. My last name isn't Doran, but if he was seeking another spiritualist named Rita, then I fit the bill close enough. Coincidence, Professor?"

Callan shook his head. "No. When it comes to schemes of the human heart, I don't believe in coincidences very often."

"I don't in this case either. This Randall Banks is a shrewd and tactical man."

"Did your friend here at the camp tell you all this?" he asked.

"Oh, no," Rita said. "She gave me just enough information for me to conduct my own research. Apparently, some of the spiritualists here had also heard of Thomas Lynn Bradford in Detroit. I just wasn't one of them."

"So what did you discover about Rita Doran's role in this man's scheme?"

"Her role was to get in touch with a spiritualist who'd put her in contact with Bradford on the other side."

"I assume she found such a person."

Rita shook her head. "Fortunately, the spiritualists she contacted refused to entertain her. They weren't interested. They considered Bradford a crackpot, someone to stay away from."

"So what happened?"

"She tried a séance of her own."

Callan chuckled. "Naturally. That would be convenient and a lot less risk, wouldn't it?" he asked. "Doing a séance herself would almost ensure her and her witnesses that Bradford would come forth from the other side."

"Yes, but it didn't happen that way," Rita replied. "In fact, quite the opposite. Rita Doran tried for days to get ahold of the dead Mr. Bradford. After she failed, other psychics joined in and claimed to have heard from him. They confirmed that Mr. Bradford must've just entered the spiritual realm, and his energy wasn't strong enough to penetrate back into the earthly realm."

Callan sighed, unable to believe the story he was hearing.

"No one else believed it either," Rita said.

"So Thomas Lynn Bradford died an obscure death, ultimately proving nothing."

"Which is all the more reason why Randall Banks is out to prove his own theories so that he can be the first," Rita added.

"In essence, also making himself a chosen one."

Callan and Rita sat quietly, staring at each other, assessing each other's thoughts. Callan desperately wanted to learn what had happened the night before in the clearing, the apparent ceremony he and Penny Donnelly had seen. He asked if she was willing to talk about it.

Rita closed her eyes to muster the courage to speak. "Professor Banks called for a séance. He invited several women and me. There were two men, but their presence was intimidating. They appeared to be personal bodyguards or something. I've never experienced anything like it at a séance before."

"Tell me about the women," Callan said.

"There were five of them and two girls. The girls were school-age locals, but the young women who attended were college-age."

"From Vermillion?"

"Yes, I believe so," she said.

"Was one of them Marissa Reynolds?"

"Her name was never spoken by the professor, but I heard other women call her by her first name. Yes, I believe they called her Marissa. We were brought together to reach a young man named Conner. I didn't catch his last name. Professor Banks wanted to know what Conner had learned in death."

Her statement saddened Callan, recalling the somber faces of Kevin and Beverly Whaite. "Were you able to reach Conner?" he asked.

"No, and it infuriated Banks. He was angry at me, at Conner, and at himself. He said that he knew Conner had not been thoroughly cleansed. Conner was the chosen one, but it didn't work out because Conner allowed doubt to affect his spirit before the cleansing could be completed. That's why he died."

"Heartless," Callan said of the professor. "Did Banks mention the name of Logan Allister, by any chance?"

Rita paused for a second. "Logan? Why, yes, he did, but it wasn't very flattering."

"What do you mean?"

She leaned closer again. "He said that Logan wanted to be the chosen one, but he wasn't clean, and his heart wasn't in it for the knowledge and the spirit of awareness."

"I don't understand what all that means," Callan admitted, "but I suppose it doesn't matter. If Conner or Logan weren't the chosen ones, then who is?"

"Oh!" Rita said, "I think you know the answer to that. The evening was centered around one woman who represented a divine star. Her court included the six other women and girls who were at the ceremony. They fulfilled the constellation he needed to reach the heavens."

"Pleiades," Callan said.

"And whatever Professor Banks believes, he believes he has the power to receive, the power to give, and the power to choose."

"And he's made his choice," Callan said somberly.

Rita nodded. "He's chosen Marissa."

CHAPTER

THIRTY-NINE

Callan and Rita finished their conversation, lamenting the sorry state in which Randall Banks had left many lives, especially those of the Whaite, Allister, and Reynolds families. After leaving the camp, Callan purchased a well-deserved cup of hot coffee, ordered it to go, and sat behind the wheel of his car, holding the cup gently on his knee as he rubbed his temple with his free hand. He'd gathered enough insight to find Marissa Reynolds, but Rita McGarry's incredible story about Randall Banks's mindset overwhelmed him. He wanted more than anything to barge into the cottage and rescue the young women inside, but doing so could potentially backfire.

He couldn't call the police either. So far, in the eyes of the authorities, evidence wasn't strong enough for Randall Banks's arrest in the deaths of Conner or Logan, and he hadn't kidnapped Marissa. She appeared to be at the cottage on Kik

Lane by her own volition. Callan didn't know enough about the other women with Marissa to make a determination about their situation. That included Arla May and the other small girl.

One thing was for certain, however: Randall Banks was more delusional than Callan had imagined. He didn't understand the man at all and certainly didn't have a clear conception of the breadth of his plans.

An image of Margot Banks flashed before him. What enormous restraint she displayed, speaking of her estranged husband without spewing anything more venomous than what she already had. Callan didn't believe he could've disguised his disdain if he'd been in her position, but Margot did so with remarkable restraint. On second thought, he recalled his conversations with her. Maybe not—maybe it wasn't restraint. Perhaps she, too, didn't know the true extent of his theories and interests. She couldn't discuss what she didn't know. Anyone could show restraint if they were oblivious. That could've been Margot. She either didn't know or chose not to know.

Callan sipped his coffee. Caffeine pulsed through his veins. The steam, rising from the rim, roused his energy. He took a deep breath, and, suddenly, he was alive and thinking more clearly. He welcomed the reawakening. There was work to do.

~

Penny Donnelly inched her way through the thick foliage of the woods behind her house. She followed the path to the clearing that she'd guided Callan on the night before and wondered how she'd found her way in the darkness. It was daylight, but the trail was overgrown and covered with ferns and twigs. More so than she remembered. Sunlight tried to reach the ground below but was blocked by the hardwoods cowering over her. Blackbirds cawed. Locusts hummed. Something furry scampered away from near her feet. She jerked toward the rustling of leaves but didn't jump. She wasn't afraid.

Callan had told her not to come to the clearing without him. He didn't trust the professor or his goons, as he called them. But she had to see the clearing for herself. The makeshift tent in the light. She couldn't wait for Callan to return from his meeting with Rita McGarry. The blackbirds, locusts and critters wouldn't deter her.

Penny looked back toward the house. She couldn't see the modest dwelling from where she stood, but she knew her home was there, where she had left her husband, Harry, in the caring hands of a neighbor who offered to sit with him until she returned. Libby was a dear friend—a new friend— recently moved two houses to the south. Penny wasn't sure where she came from. Libby's past seemed ambiguous to Penny, but she didn't care. A heart warmer than her hugs, a kind word when Harry was at his most difficult, and eyes that understood the patience required to deal with a loved one with dementia were Libby's gifts. If angels came to earth disguised as people, then Libby Hartman was surely one of them. And Penny was grateful.

She turned off the path and trod through thicker vegetation to get to the fence line that separated her property from the Wainstetter land that Randall Banks rented. Penny tucked strands of loose hair under a worn garden hat and wiped perspiration off her brow. The autumn equinox was near, but the summer air was still warm, drawing sweat bees around her face to swat away.

Penny drew near to the spot where she and Callan had stood before just in time to see two cars kick gravel down Kik Lane. If she'd hurried faster through the wood's thickness, she might've been able to see who and how many got into the cars. But she was too late. The only car she could see still near the cottage by the clearing was a dirty tan one. A man in dark clothing stood in front of the car, leaning his butt against the grill, smoking a cigarette and checking his fingernails as if he was waiting for someone to come out of the cottage.

To the right, a flap opened on the tent and two young women emerged. Penny couldn't tell if she recognized either one of them from the night before. Odd, high-pitched tones emitting from the opening softly faded away when the women let the flap close gently behind them. She watched the women as they strode toward the cottage, speaking discreetly, until they reached the door and went inside.

Soon, another woman emerged from the tent. She hurried away but didn't go inside. Instead, she walked down the side of the cottage to the man leaning against the tan car. She said something to him, and he pointed toward the cottage. She made a comment that didn't appear to faze the man and hurried out of sight to the front of the house while he took a puff and kicked a couple of rocks underfoot.

Suddenly, the man looked up and came away from the grill, anticipating someone who'd obviously come out from the door out of Penny's line of sight. He stepped around the side of the car and opened a back passenger door, but the people who'd now come into view weren't interested in getting in the car. The man hollered for them, but he was ignored.

Penny gasped. A man and woman, holding the hands of a little boy between them, walked past the man holding the car door open and continued down the lane unintimidated by the man's ranting at them to get into the car. Penny's gaze darted around the property from the tent to the house to the car and down the lane. She expected—no, she hoped—to see Arla May with them, too, to be relieved to know the little girl was safe with others. The thought that she was inside the cottage with such an odd group of people as who'd come out of the tent and into the house caused her to shudder.

Penny reached inside a pocket to pull out her phone to call Callan, to tell him about what she was seeing, but felt emptiness instead. She must've left her cell on the counter in the kitchen.

She remembered Harry telling her one time about seeing the couple and the little boy. She thought her husband was having a delusion. His description of them being sure of where they were going but disengaged with their surroundings was exactly what she'd just witnessed. "They're not of this place," he said to her. Penny didn't know what he meant at the time, dismissing it to dementia, but now she understood. She saw it herself.

Penny squinted. Still, no sign of them. Gone. Wherever they were, they'd fled to a place where she could no longer see them. The man had lost interest, it seemed. He slammed the car door shut, flicked his cigarette onto the dusty drive, and meandered toward the cottage, hands in his pockets, not giving the couple and their strange little boy a second thought.

~

Callan seethed upon hearing that Penny had gone against his wishes and surveyed Banks's clearing alone. She confessed immediately upon reaching her house, calling him when she found her cell. He scolded her repeatedly, reminding her that

Randall Banks had at least two men at his disposal, and he'd use these men in any capacity he could to reach his destiny. No harm had come to her, but harm could easily have been done.

He shouldn't have been so brash with Penny, but her bold independence alarmed him. Randall Banks wasn't a man to be trusted. Callan didn't believe for one second that he'd care that Penny was a woman up in years. He'd hurt or kill her if he had to. And he was a liar. He'd disguise the truth with false alibis and witnesses. Conner and Logan were proof of that.

Randall claimed he wasn't at the sweat lodge when Conner Whaite was killed, even though circumstantial evidence indicated that he was not only there, but he directed the cleansing. He claimed he wasn't at Mount Nebo the day Logan Allister was killed, but he was seen by two geocachers, searching for a document that Logan placed into a cache on the prominence. He also claimed to be Thomas Bradford to Penny Donnelly and Rita McGarry to mask his experimental theories at the cottage he rented from A. D. Wainstetter.

There was no doubt that if Penny had been caught spying on his enclave in the clearing, harm would've come to her, and Randall Banks would've been nowhere in the vicinity, according to his testimony.

Callan needed backup before he proceeded further. He couldn't do it alone, and he needed more than Penny and Rita to bring Marissa home. Before pulling out of the coffee shop parking lot, he made an urgent call to John Steinmeier. John was preoccupied and unavailable, assisting authorities with the sweat lodge incidents. He tried Leah next. Fortunately, she answered soon after he rang.

"You want what?" she asked when he asked if she'd be able to help. "Come to Chesterfield? Oh, I just can't, Professor. I have so much going on with my classes. Don't you need the police?"

"No," he replied adamantly. "I don't have enough proof to call them yet, and, besides, the authorities here aren't up to speed about the activities in Chesterfield as they are in Vermillion or Benton counties."

"Okay, I get it, but I really can't, Professor. I'm sorry. I just can't make it."

Callan said he understood, dejection in his voice.

"You could try Mitchell," she said.

"He has classes too."

"Yes, I know, but Marissa is all he talks about. I don't think he's been going to class. I don't think he's been doing much of anything since Marissa stopped contacting us. He'd feel better helping you out rather than being here."

"He hasn't heard anything from her?"

"No," Leah replied, her voice trailing.

Callan detected a hesitation. "But what?" he asked. He suspected the hesitation wasn't about Mitchell. "Have *you*?"

"Yes," she said meekly, "but I doubt if I'll hear anything more. I told her what I thought of what she was doing with Professor Banks. About being the chosen one and how stupid the whole thing sounds. I told Mitchell what I said to her, and he got pissed. I think I made things worse for him."

Callan paused. "Then I shouldn't call him to help."

"But he'd really like to," she added.

"I'm sure he would, Leah, but I don't know where his head is. He'll need to focus. I can't put him in a situation he can't handle. Besides, I need more than Mitchell with this situation."

"Have you tried Professor Fordworth? I saw her crossing the campus today. She asked how it was going. I didn't know enough to tell her anything. She said if there's anything she can do . . ."

"Yes, yes," Callan said, thinking seriously about her as a possibility. "She'd have a level head. If I'm able to get to Marissa, she may even be able to coax her into returning to Vermillion. I'll give her a call."

~

Callan downed the last of his coffee. He sat in his car, now stuffy and warm, rolled down the driver's side window and rested his head against the headrest, contemplating his dilemma. *Mitchell Dells.* Could he trust Mitchell with his current state of mind? Would he be objective and disciplined enough to follow orders? Callan wasn't sure. During their last meeting, Mitchell had been in a terrible state, guilt-ridden over Logan and concerned for Marissa. Callan couldn't remember the last time he'd seen someone so long-faced and heartbroken. No, Mitchell wouldn't do. He couldn't be objective.

Callan remembered a time when he worked as the audit executive at a bank in Indianapolis. He had assigned a staff member to a financial fraud case, involving four elderly couples. The young woman worked diligently against a particular suspect she believed duped the couples, scraping together circumstantial evidence, altering documents, and creating suspicion that wasn't there to nail the guy into confessing. He didn't confess. The true suspect was someone else, but his staff person was so sure. She wanted it to be true; she just had to find the guy behind the scheme to make sense of the victims' loss. Her grandparents were two of the victims.

Never again, Callan vowed. A person intimately involved with a case is never a good idea in reaching the truth; their focus taints their objectivity.

But then again . . .

He thought of Banks and his men, brazen enough to follow him to steal his briefcase, to intimidate Rita McGarry into doing what the professor wanted. Mitchell was young, strong, athletic. He had a martial arts background. A very good one, if Callan remembered correctly. Mitchell's brawn and tactical skills could come in handy.

He grabbed his cell from off his lap and punched Glynis Fordworth's number.

"I thought you'd call," she said when she answered. "I saw Leah today. I figured it was a matter of time before I heard from you."

"She said you offered to help me."

"What do you need?" The warmth in her voice hinted of a smile on the other end of the phone.

Callan told her that he'd be grateful if she could come to Mounds Park for a day or two to watch Randall Banks's clearing as the equinox approached.

"If it can be tomorrow, I can," she responded. "I have an evening class tonight. Then I have nothing for a couple of days. Will that work?"

Callan said it would. "And Mitchell Dells? What do you think about him, coming along?"

She hesitated. "The Adonis?"

"Yes, I suspect, or so women believe."

Glynis snickered. "You trust me alone in the woods with him?"

"He knows martial arts."

"Then I'll behave," she said.

CHAPTER FORTY

When Callan called, Mitchell Dells pounced on the opportunity to help Callan at Randall Banks's clearing. He was feeling better, he told Callan. Their last conversation had helped him to reflect on his involvement in Logan Allister's death more rationally. He thought he was responsible for Logan's death directly by his words to him, but now realized his feelings were simply guilt, penetrating his core, poisoning his perspective. "I wasn't even there," Mitchell said to indicate to Callan that he was fine. "I wasn't the one to pummel Logan, so why should I feel guilty?"

"That's the spirit," Callan said.

That's exactly what Callan wanted to hear from the young man, that he was better and thinking clearly. Callan told him that he wanted Banks's clearing observed prior to the equinox to thwart possible harm to Marissa.

"Why? Is that a possibility?"

"Given what I know now of the circle he's created, I believe it's more than a possibility, Mitchell; it's inevitable. Are you up to the task?"

Mitchell gave Callan his word. "And thanks," he said, before hanging up.

Satisfied, Callan drove to Harry and Penny Donnelly's home across from the park. Penny was out front, picking dead and drying foliage from out of her September flower beds. Callan imagined them once brimming with color and splendor. Now, only mums in rust, yellows, and oranges cast a golden hue against the home's shaded lawn.

Upon seeing Callan drive up, Penny rose from a stooped position, gloved hands on her hips, a trowel hanging from her side. She watched him as he closed the car door and meandered toward her.

"If you're here to admonish me in person, don't," she said gruffly. "It's my property, and I'll do what I want on my own property."

Callan raised his hands to surrender. If he had a white flag, he'd have waved it too. "I don't blame you," he said. "If I said harsh words to you earlier about being alone at the clearing against my wishes, I apologize. You're a grown woman, and it's your property, as you say. I was out of line."

Penny took a deep breath, taking in the apology and exhaling her anger. She dropped the trowel and removed her gloves, letting them fall to the ground as well. "That's not why you're here, to apologize. There's something else on your mind, isn't there?" she asked.

He spoke briefly of his conversation with Rita McGarry.

Penny frowned and motioned for him to come into the house where they could talk more comfortably and over a cup of something soothing.

Harry Donnelly sat in his recliner in the living room, television blaring, eyes fixed on a game show. Callan greeted the old man, but Harry ignored him. Penny walked through to the kitchen, paying no attention to her husband. Callan figured she knew enough of Harry's illness to know when his mind was so deeply entrenched in his own world that no communication was going to arouse him.

Penny reached for the can of coffee from an overhead cupboard as Callan explained in greater detail what Rita relayed to him. He added that he had invited Glynis Fordworth and Mitchell Dells to the clearing the next day.

"Reinforcements?" she asked. "Still afraid I'll do something rash on my own?"

"No," Callan said, smiling, "but reinforcements are a good idea, don't you think? I'm not sure authorities in Vermillion County are giving what I've found here in the Chesterfield area much credence."

"Oh, you've been in contact with them?"

"No, but John Steinmeier, our Director of Security, has. He wasn't crazy about me being here, but knowing John, he's kept authorities in Vermillion updated."

Penny filled the coffee maker with water and turned, shifting weight to a hand braced on the sink counter. "If you've mentioned anything to your Mr. Steinmeier about our idiosyncratic folktales around here, I'm sure they'll count us all as crank pots, and you'll never get their attention."

Callan waved her comment away.

"Oh, please, sir, don't tell me my talk of pukwudgies, fairy circles, Arla Mays, dynamited caves, and what Rita had to tell you of the spiritualist camp hasn't tainted your thoughts of us in Chesterfield," she said.

"Don't give it a second thought."

"But I do. Things that go bump in the night make us sound foolish and uneducated. Some of us *are* foolish, Callan, but we're not daft. There are real stories behind folklore, you know. People nowadays forget that." Penny turned toward the living room where the television continued to blare. "Harry speaks of those stories and superstitions from his childhood here. I feel bad for him. Makes him sound stupid and foolish sometimes. But he's not, he's really not, Callan. Harry was a fine, strong husband and father, a pillar around these parts and for his family. His talk now, though, makes him sound . . . makes him . . ."

"It's his illness," Callan said. "And he's down home, like many of us. He grew up with these stories he tells. He doesn't have to believe them to tell them. They're a part of where he came from."

Penny sighed; sadness filled her eyes as she approached him.

"Look," Callan said, reaching for her hand that she rested on the back of a kitchen chair. "I remind myself that Chesterfield is a community different from most communities. Think about it. There's ancient history here. That's very rare in this country. Not only that, but Chesterfield's history has been preserved and kept alive through folklore and research. The spiritualist camp isn't ancient, but it's been around since the late eighteen hundreds. That's a long time. When you have as much history as Chesterfield has that's been preserved—ancient at that—there are bound to be tales that sound stupid and foolish, but it makes the place that much more interesting."

Penny nodded meekly. "It doesn't mean that we believe in them though," she said.

"Precisely. It simply means that they are engrained so deeply as part of the town's culture that you accept them for what they are and with that in perspective. Kind of like our belief in Santa Claus. We know there is no Santa, but he's tradition, and each of us would be hard-pressed to ignore him as a figment of our imagination. It's the same thing with the mounds, the dynamited caves, the camp, and the pukwudgies. The tales are odd to most outsiders, but they're unique and an important part of Chesterfield's history, tradition, and culture."

Penny smiled for the first time. "You forgot ghosts," she said.

"You have those too?" Callan asked amused.

She shrugged. "Some say they wander in some of the old houses."

"Do you believe in them?"

"Ghosts, you mean?"

He nodded.

Penny smiled again. "I'm probably more open to supernatural occurrences than to ghosts just by my living here for so long."

"What's the difference between a supernatural occurrence and a ghost?"

"I'm not sure there is a difference," she replied, "but the supernatural seems to cover a much larger spectrum. For example, I know Rita believes in spiritualism and the paranormal, but I'm not sure that boils down to ghosts."

Callan nodded, trying to understand but unable to fully. Instead, an image of Arla May came to mind, youth shrouded in mystery.

Penny slid into the chair in front of her and focused on his eyes. "She's rather hard not to think about, isn't she?" she asked.

Callan came to. He twitched and met her gaze.

"I had a hunch that's who you were thinking about," she said.

"Yes, but I'm not sure what to think."

"Don't you?" Penny asked. Something in her tone

indicated that she hoped he did.

"She's a child, Penny." He didn't mean for it to sound flippant, but that's how it came out.

Penny sat back. "You don't mean that."

Callan sighed. He didn't know what he meant exactly, but he wasn't in the mood to discuss it. Doing so would lead him back, he feared, back to a night he accepted in faith whether he understood, a night harder to explain than to believe.

"Just answer me this if you would," Penny said. "I'm only asking because it concerns me so. Is Arla May a lost soul, do you think, roaming the earth until she finds what she's searching for? If it's not the case, then I don't know what to think of her myself."

Callan reached for her hand and squeezed it gently. "I don't believe in lost souls in the sense you're speaking of, especially not with children."

Penny didn't look convinced. "How can you be so sure?"

"I can't entirely," he said, "but my faith is in a God who is much more merciful than to allow children to be lost like that. He takes them home to be with Him, gives them the love they didn't receive on earth. I believe that."

Her eyes widened. "Then who is she?"

There it was. The question he hoped to avoid. He released his hold on Penny's hand and squirmed, rubbing the top of the table before him for something tangible. *Who is she?* Who was the bronzed spirit that held him tightly, gave him love like he'd never felt before, reassured him when the bottom of his own world had fallen out?

Callan didn't mean to say what he believed Arla May was just yet, not until he'd gathered his thoughts completely, but he must've done so. The gasp from Penny's mouth, her palm to the side of her face, and exclamation that she hadn't thought of Arla May in that way told a different story.

"Yes, yes!" Penny said. "An angel. I'm much more inclined to think of Arla May as an angel than a lost soul, yes. Angels do come in different forms, don't they? And there's so much more she could do as a child than she could as an adult. There's an innocence in children. Someone like your Marissa could trust a child, couldn't she? Oh yes, I like the idea that Arla May's an angel, Callan."

Callan nodded, relieved she accepted his thought, but there was something else.

Her eyes narrowed; she bit her lower lip. "But I wonder . . ." she said, her voice fading. "Who is she here for? Do you think it's for this student of yours at Vermillion?"

"It could be anyone," Callan replied, secretly hoping Marissa had such a guardian.

"And what about the family?" she asked. "What about that man, woman and little boy? Do you believe they're angels too?"

He lifted his hand for patience. Callan hadn't quite grasped the concept of Arla May yet. Still, he answered candidly. "Why not?"

Penny tucked a strand of gray hair behind her ear. "I don't know, it's just, well, it's just that they don't look like what I think of angels. I mean, Arla May fits more in line of who would represent an angel to me."

"Is that so?"

"Well, don't you think?"

Callan shrugged. "Who says angels have to look like winged little girls as we see in storybook pictures, or slender young women with porcelain white skin, blond hair and blue eyes?"

"They don't, I reckon," she said. "I've not given it much

thought. I suppose angels need to come in all sizes, in both masculine and feminine forms, to do their works completely."

"That's what I'm getting at."

"But they seem to be a family, Callan."

"Yes, I know," he said, "but they aren't, are they? Even Arla May said so to me in so many words on Fiddleback Mound when I saw her. She told me the man and woman weren't her parents."

"That doesn't make sense."

"Not from an earthly standpoint, I'd agree with you, but each one of them could have a different mission and be called for a specific purpose, perhaps for a different individual. Even though their tasks may be different, being together allows them to fulfill them more effectively."

Penny smiled, admiring Callan's thought process. "You've really thought about this, haven't you?"

He grinned. "Yes and no."

"You can't have a 'yes and no' answer to that question, Callan. You simply can't. I won't accept it."

"Okay then, you're right. Regarding Arla May, no, I haven't spent much time thinking about what or who she is, but as far as angels in general, I've given it a great deal of thought. I've had experiences in my life that I can only explain as having been assisted by angels—each called to help me based upon their purpose at that specific time."

Penny held her breath. She stared intently at him.

"I didn't mean to alarm you," he said.

"No, you didn't. I just don't normally think of men— of men with the kind of inner strength and confidence you have—as having divine revelations such as that."

"Yes, well, we are often underrated, we men, at least the ones you speak of, with true inner strength and confidence."

"And soul," she added. Penny looked into his eyes for several more seconds but remained silent.

Callan didn't add anything to what he'd already said. He sensed she wanted him to, however. He was sure Penny wanted to know more about his experiences, about his thoughts on angels and how they worked in his life. Penny didn't ask any of those questions. Instead, she turned sadly toward the man in the living room who drifted placidly in front of the television, lost in time and space.

"He has an angel, too," Callan said, reaching for her hand again.

"Do you think so?" she asked. A lip quivered. "Sometimes I'm not so sure."

Callan could only nod and tell her that he was sure of it.

She suddenly placed both hands on the table to help her rise then focused her attention away from sadness to the kitchen counter. "Speaking of angels—of mercy or death as the case may be—I've neglected our coffee. You take cream, don't you?"

CHAPTER

FORTY-ONE

The next day, Glynis Fordworth rolled to a stop in front of Mitchell Dells's dorm and spotted Mitchell sitting on a ledge outside the entrance. He nursed a fountain drink with one arm entwined in the straps of a swede backpack. A scowl on his face confused her. Was he angry? The young man tried to disguise his disposition with a pleasant greeting, but Glynis could see through it.

Outside of town, she pasted a smile on her face and said, "Professor Morrow wanted me to thank you again for coming with me."

Mitchell nodded, but his focus remained on the road ahead.

"How were your classes?"

There was a long pause before he finally said, "Good." Then, as an afterthought, he added, "Yes, going very well. Thank you."

A couple of miles passed on the narrow state highway that rose and dipped with the terrain. Mitchell turned his head toward her. He didn't say anything until Glynis turned to face him. "You haven't heard anything from Marissa, have you?" he asked.

"No, nothing," she replied.

"Has Professor Morrow?"

"No, I don't believe he has. I don't believe anyone has lately."

"That's not true," he said sharply. "Leah spoke with her."

"Oh," Glynis blurted, surprised. She'd heard but wanted his take. "I didn't know. What about?"

Mitchell sneered. "That's just it," he said.

Glynis waited for more, but Mitchell chose to sit, content with silence being his response. He seemed calm but his lower jaw ground side to side. "What's just it?" she asked. "What's happened?"

"Nothing's happened. In fact, I don't think anything is going to happen now," he said. "Not the way we want anyway." Mitchell sighed, then rested his head back and closed his eyes. "Not anymore."

~

Combines hummed in the distance, gathering the fruits of a plentiful Hoosier harvest. Callan drove from the studio room he rented in the country south of the park to the Donnelly home, admiring the sun glistening off the massive machines. Glittering rays, softened through tiny shreds of grain dust blown into the air, created halos around the machines as they ground tirelessly through the fields.

The landscape was flat to gently rolling, not particularly

interesting to an outside visitor, but Callan believed strongly that Indiana's gifts weren't in bright lights and attractions. Simple pleasures and good acres of land were overlooked.

That's how Callan felt now, overlooked by the authorities' investigations into Conner Whaite and Logan Allister's deaths. Underestimated by Randall Banks's grand theories to predict the future. And underappreciated by John Steinmeier's skepticism of Mounds Park. John would think even less if he knew pukwudgies roamed the overgrown foliage and dynamited caves where Banks had taken residence.

They may be right, he thought, but there was one important aspect Callan believed they all overlooked. Today was the autumn equinox, a point of balance in the earth's tilt at the equator, where space and stars transition to a new position in the celestial heavens. Beyond marveling at standing an egg or broomstick on end, civilizations had celebrated the autumn equinox for centuries with deeper meaning. Stonehenge was positioned according to the equinoxes and solstices. Machu Picchu in Peru and Chichen Itza in Mexico, the same way. The Great Sphinx and Pyramid of Khafre in Egypt, Newgrange in Ireland, Serpent Mound in Ohio, and Chaco Canyon in New Mexico were all significant in that regard.

Add the Great Mound near Chesterfield, he believed. Why not? Unassuming but enormously complex, the mound and its system of hundreds of additional earthworks around central Indiana were built to honor the sun and the earth's majestic power in the skies. It was no wonder Randall Banks was so attracted to Mounds Park and the unique spiritualism and folklore of the area. Out of the obscure fields and glacial prominences of Indiana, he planned a legacy to be marveled at by humankind and to ennoble himself in the heavens.

Callan pulled into the Donnellys' drive with a new

resolve—to beat Randall Banks in his quest for immortality before anyone else was killed. He was still seated in his car when Glynis and Mitchell pulled in beside him on the double driveway. Callan greeted them with reserved gratitude, grateful for the assistance but cognizant of the potential danger ahead. He introduced them to Penny and Harry and led them through the backyard to the edge of the woods, giving brief instructions regarding the purpose of their tasks.

He noticed Mitchell's subdued demeanor but thought nothing of it until he caught Glynis's apprehension.

"We're not here to be heroes, Mitchell," he said, believing it to be the reason for her warning expression.

"I know," he said bluntly, a tone close to indignant.

Callan paused to study his deep-set eyes and drawn brows. "And you're okay with being here, to watch over the clearing while I attend to Ms. McGarry in case Professor Banks tries to contact her?"

"I said I was."

"Yes, I know, of course, but I want to be sure."

Mitchell extended his hand toward the path, leading into the woods. "I'm sure. Is it this way?"

The young man walked around Callan. The lack of eye contact and clenched jaw caused Callan to look at Glynis for assurance that Mitchell was going to be able to stand watch without blowing their cover.

"I'll look after him," she whispered, patting Callan's shoulder as she passed to catch up.

Callan hurried past the two into the woods, raising a finger to his lips for silence. He showed them the less obvious path to the fence line where they could get a good view of the cottage, the lane, the clearing, and the lodge. Penny Donnelly had set chairs, a cooler, and other amenities to make their stakeout more comfortable.

"It's the equinox," Callan whispered, pointing out the various landmarks on the property, "but Penny and I haven't seen any evidence that there's been a cleansing for Marissa or any other woman who may be in line to be the chosen one."

"You make it sound like there'll be another ceremony after the cleansing," Glynis said.

"I expect one, yes. One that offers a woman, probably Marissa, to the heavens for Professor Banks to contact in the afterlife. But a cleansing must occur first. That's what I don't understand. Why hasn't there been a cleansing? Why isn't there a fire in the pit to heat the rocks yet? That's what I need you to look out for this morning and afternoon."

Callan lifted the lid to the cooler and pointed to sandwiches, canned drinks, apples, and carrot sticks inside. A sack of pretzels and cheese crackers sat on the ground nearby.

Glynis nodded her approval.

Mitchell glared defiantly at the refreshments. "I'm not very hungry," he said.

"Not now, but I want you to eat something after a bit anyway," Callan responded. "I need you alert, and I know young men. I raised two sons. They got grouchy when hungry. I can't have you disagreeable today."

Callan side-glanced at Glynis who exhaled frustration but agreement. He checked his pants pockets for the car keys.

"Anything else we should know before you go?" Glynis asked.

"Yes," he replied, grateful for the reminder. "There shouldn't be too many people coming and going from the cottage or the cleansing lodge. Penny and I have noticed only a few, but they're the same ones each time. There's Professor Banks, of course, and Marissa. Two women about Marissa's age often accompany her. You may recognize them as VC students, Mitchell, so let me know if you do. We've seen two smaller girls, about eight or nine years of age. Not sure what their role is in all of this. Then there are two other men. They drive that tan car you see beside the lane, the one that hasn't been washed. You may recognize them too, Mitchell."

Mitchell stared at Callan, unsure why he'd know them.

"Maybe not their faces, but you may recognize their voices if you're able to hear them from here."

He shook his head, still not sure why Callan would mention the men.

Callan paused to give him the once-over. "When you were ambushed at the sweat lodge outside of Vermillion," Callan said to remind him.

"What . . . oh, that. Yeah, no," he said, shaking his head. "I don't remember much from that night."

Callan hesitated again. "But you remember something, you remember the men, surely."

"What?"

Callan turned toward the cottage and pointed to the car, his voice stern. "I'm talking about the men that drive that tan dirt-buggy over there. They're probably the same men who ambushed you that night, Mitchell. I want you to be vigilant, not just for Glynis and Marissa, but for yourself."

Mitchell looked away but nodded.

Callan looked at Glynis. This time, she bit her lower lip. Callan didn't feel he had any choice but to let the two of them remain at their post in front of the clearing. He was in a bind; he hadn't developed a Plan B. Callan looked at Glynis again. This time, she nodded.

"We got this," she said, then gestured that it would be okay for him to go.

Callan hurried to the Donnelly house, did a wellness check on Penny and Harry, and told them it was important for him to know if Rita McGarry contacted Penny during the day. He needed to stay in touch with the medium. Callan was sure something was bound to happen with the equinox upon them, and he wanted to know sooner rather than later if anything did.

He'd just finished the conversation with Penny when his cell buzzed from inside his pants pocket. Callan answered immediately.

"Professor Morrow?" the caller asked. "This is Rita McGarry. I'm sorry to call you this morning."

"I was hoping you would," Callan said.

"Yes, well, I received a phone call not long ago from Professor Banks. It sounded urgent. He'd like to meet with me at Camp Chesterfield soon."

"Just you?"

"That's what he said because I'm fairly certain he knows you're in town. That's my fault, I'm afraid."

"How's that?"

Rita sighed. "When he requested to meet me, I asked if he'd like someone else in attendance. He sounded alarmed and asked who else should attend. I told him another medium."

"Why did you suggest that?" Callan asked.

"Because I didn't leave on good terms with him at our last meeting. I thought he'd prefer it that way."

"Did he buy it?"

"I don't think so. Not completely. He hesitated for the longest time," Rita replied, "then he asked if this medium would be coming from Vermillion, hinting that it could be you. See what I mean?"

"Yes, I understand, but I don't know what to think exactly."

"I don't either. I let the comment pass and asked what time he'd like to meet. He said he'd like this afternoon, maybe even late this afternoon."

Callan paused. "That doesn't make sense."

"In what way, Professor?"

"It's the equinox. This evening is what he's based his whole theories on. It's important to him. I'd think he'd be preparing for his sacrificial ceremony if there's going to be one. Later this afternoon with you doesn't give him much time."

"Then I'll call and ask if we could make it earlier."

"Yes," Callan said, giving Professor Banks's unusual request more thought. "Yes, but don't tell him that I'll be there."

A grave tone resonated in Rita's voice. "I won't, but please come. I don't want to be alone with that man."

CHAPTER

FORTY-TWO

Glynis studied Mitchell's intense expression as they sat eager, but quiet, secluded behind the barbed-wire fence line. He hadn't taken his eyes off the cottage or tent since they nestled into their hideout. Back and forth, his gaze darted between the two, occasionally shifting to the tan car on the lane. She reached down to rifle through the sack of snacks Penny had provided, then peeked inside the cooler.

"Very nice of Mrs. Donnelly to do this for us," she said.

Mitchell glanced at the open cooler. Her comment didn't register. "Do what?"

"Sandwiches and snacks."

He nodded then turned back to the clearing.

"Something to drink?"

"Nah, I had a sugar-free on the trip. Shouldn't have done that."

Glynis shrugged. She didn't understand.

"I'm in training," he said blandly. "I don't drink shit when I'm in training."

She stared at him blankly.

"Krav Maga," he explained. "I can see you don't know what I'm talking about."

"No, but I'm sure you're very good at it, and from what I know about any kind of training, one has to eat and drink to stay strong," she replied. "You'll have a sandwich, won't you? Penny's gone to a lot of trouble; looks like she's been to a deli."

He turned up his nose. "I don't *eat* shit either."

The comment stung. "Mitchell, Professor Morrow would like you to have something to eat and drink. He said so himself. You can't stay out here all day without something to sustain you."

He looked away.

Glynis closed the lid to the cooler, folded her hands in her lap, and took a deep breath of restraint. It didn't last long. "I'd like to know what's bothering you. Nothing good can come from us being here if you're upset."

No response.

"What did Leah say to you when you talked to her? She must've said something for it to have affected you this way."

Mitchell looked down, closed his eyes, then slowly lifted his head to face her. "You're not going to give up, are you?"

She shook her head, conviction radiating from the expression on her face.

"Okay. It's not what Leah said to me; it's what she said to Marissa."

Glynis couldn't hide her alarm. "Marissa?"

"Yeah, I told you in the car that Leah talked to Marissa. She's the last person to do so. It's what she said to her that makes this whole stakeout meaningless now. Marissa's never going to leave Professor Banks. Not now, not anymore. I know Marissa. She won't."

"I don't understand. What did Leah say to her?"

Mitchell snarled. "Leah told Marissa she wasn't the chosen one. Professor Banks had already chosen Conner for that spot, but Conner's cleansing failed, so that's why Banks picked her. Leah pointed out that if Conner was the chosen one, then she was runner-up. She was number two. She said Banks was using her, but Marissa was too vain and self-centered to see it."

Glynis's heart pounded, still not quite sure why he was so upset. "What Leah said makes sense though."

The young man scoffed and clenched his jaw.

"No, think about it, Mitchell," Glynis said. "Marissa's an intelligent woman. What Leah said would make sense to an intelligent woman. All she was trying to do was reach out to Marissa on her level to help her see the fallacy of what Professor Banks was doing. Can't you see?"

Mitchell turned so fast Glynis started. "No, it's *you* who can't see. You don't get it. That's because you don't know Marissa like I do. You haven't studied with her or talked with her or listened to her inner thoughts and beliefs. You don't know how she thinks, what she feels, or what she wants. You don't even know what makes her tick. You don't know any of that."

"What's your point?"

"I'm saying that you, Leah, and Professor Morrow have it all wrong about her. It's the same reason why she hasn't reached out to her parents. Her parents are helicopters, Professor. They hover over her, sheltering her every move, protecting her from the outside. I remember once when we went to a concert in South Bend. Oh my God. Her mom was a nervous wreck.

She was sure I'd never find their house, like it was out in the boonies somewhere. Then she was worried that Marissa and I would never find the concert venue, as if Marissa doesn't even know her own hometown, what's up or down, this way or that. She was constantly asking me if I knew where I was going and what I was doing.

"And her father is just as bad—harsh and controlling. I could tell in just one evening with those people what she was going through. So yeah, Marissa wants her own space, to find her own being. She knows all about Professor Banks. No one needs to tell her. She's weighed the pros and cons, and she's made her decision. Marissa's made the choice to go through with the Circle of Chesterfield that Banks has envisioned. And she made that decision on her own. Now do you get it?"

Glynis couldn't believe what she was hearing. "Are you saying she's doing this to defy her parents?"

Mitchell placed his head in the palms of his hands and rubbed his face, flicking his sandy hair out of the way. "Not entirely, but if someone says she should, she won't; if someone says she can't, she will. She's sick of people telling her what's good for her. People don't understand that, not her parents, not Professor Morrow, not you, not Leah. Oh God. What Leah said to her was devastating. Using reverse psychology by telling Marissa the fallacy of Professor Banks's theories to make her change her ways wasn't going to work. I know Marissa. It backfired!"

He buried his head in his palms once again. "Instead of coaxing her away from the circle, Leah may have driven her closer to it," he said. "And if that happens, Professor, she's never coming back. Never."

Mitchell emerged, eyes swollen. He wiped drips coming from his nose with the back of his hand. He sniffed and tried to hide the pain stabbing his heart, the humiliation of a young man blubbering in front of a respected professor.

Glynis's eyes softened at the transformation. Mitchell Dells had come to the clearing angry and defiant. Combative. Sharp-spoken and disrespectful. Now, just minutes later, not only was the source of his emotions understood, but his response to the danger of losing Marissa forever was also clearer.

She reached and gently rubbed his back.

He sobbed again.

"You're in love with her, aren't you, Mitchell?"

Chapter

Forty-Three

Callan arrived at Rita McGarry's modest cottage along Eastern Drive in Camp Chesterfield. Fall decorations of pumpkins surrounded by brown, dried cornstalks and gourds of various shapes, colors and sizes adorned the short walk to her front door.

Rita greeted Callan warmly. Her smile was genuine, her voice soft and appreciative. She led him into a small, white kitchen with a round, white, Amish-made table on one side of the room, against a wall.

"I can make you tea," she said. "I only drink green tea, I'm sorry."

Callan declined politely. He'd had enough coffee on the way to keep him wired. He didn't need anything else.

"You probably think it's silly to be so apprehensive about seeing Professor Banks alone again," she said, avoiding eye contact. She gestured for Callan to take a seat at the table.

"No, not at all," he replied. "Your experience with the professor hasn't been a pleasant one. You can't trust his lies, who he portrays himself to be, or his motives. I'm right with you."

She smiled, grateful for his understanding. "It's all rather surreal, isn't it? Being a medium, you'd think I've run into crazier situations than this and would be used to it, but I'm not. I haven't had such an experience before. My clients are very generous and grateful for the information I provide. Their motives are pure, even if misguided sometimes."

Callan reassured Rita that he wasn't there to judge. What she did wasn't his bailiwick, but that didn't make her beliefs any less valid to her.

Rita folded her hands in her lap, leaned forward, and studied his face, especially his eyes. "May I see your hands?" she asked sincerely.

He shook his head. "I'd rather not."

"Any particular reason?"

"No, I'm just not sure what you're looking for, and I'm not interested in knowing. I assume you want my palms for some sort of reading, to foretell what's going to happen to us. Forgive me, but I'm apprehensive and nervous. Whatever will happen today, and this evening, won't be resolved by the lines in my hands. I'm sorry. I'm giving this situation to a higher power, and I'd like to keep it that way."

She sat back and nodded, respectful. "Then I don't suppose you'd be open to a Tarot reading."

An image of an elderly woman came to mind. He smiled, recalling her hands, gnarled but gentle. Her face, dry and creased, but soft and warm. "I knew a grandmotherly woman in Chicago once who dabbled in Tarot," he said. "Bernadette

Powers was her name. I'm very fond of her. She used the cards to determine the outcome of a certain case we were involved in, and . . ."

Callan drifted back to a dark room in Oak Park, Illinois. He could still see the Tiffany-replicated lamp on her wooden nightstand. He could still hear the creaking of the drawer in the nightstand, opening to retrieve her cards. The mustiness of the room, the clutter of magazines on top of aged, faded doilies, her dry, gray hair wrapped in a bun on top of her head . . . it was still vivid in his mind.

"And what, Professor?" Rita prompted.

"They didn't help at all," he said, returning to the present. "The cards only made her more anxious and afraid. In fact, her belief in the cards' outcomes practically had her bedridden with fear. I'll never forget what they did to her," he said. "If you're a devoted Christian as you say, Ms. McGarry, I don't understand why you rely on such things yourself."

Rita's face hardened. She took a deep breath and held it in. "Then you *are* judging me," she finally replied.

Callan looked away. "Yes, I suppose it looks that way to you, but it's a fair question. You're confusing my candidness with judgment."

She bit her lower lip.

"Go ahead," he said. "Your turn. Ask *me* a candid question. Anything. If I have no response for you but feel defensive, then you have a right to judge me on my beliefs. But if I answer you honestly and straightforwardly, and you have nothing to retort, then I don't call it judgment. I call it affirmation."

Rita looked closer into his eyes. "Do you mean that?"

"Yes, certainly."

"No, I mean, about asking you something candid."

Callan paused, realizing he'd opened himself to a

conversation he may not want to have. He arched his back and waited for the question. Apprehension welled. He was surprised when she leaned in and asked, "Do you believe in angels?"

~

Glynis glanced at Mitchell to see how he was doing. He stretched, extending his legs beyond the lawn chair, straightening his back, and drawing his arms behind his head. He yawned, then caught himself, wondering if he yawned too loudly. Glynis said she thought no one on the other side of the fence heard him. Not much was going on at the cottage, clearing, or tent.

"I haven't done anything but look straight ahead, yet I'm exhausted," he replied.

"Try not to worry," she said. "Worry just saps the energy out of a person."

"But he's a madman, Professor."

"Yes, I know, but . . . just the same, try not to worry."

Mitchell ran fingers through his hair to invigorate his scalp, get the blood flowing. "Have you heard anything from Professor Morrow?" he asked, shaking his hair back in place. "I'm surprised nothing has happened yet."

Glynis was surprised also. She glanced at her phone. No messages.

"When did he expect things to happen?" he asked.

She confided that she didn't know.

Mitchell squirmed in his seat, stood and stretched again. His impatience alarmed Glynis. She asked him to sit down.

"I'll contact him now," she said. Glynis thought about calling but wondered how far her voice would carry across the clearing. She decided to text Callan instead.

Nothing yet, she typed.

A few seconds later, a text returned: *It will soon.*

How can you be sure

It's the equinox

Still not sure I understand it all, she replied.

There was a pause. Soon, the following appeared: *You will.*

She reiterated to Mitchell what Callan had texted. The response seemed to satisfy the young man for the time being. She watched Mitchell carefully. Still agitated. Impatient. She picked up her phone again.

A bit of an issue here

Callan replied with a simple question mark.

Love is in the air

What? With Banks and Marissa? Is there not going to be a cleansing but a wedding?

Glynis realized immediately her choice of words were wrong. *No, sorry. Nothing like that.*

Double question marks.

It's Mitchell. He's in love with Marissa.

Pause, then: *Oh shit. You're kidding me, right?*

I wish I were

Get him out of there

Glynis nearly dropped her phone. She caught it midair then replied: *Where's he to go*

Do I need to come there

No, we're fine for now

Let me know if I do. Call don't text. I want to know if he does anything stupid. I'll be right there.

Glynis set her phone in her lap and turned toward Mitchell. He yawned and tapped his right foot with anxious repetition, staring ahead into the clearing.

~

"Trouble?" Rita McGarry asked when Callan set his cell on the table in front of him.

"I don't know," he said. "I don't know what to make of it. I shouldn't say until I've had time to process what I've just heard."

She rose from the table to give him privacy, but Callan requested she stay.

"No," she replied, "I know when someone needs time alone to think, and you need time." Rita side-glanced at the door leading outside. "Besides, I have some nervous energy myself. Piddling in my garden will help." She left the kitchen, stepping into the bright sunshine to pluck brown petals from her potted geraniums.

Callan sat alone at the kitchen table. A clock ticked from another room. The refrigerator hummed. A car passed on the lane out front. Muffled hellos from Rita to a presumed neighbor were short and sweet. He sat with nothing more than his thoughts to confront.

He wasn't sure what to make of Glynis's text messages, especially not in the scheme of things. Did Mitchell's feelings toward Marissa connect anything with Professor Banks? Callan thought back to the beginning when Conner and Logan were found in the first lodge. If Conner had been researching Banks's theories to disprove them, then why did he allow himself to be drawn into the lodge? Was he gathering additional information to use against Banks? If so, did Banks suspect Conner's plans and purposely make the lodge unsafe? Then why put Logan at risk as well? It didn't make sense. No, Conner must've had a change of heart. That leaves Logan in the lodge. He may have been the intended target from the beginning. He was more outspoken than Conner, killed at

Mount Nebo as he planted a handwritten note explaining Banks to be a hoax, hours after Dana Weiss turned down a relationship with him. She was despondent, mostly out of guilt, but not as despondent as . . .

Callan's eyes widened. He held his breath, reaching for his phone on the table. He rose and stepped toward a window, looking out over Eastern Avenue, a cluster of sunflowers towering nearby. He could see Rita, hair glistening in the sun, reaching for her phone also. Callan turned away to punch John Steinmeier's office number into his cell. Travis Wellman answered.

"Is he there?" Callan asked.

"Just a sec."

Callan stepped back to the kitchen table as the phone exchanged hands.

"Yeah, this is Steinmeier," the security director said. "Is this the wandering astronomer?"

"Very funny. Hey, I have a quick question for you, but it's important. Have you received word from Benton County on what they suspect killed Logan Allister?"

"Sure have. Killed by blunt force injuries to his head and abdomen. Split his spleen and his head . . ."

Callan stopped him. "I don't need to know the details. What weapon was used?"

"Didn't find a weapon."

"Wasn't there one found at the scene?"

"No, why? Have you heard differently?" John asked.

"Just asking," Callan replied. "Do they have any idea what was used?"

"Not a clue yet. Still looking into it. Not sure there's been an official word from the medical examiner."

"Are you sure?"

"I'm always sure when I don't know something, Cal. Not hiding anything from you. The investigation is still ongoing up there."

Callan sighed. "That's what I was afraid of."

"Afraid? That's a strange word coming from you," John said, sarcasm thick.

"Yeah, well, not this time, John," he replied solemnly. "Fear is exactly what I'm feeling right now. I'll need you to stand by, close to your phone."

~

Rita entered the cottage, meeting Callan at the doorway, her hands shaking. Flight rather than fight radiated from her eyes. She lifted her phone in front of her. "I just received a call. Professor Banks. He has something he has to do yet, but he still wants to see me."

"What did you tell him?" Callan asked. "Did you mention I was here?"

"No, I didn't want him to know. I told him to call when he gets close."

Callan stepped toward her. "Stay calm, okay? I'm here. I'm going to stay here."

"But what does he want?" she asked, voice quivering. "Oh, I thought I could do this, hoping I could do this, I mean, see him again, but I can't. I don't want to."

"I understand, but any chance to negotiate with him for Marissa's release is a chance we must take. For whatever reason, he still trusts you and believes you're key to his plan. Apparently, whatever you've said or did to him in the past doesn't matter, Rita; he still trusts you. For Marissa's sake, please, do this for her."

CHAPTER

FORTY-FOUR

Mitchell saw the door to the cottage open. Earlier, he'd watched two men build a pyre just yards away, then carry the hot stones one by one, protected by blacksmith gloves, into the domed lodge. Now, the same two men, dressed in black, stepped out of the house on Kik Lane and walked across the lawn side by side without speaking. They stood outside the flap to the lodge, one man on each side of the entrance. Professor Banks followed, holding a lighted candle, its flame lost in the rays of sunlight, while he held a black leatherbound book in the other. He strode more slowly than the men, taking each step deliberately, ceremoniously.

Two young girls came out next. They wore white gowns with halos of white flowers encircling the tops of their heads. Each girl carried a bouquet of autumn flowers in their small hands and stepped expressionless across the yard toward

Professor Banks. They stopped short of entering the lodge, one girl on one side of the entrance, the other girl on the other side, facing the tent.

"What's going on?" Mitchell whispered to Glynis.

"The cleansing must be starting," she said.

Next came two young women, dressed in white, flowing gowns, each holding a bouquet of similar flowers, with a halo of white flowers crowning their heads. They walked in sync toward the lodge.

Mitchell gasped. "I know those girls. They go to VC. They've been in some of my classes. I've seen one hanging around with Marissa sometimes."

Two more women exited the cottage in much the same way as the first two, dressed similarly.

"Do you recognize them?" Glynis whispered.

"No," he said. "Not at all."

The four women took their places behind the small girls, facing the tent.

Finally, Marissa emerged. She also wore white with a halo of flowers encircling her head. She held a lighted candle rather than a bouquet of flowers and stepped toward the tent with an air of grace and divine royalty as if fully aware of the ceremony's importance. Determined and resolved, holding her head high.

Mitchell nearly sprang from his chair, ready to rescue Marissa when he saw her. Glynis grabbed his arm and pulled him back, pleading for him to sit down.

"What's going to happen?" he asked, eyes wide with alarm.

"Nothing yet," she reassured him. "Professor Banks is simply assembling his court."

Mitchell fell back into his seat. Confusion raced in his mind.

"Pleiades," Glynis whispered. "Seven divine sisters. They're finally in place."

~

Marissa proceeded into the tent without hesitation. Professor Banks followed her inside, closing the opening after doing so. Marissa crouched and shuffled the pile of hot stones, glowing in the center of the lodge, with a metal rod she picked up from the floor. The embers grew brighter. Already, perspiration formed on her forehead and neck. Her white cotton gown clung to her back.

Her gaze darted around. Crudely constructed from five-foot branches corded together at the top and along the side supports with strips of willow bark from the branches, the dome was covered in white blankets, layered from the bottom, leaving no space at the top for steam to escape.

Professor Banks kneeled on the other side of the stones, facing her. He extinguished his candle and lifted his right hand, making a large circle in front of him. Marissa realized he was drawing a circle around her body, a symbolic gesture of wholeness.

She kneeled and extinguished her candle.

"During this time, think of healing," he instructed her. "Be reverent, be silent. Pray for guidance and enlightenment. Be cleansed and purified so that your prayers will be heard and answered accordingly. Most of all, be humble. You are the chosen one, Marissa, but there is no reward for arrogance. Do you understand these things?"

Marissa nodded.

"Then let the cleansing begin."

Professor Banks rose slowly and left the tent as

ceremoniously as he entered.

A sweet waft of fresh autumn air rushed in, cooling Marissa's saturated skin for just a moment. She stared at the glowing stones, captivated by their mesmerizing hue and crackling sounds. The tent was dark except for the stones. There'd be a break, she reminded herself. Professor Banks promised her a break. After the break, there'd be another round of purification and cleansing. Another break and then the last of the process. Three rounds in all. Three divine rounds, then she'd be cleansed, worthy of receiving the fruits of the circle's promises.

The Circle of Chesterfield.

How honored she was to be chosen, to be the one purified by the circle to receive its gifts. She sang in her head hymns of praise. Marissa wasn't sure what the words meant, but it didn't matter. She was filled with joy. The joy kept her mind off the heat and the drenching sweat, rolling off her forehead and into her eyes, from between her shoulder blades to the small of her back. Her gown, now completely saturated, weighed heavily upon her weakened frame.

In the middle of a verse, Marissa stopped singing. Something moved in front of her. She looked up and saw a blurred image of her grandfather repairing a chair leg on his workbench. Marissa extended her hand to touch him. She missed him so much, longed to see him, but he was out of reach. No, that wasn't true; he wasn't even there. Her hand felt nothing. The image wasn't real. Marissa couldn't understand. She was so sure he was there for her to touch and to be held on his knee as he had when she was a child. Love pure and simple. Unconditional affirmation. That's all she wanted from him. That's all she wanted from her parents and friends around her—all she wanted now.

Stop. I'm losing it, she thought. *I can't lose it.*

But what did she have, she wondered? Was it what she wanted? She recalled her last conversation with Leah Carver. Leah told her the Circle of Chesterfield wasn't real. The cleansing meant nothing; her sacrifice would not lead to a promise. Marissa snarled under the sweat that dripped from her nose, clogging what breaths of air she could feed into her lungs.

She tried to push Leah's harsh words from her memory, to think of anything that could keep her from losing determination and consciousness. Trying not to concentrate on the heat and her own misery was harder than Marissa thought it would be. Was it because she was so focused on her own comfort in life that she couldn't bear a few minutes of an intolerable trial for a larger prize? Or was Leah right all along? Was this a sham? Was Marissa the impostor, believing that she was the only one destined to fulfill the circle's raison d'être? Suddenly, she wasn't sure, but it didn't matter anymore. Just a few more minutes was all she had to endure to know the truth.

Marissa smiled, staring into the silvery stones. *At last,* she thought, *the world will know, including Leah, that I'm the chosen one.*

"How long does this take?" Mitchell asked Glynis, weary and frightened. She sensed he was becoming more agitated, watching the tent, only being able to see Marissa when she had come out of the flaps two times since the ceremony had started.

Glynis turned. "Weren't you forced into one of these sweat lodges? How long did it take *you?*"

Mitchell shook his head. "Mine wasn't like this."

Glynis didn't question. She watched as Professor Banks turned from his stance outside of the tent and went inside for the final time. When he emerged, Marissa's limp body was cradled in his arms. Limbs hung over his arms, swinging like those of a sleeping child being carted off to bed. The professor hurried to the cottage. Behind him, the women, the two little girls and the men followed close behind. Professor Banks stopped suddenly.

Marissa moved. She wanted down from his arms. She pleaded to walk on her own, to show the world that Marissa Reynolds was worthy of what had transpired. He resisted, but soon relented, and the young woman stood uneasily on her feet, holding onto his shoulder for support. Marissa stumbled several times before gaining a foothold, finishing her trek from the lodge and climbing the steps to the cottage on her own.

When the last of the entourage had entered the cottage, Glynis picked up her cell and texted Callan: *It's over. She's okay.*

Chapter

Forty-Five

Glynis felt her cell vibrate with a return text from Callan, relaying to her that he and Rita McGarry were still waiting at Rita's home in Camp Chesterfield for Randall Banks to arrive. Glynis texted back that she suspected the professor was waiting to see if Marissa would fully recover after the ceremony. Glynis didn't know how long it might be because she wasn't sure how Marissa was, but by the looks of Marissa climbing the steps to the cottage, she didn't believe she'd be long. It didn't appear she required medical attention.

Glynis was right. A blue sedan came up the lane and parked next to the dirty tan car. They couldn't see well, but the car only had one occupant, the driver. She tapped the horn lightly three times. Upon doing so, the four young women that Mitchell recognized as possibly coming from Vermillion

College and one of the small girls came out of the cottage and climbed into the car. The driver backed out and sped away.

"There go the women," Glynis said.

"Weren't there two little girls?" Mitchell asked.

Glynis thought for a second. "Yes, you're right. One must still be inside."

The two didn't have to wait long for more people to come out of the cottage. Three men and Randall Banks hurried from the cottage door to the tan car. The two men who were dressed in black got in first, climbing into the front seat as they flicked their cigarettes onto the gravel. Randall came out with the third, opening the back passenger door for him to scoot in. He jogged quickly around the back of the car to sit behind the driver. The driver revved the engine and careened down the lane, leaving a trail of dust.

Glynis picked up her cell again and texted Callan that Randall Banks was on his way.

He texted back: *Is Marissa with him?*

No, she replied.

A simple, one word *Damn* followed. Callan didn't add further instructions.

Glynis rose. "I gotta use the bathroom. I've sat here long enough."

"Wait," Mitchell said.

"No waiting," she blurted, using her thumb to point behind her. "You were able to go in the woods. I need better facilities than that."

"Marissa hasn't come out yet. That means she's still in the cottage."

Glynis glanced toward the house. He was right. They didn't see her come out and get into the cars that left. She sighed. "But I gotta go, Mitchell. I can't wait any longer." She peered into his eager eyes and raised her hand, commanding as though training a puppy. "You stay. Hear me? Stay put until I get back."

"But . . ."

"No, I mean it, Mitchell. Don't do anything until I return. I'll only be a moment."

Glynis turned and hurried through the foliage toward the path that led to the Donnelly home.

Mitchell watched her go, but he felt trapped. Caged. Marissa was inside, so close to being rescued, yet there he sat, chained to instructions that could cost them valuable time in getting her safely back to the college. Without hesitation, he leaped from his chair, found a small opening in the barbed wire, and crawled through, tearing a hole in his shirt and scratching his shoulder blade. He ran swiftly across the clearing to the door of the cottage. The screen door opened easily, but the wooden inner door was locked.

Mitchell stood back. Using power and skill from his martial arts training and knowledge on where to kick for maximum impact, he burst the door open with one thrust from his right leg. He raised his arms to defend himself as he peeked inside. No movement, no sound. Mitchell inched into the kitchen. Dirty cups, plates, and saucers were strewn about a small 1950s-style metal table with a Formica top. The doorway on the other side of the kitchen led to a living area much larger than what the outside of the cottage led him to believe.

No one was there.

"Marissa!" he called.

No answer.

Compared to the kitchen, the living area was relatively tidy. The television was on, however, as though someone had been watching it but left the room. He craned his head toward the hallway he presumed led to the bedrooms.

"Marissa!"

Three steps were all he took before he was abruptly stopped. A small girl, wearing a gray jumper suit, stood directly before him, blocking his way.

"You shouldn't be here," she said.

"Where's Marissa?"

"She isn't here," the girl replied, cold and expressionless.

"Where are the others?"

"They aren't here either."

"Where are they?" Mitchell stepped closer, his voice more demanding.

"You shouldn't be here. No one is here."

Mitchell's eyes darted around him to check the surroundings. He detected no movement, no sounds. No one, just as the girl indicated. "Did Marissa go with them?" he asked.

The girl laughed.

"Tell me! Where's Marissa?"

"She isn't here," she said snidely. "I told you she isn't here."

"Did they all go back to the college?" His tone softened.

The girl didn't laugh or shrug, she simply smiled as if Mitchell had been outsmarted. "I saw you in the woods," she said.

"When?"

"Just now with that other lady. You saw everything yourself. Why are you asking me?"

"But I didn't," he said. "You don't know what you're talking about." Mitchell glared into her eyes, wondering if they held answers he couldn't conceive.

She stepped back, revealing nothing. "Yes, you did. You

saw all that you need to know from the woods."

Mitchell glared at her, refraining from grasping her small frame and shaking her into submission.

She smiled coyly. "*Love must be sincere,*" she recited from *Romans.* "*Hate what is evil, cling to what is good.*"

A combination of anger and fear welled in his core. "Get out of my way!" he yelled.

"Do not repay anyone evil for evil."

Mitchell tried to push the little girl out of his way, but she didn't budge. Cemented in place by a power he hadn't mastered. He scurried around her, squeezing between her and a wall, then rushed down the hall to a bedroom. No one was there.

"You should do right," she said. "Live with peace. Do not take revenge."

Mitchell hurried to the second bedroom. No one was in that room either.

"Do you hear me?" she called. "Do not take revenge. Haven't you heard it said that if your enemy is hungry, you should feed him; if he's thirsty, you should give him something to drink?"

Mitchell peered down at her porcelain face. "Shut up! Shut up, you creepy little freak. Shut the hell up. I mean it!" He ran to the third and smallest bedroom. Still, no one was there.

"Did you hear me tell you that love must be sincere?"

"Where is she?" He lurched at her, stopping just short of grabbing her. Spittle foamed from his mouth. "I mean it. Tell me! Where's Marissa?"

The girl stopped reciting and smiled. "Did you not pay attention?"

"What are you talking about?" Mitchell wiped his mouth

clean with the back of his hand.

"Attention to the details around you."

"I listened to every word you said," he spouted. "I heard every word that came out of your damn mouth, but you said nothing that made any sense."

"Think," she replied. "If your love is sincere, you will think."

Mitchell paused, darting his focus to different points within the hall, shaking his head in frustration. "I am thinking! I told you. I've heard every word you said."

"But I didn't say anything except to pay attention to the details."

Mitchell took a deep breath and scrambled for clues in his head that made sense. *Think?* He wasn't sure what to think about or where to begin. *Think!* He looked down. "Was she with the women that left minutes ago in that blue car?" he asked, hopeful.

The little girl stared expressionless at him.

"No. That's a no, isn't it? She wasn't with the women in the blue car. She's not here though. When did she leave?"

"You're not paying attention."

"But I am! Please, stop this foolish shit, and just tell me."

"No, first, what did you see?"

"What? When? A few minutes ago?" He spun in place, thinking. "I, well, I saw a blue car drive up and the women and a small girl climb in."

"And?"

"They drove away. What else? Oh, and then Professor Banks and his men came out and got into the tan car."

"And?"

Mitchell glared at her. "What do you mean 'and'? There is no 'and'. They drove off, but I don't care about them. I only care about Marissa. I can't find Marissa!"

She smiled.

"No, I'm telling you everything," he pleaded. "What I just told you is what I saw."

This time she laughed.

"Why are you laughing at me?" he asked, half-crazed. "I saw a driver, three men, and Banks. I saw . . . oh, shit." Mitchell remembered the scene perfectly now. "There have never been three men before," he said, looking down at the little girl intently. "Am I right? There have only been two plus Professor Banks . . . but today he had three. Oh my God! Marissa! She was one of the men in disguise."

The girl smiled broadly and nodded. "There are some things you must work out for yourself. Not everything can be handed down to you, nor should it be, especially when you can think for yourself."

Mitchell let out a string of expletives at his naivety.

The young girl stepped into the living room, sat on the edge of a chair, and watched television. "Be blessed and do not curse," she said, staring at the screen.

Mitchell scoffed, rushed through the kitchen, knocking over a chair around the Formica table, and burst through the screen door.

Glynis saw Mitchell running frantically toward her across the clearing just as she returned to their setting. She knew something was wrong, but she didn't understand what it could be other than to realize that Marissa wasn't with him. Before he reached the fence line, Glynis turned toward the lane, movement coming from the corner of her eye. Walking casually down Kikthawenund Lane away from the cottage were a man and a woman, holding the hands of a small boy between them. Several yards behind, another child followed—a young girl in a gray jumper suit, plain and expressionless.

CHAPTER

FORTY-SIX

Rita McGarry stirred honey into a cup of hot tea as she and Callan sat with nervous tension at a small table on the porch of her camp cottage. Callan refused any refreshment. Rita listened to the wind, rustling through the dry late-September leaves in the trees that canopied her home. The sound calmed her. The warm breeze soothed her. Only the thought of meeting Randall Banks had her on edge.

"I was hoping he'd stop these shenanigans on his own," she said, setting her spoon on a saucer.

"I was too, but the phone call I just received from my colleague, Glynis Fordworth, indicated that he's no longer at the cottage. He's apparently on his way." Callan shifted in his seat.

"And?" she prompted, suspecting more that he withheld.

"Marissa was with him."

Rita scooted to the edge of her chair, encouraged by the news. "That's a good sign, isn't it? You'll be able to see for yourself that she's okay."

Callan shook his head and shifted again. "He's too delusional to know what it means," Callan replied. "The cleansing is done; he's ready for today. I don't know what he could want from both of us this afternoon."

"To reconcile with me, I'm sure," Rita said. "His theory can't be proven without a medium's voice to reach a saint."

"True, but he's cutting it rather close."

"What do you mean?"

Callan raised his brows as if he thought the answer was obvious. "Today is the equinox. He must be very sure of his ability to talk you into helping him after the row you had, or I'd have thought he would've called you sooner to make sure you'd be there for him."

Rita sipped her tea. What Callan said made sense. She replaced her cup and glanced at her watch. "It's ten after," she said.

Callan frowned. "It's only a couple of miles from Kik Lane to here, isn't it?"

"Three at the most."

"He should be here," he said. Callan stood to get a better look out of the porch's screened windows. Randall Banks was nowhere in sight. "Glynis texted me quite a while ago that he'd left the cottage."

"Perhaps he changed his mind."

Callan nodded but didn't appear convinced. "Or perhaps he never had any intention of showing up. Maybe he didn't want to take the chance that I'd be here."

Rita's face paled. "Or maybe he did know you'd be here."

"What do you mean?"

"He knows where we are now. Both of us. Perhaps we were manipulated to be out of the way here at Camp Chesterfield. He's free now to do what he intended to do all along without interference."

Callan's heart dropped to the bottom of his stomach. "You're right," he said. "You're exactly right. He's doing just that, preparing for the equinox without us."

He reached for his cell. Rita heard few introductory words before Callan spouted instructions for Glynis to meet him at the Great Mound as quickly as possible.

"I'll stay here just in case he shows up," Rita said. She gave Callan a sorrowful look, knowing full well he wouldn't show. It was Callan who'd have to face him without her.

~

Callan careened into Mounds State Park and parked near the entrance to be close to Trail 1, the easiest and shortest trail to the Great Mound. He ran faster on the trail that he'd run in years, racing to beat his nemesis before an equinox ceremony could begin. It was still early. The sun wasn't positioned properly on the mound yet, but Randall Banks had managed to surprise him more than once. Callan left nothing to chance.

He barely noticed the stately Bronnenberg House as he ran. His sight was on the trail as it turned toward the river, passed the house and headed for the mound. The closer he got to the brown log fence that surrounded the Great Mound, however, the less impressed he was that a ceremony of any kind was going to take place.

Three individuals—and only three individuals—stood at the entrance to the mound with their backs to him. They apparently heard his panting and the kicking of loose gravel from the path, and turned in unison.

"We haven't seen him yet," Mitchell called out, the first to do so. Glynis and Penny stood by his side.

Callan stopped to catch his breath and scan the area. He didn't see Randall or anyone else who appeared connected to the equinox ceremony.

"Are we too early?" Penny asked.

"We may be," Callan responded, "but he needs time to set up to deliver Marissa. Where else could he be?"

"This is unreal," Mitchell said, arms outstretched, spinning full circle. "Oh my God, this is freaking *Indiana Jones* stuff, Professor. I can't fathom this. I can't believe Marissa's involved in this kind of shit."

Callan approached the young man and put his hand on his shoulder to ground him. "Calm down. We'll find her."

"But will it be in time?"

Callan shook his head. He didn't know. He didn't even know if Marissa understood how much her life was in danger, being with a man like Randall Banks.

"If she's not here, where could she be?" Mitchell asked. "They left the cottage on Kik Lane a long time ago."

"Surely, they have to be here shortly," Penny said.

Callan turned toward her. He heard what she said, but, somehow, he no longer believed it to be true. "Does he?" he asked.

The three stared at him blankly.

"We have to ask ourselves," Callan replied, "Why must he be here? I've been thinking about this ceremony all wrong. I can't believe I've been so stupid! He's tricked me again! I've tried to stay one step ahead of Banks and his theories, but, by damn, the son of a bitch has tricked me again!"

"What are you talking about, Callan?" Glynis asked. She

stepped closer, a grave expression shrouding her face. "He has to be here, doesn't he? It's the equinox. You said so yourself."

Callan laughed. "No, he doesn't have to be here." He turned toward the Great Mound and lifted his hands in the air. "I've been an idiot! He doesn't have to be here for the equinox at all. Don't you see? The equinox will come over the Great Mound whether Randall Banks is here or not. But like Moses had to be on Mount Nebo to see the Promised Land, Professor Banks must be on *his* Mount Nebo to receive the knowledge he desires."

"You mean he's on his way to Mount Nebo?" Mitchell asked.

"That's exactly what I mean."

"Then what are we waiting for? Let's go!"

"Stop! No, not without backup," Callan said. "I'm not going to be a fool for a third time. We'll go all right, but first, let me call John Steinmeier to have authorities in Benton County be there ready for us. It'll take a while for us to drive from here and for John to drive up from Vermillion. It'll also give the Benton authorities time to set up."

The three didn't appear convinced. They stood, mouths gaping, eyes bulging. "But won't we be too late?" Penny asked.

Callan shook his head. "On the contrary, I believe we should be just in time."

CHAPTER

FORTY-SEVEN

There wasn't a shortcut to Benton County. No interstate access from east to west across the state, not a divided highway that would make their journey faster from Mounds Park to Mount Nebo. Callan and Penny arrived ahead of Glynis and Mitchell. Callan didn't see law enforcement at the scene, just a dirty tan car, parked along the county road near the path's entrance to the Mount Nebo prominence.

Darkness loomed to the east. The west was dimming with a watercolor canvas of oranges, pinks, sky blues, and purples. Callan gazed at the beauty in the face of horror. Adrenaline rushed through his veins as they trod up the path. Penny struggled to keep up, apprehension holding her back. The trail to the prominence seemed even longer than Callan remembered. He looked back often to see how she was doing. Penny reassured him with halfhearted gestures that she was keeping up the best she could.

Callan suddenly stopped.

The silhouettes of two people loomed ahead, both in prayer, one cloaked in a long, dark robe, the other in a soft, flowing gown. Each held candles as their only light. Callan scanned the brush on both sides of the path. The silhouettes were those of the professor and Marissa, but where were his two guards? Did they pass them on the path unknowingly? Were they watching from a distance? Cold chills crept up his back.

His caution was interrupted by Randall Banks's voice, bellowing from the prominence to the heavens, pleading for clarity and mercy. Randall reached for the sky toward the setting sun in a dramatic exhibition of their pure hearts and openness.

Randall took Marissa by both hands and pulled her in front of him. He lifted her arms so that they, too, reached the sky. He sermonized a song of thanksgiving, proclaimed their innocence, and urged compassion and generosity. Marissa couldn't see the professor drawing a blade from within his cloak, but Callan could. Randall held it over the young woman's head. His voice rasped, proclaiming acceptance of God's gifts and offering his sacrifice in return.

"Banks!" Callan yelled, fearing what might be next. "Stop! Let her go!"

Randall turned abruptly.

"It won't work!" Callan said.

The professor pointed the knife at him, vile words spraying from his lips. "Leave at once, Morrow! You don't understand. You're not willing to believe."

"But I speak the truth."

"And so do I," Randall responded. "What makes you

think the truth isn't in my work, only in your beliefs?"

Callan didn't have time to rush him. The couple were too far away. Randall would be too quick. He feared harm to Marissa. Callan thought of another approach. "Because it's flawed," he said. "I do believe in you. You've convinced me, but your theories have errors in them. Please! Let's talk about it. Put the weapon down, and let's discuss. I know you don't want to find out what went wrong after it's too late. The equinox is upon us. There's no time for error!"

Two sets of footsteps approached from behind. Penny screeched. Callan whisked around. Two men, the two who'd been at Randall's side since Conner Whaite's death, confronted them, one of them snatching Penny and pulling her arms back into a crisscross.

"Don't hurt her," Callan pleaded.

"Then get the hell out," he said.

Callan froze, staring the man down but speaking to Randall. "You realize it, too, don't you, Banks?" he yelled. "You must realize it. You're too bright, too brilliant, too clever not to see that even with Rita McGarry as your conduit to the heavens, God isn't going to reveal to you what you want tonight."

"That's not true!"

"It is. You certainly realize it. He isn't going to reveal *anything* until you perfect your theory."

"But it is perfect!"

"It can't be. Don't you see? You have the wrong medium."

"No, no," Randall replied, "it's too late."

"No, it's not! Rita McGarry isn't the right medium for you. She doesn't believe; she practically told you so, and you know it. You need a medium who truly believes, Banks, or your plan won't work. Rita McGarry isn't that medium, just like Rita Doran wasn't right for Thomas Bradford."

"She betrayed me!" Randall blurted.

"She didn't betray you. All she did was see the disconnection of your plan from the Bible, but she didn't betray you. You just have more work to do. Please, Banks. Release Marissa, and let's go home and think about this. Let's tweak this plan—a better plan. Together we can do this."

The professor stood stoically on the prominence, gazing at the falling sunset, holding his divine chosen one tightly, the knife still precariously close to her throat.

Marissa began to tremble. Her knees shook. A tear streamed down her face in the near darkness, glistening from the red in the sky and the small flame of her candle. "Please!" she cried to Randall in a voice that even Callan could hear from where he stood.

Randall clasped her tighter, promising nothing.

"What of it, Banks?" Callan called. "Will you let her go? Will you perfect your theories for the solstice? Forget the equinox, Randall. The solstice! Think of it. The winter solstice is the grandest of them all."

"Please!" Marissa begged again.

Callan saw Randall shake. He wasn't sure if it was anger or frustration, but the professor's body shook violently from within, nicking the area around Marissa's clavicle, soaking her white gown with blood. She trembled more. He told her to stop. When she couldn't, he grabbed her arms and twisted them painfully tight behind her.

"Banks!" Callan called in fear. He lurched toward them.

"I wouldn't," the man holding Penny said as he tightened his grip.

Callan paused and glanced back.

The man snarled, craning his head around Penny's to show

his teeth. The other man stepped forward, placing his hand around his belt, brandishing a firearm underneath.

Callan submitted, raising his hands, glancing at a figure crouched below the brush hidden by dusk, approaching slowly and silently on the path from the road. Callan raised his hands higher to be sure the men saw that he'd surrendered.

Marissa nearly fainted. Strength held her no longer.

Randall kept her up, told her to stand on her own, then peered through the darkness to the four below. "Get them out of here!" he yelled to his men.

Before either man could step forward to do as they were told, in a split-second move, a foot swung across the side of one man's face, knocking him to the ground. Another foot swung the other way, hitting the other man, dropping him decisively, so that Penny could drop to the ground, out of the way. Without losing momentum, the figure swung again, this time snapping the arm of the man who held the gun. It tumbled off the side of the path into the brush.

Mitchell Dells didn't let up. Using every martial art skill he knew, the young student pulverized both men.

Blue lights appeared from the road; deputies surrounded and secured the area. Callan exhaled a sigh of relief as he reached for Penny to comfort her. He turned in time to see Banks drop the knife that had only moments ago held Marissa at ransom. Banks raised his hands in defeat, releasing Marissa, allowing her to run toward Callan with the remaining strength she had within.

Chapter

Forty-Eight

Callan, Penny, Mitchell, Glynis and Marissa spent a good portion of the night and wee hours of the next morning providing statements and answering questions to Benton County authorities. John Steinmeier appeared early in the morning to offer support at Calan's request. Hour after hour of intense questioning took its toll on the five of them. They were not prepared and were too exhausted for the emotional reunion when Marissa's parents hurried through the station to reunite with their daughter.

Callan saw them first and rose to meet them, saying a few words to ground their emotions and to preface the traumatic state in which they'd find Marissa. As Marissa and her parents embraced, Callan fought back a lump in his throat, and tears formed in the corners of his eyes. He hadn't taken his eyes off Marissa since their interviews were over. Grateful and relieved.

He felt that now. Finally.

John saw his colleague and friend choke back tears. He inched toward him silently and placed a kind hand on his back, allowing Callan to release what had been pent up for so long.

~

Marissa saw Callan too. She squeezed her father's hand and asked for a moment. Greg didn't want to let her go, but she insisted.

"Just for a moment," she said. "It's something I have to do."

He relented, and she shuffled toward Callan. John stepped away to give her room. Marissa hesitated, standing face to face, not knowing what to say, hoping the right words would come to her to express her gratitude and to tell him what she wanted—needed—to say.

"I suppose you'd like to know why," Marissa said.

Callan nodded. "I would, but it's not what's important right now."

"Oh, I think it is. You worked so hard, so tirelessly, to find and protect me from what I got myself into. I owe you an explanation, and, quite frankly, I don't think I could return home with my parents without telling someone what's welling up in my chest. I'll burst. I'll simply burst."

"What about?"

"How enthralled I got with Professor Banks and his celestial theories, his hopes, and the glorious revelation that only I was to receive."

"Perhaps your parents are the people you need to tell."

Marissa looked back over her shoulder at them and shook

her head. "No, they aren't ready for that, Professor. I couldn't do that to them right now. Not yet anyway."

She didn't know where to begin. Marissa saw a tear glisten in a corner of his eye. She had underestimated the emotional toll the investigation must've had on him.

"Maybe this isn't the right time or place to do it either," she said, "but I feel so ashamed and stupid right now. I was so naive and ignorant about what happened to me."

"No, you just got caught up in Professor Banks's experiment, Marissa. You need time to process what happened and to heal. It occurred before you even knew what was happening."

"Oh, no, Professor Morrow, no. I knew exactly what was happening," she said adamantly. "That's what I can't believe. I believed wholeheartedly that I was going to be a part of a wonderful prize that would astound the world and immortalize me. Not only that, but I was captivated, knowing that I was the only one who could fulfill this wonder. It was a feeling I've never had before. It was euphoria and fulfillment that overpowered me completely."

Callan's brows raised. "So you truly believed that you were the chosen one?"

"Yes!" she exclaimed. "It was such an honor."

Callan stepped back. "But Conner died, Marissa. He died being cleansed for the very same purpose."

Marissa glanced away in thought, smiling as she did so. "I know, Professor, but that's because he was wrong. He wasn't the right person to fulfill the glorious mission we had. Leah tried to tell me that if Conner was the chosen one, then how could I be the chosen one too. There is only one chosen one, she said, but she said that because she couldn't see the big picture like I could. Professor Banks told me that Conner wasn't right. He'd made an error in choosing him."

"Because of Pleiades?"

"Yes, of course. Professor Banks ignored the Pleiades constellation in his theory. He realized that he'd made a mistake when Conner died, by choosing a man over a woman."

Callan frowned. "And that made sense to you?"

"Absolutely."

"I don't see how it could, Marissa."

"Because I wanted it to make sense. I wanted to be chosen over someone as worldly and as intelligent as Conner Whaite. We do that, you know. I mean, as people. We want something so badly that we're willing to make choices we wouldn't normally make. I thought for sure Conner's death meant that I was destined to be the one. Professor Banks's Pleiades theory made complete sense to me."

"When did it not make sense?" Callan asked. "Surely, it dawned on you at some point that you had to die for this experiment to work. Weren't you scared?"

She shook her head. "No, I think the scary part is that I *wasn't* afraid."

"Not at all?"

Sadly, Marissa shook her head again. "I was totally brainwashed. The other students' involvement in the circle encouraged me and strengthened my resolve to go through with the experiment. It was glorious, Professor. I can't describe it any other way. To be the chosen one—the one and only one—to know in your heart the day and hour Christ would come again; it was magnificent."

Marissa breathed deeply, smiling broadly. Moments ago, she was ashamed and bewildered. Now, pride welled in her chest as she talked about the experience. Euphoria returned. She felt it again.

Callan's expression turned grave.

"What?" she asked. "What's the matter?"

"You talk of glory and euphoria, but it was also something else, wasn't it?"

Marissa lost her wondrous glow. His tone resonated judgment and skepticism. She raised her chin and set her jaw.

Callan wouldn't let go. "Surely, it wasn't as grand as all that, Marissa."

Images of her experience flashed in her mind. Her emotions and feelings came to the forefront. She took a deep breath and admitted, "You're right, it wasn't all glory and wonder." Her words became harsh. "It was self-righteous. It was arrogant. Most of all, it was a lie, a horrific lie."

Callan nodded as if that was what he wanted to hear. "Because I saw you, Marissa, standing on the prominence in front of Professor Banks, the sharp edge of his knife against your throat, cutting you without concern or compassion. You didn't appear to be a woman committed to dying for a glorious cause."

Marissa hung her head. A tear formed and dropped down the side of her cheek. What was euphoria a moment ago was now regret, remorse and shame once again. "You could see that on the mount?" When he nodded, she said, "You're right. I was far from being that woman Professor Banks said that I was. I was frightened and alone. I'd turned away my parents and my friends. I had no one to turn to. I was going to die, and what would I have? Would I have a glorious revelation of the Lord's coming or would I have a God that I loved and believed in who would grieve because I gave in to my self-righteousness and greed?"

"Did you come to that realization on Mount Nebo?" he asked.

Marissa looked away and smiled. "No. Mount Nebo only

solidified what I had felt during my cleansing in the afternoon. The cleansing got me to thinking. I was miserable in that tent. The process isn't all that Professor Banks built it up to be. I was suffocating and praying . . . and I saw my grandfather at his workbench. My grandfather. He came to me."

"Like in a mirage?"

Marissa hesitated, looking away again. "I suppose, but not really. He was actually in the tent with me, Professor. I don't know how to explain it."

"Perhaps you shouldn't," Callan said, thinking back of his own experience the night his parents died.

"Then there was Ms. McGarry, Professor," Marissa added. "Her defiance against a powerful man like Professor Banks helped me see the fallacy of his teachings. It was her adamant conviction during the so-called séance we had that made me realize the circle was wrong. Ms. McGarry recited the truth, but I could see that it didn't change the professor or his thinking. He was as committed as ever to his theories. The truth was never going to change him."

"But, thank God, it changed you," Callan said.

Marissa took his hands. "Yes, because there was one other person who changed my mind. You never gave up. Even though I wouldn't talk to you, I knew through Leah and the others within the circle that you continued to search for me. You were my guardian angel, Professor, looking out for me when I wasn't looking out myself. I'm so very grateful."

Chapter

Forty-Nine

Callan watched Mitchell stumble from an interview room, the last to make a statement to the sheriff and his deputies. The young man's eyes, dull and sunken, carried the toll of an endless night of questions and interrogation.

"Where's Marissa?" he asked Callan immediately upon his release.

"She's left already," Callan replied. "She went back home with her parents."

Mitchell's shoulders dropped, his expression dimmed.

"How about some pancakes? Maybe more," Callan offered. "You must be famished. We all are."

John Steinmeier heard the word pancakes and scurried to their side, mentioning a place recommended to him by several of the officers.

Callan pulled John aside and said, "Sounds good, but I

want to follow up on a couple of more details here."

"I think they have it," John said.

Callan gave him a second look to see if John caught what he was saying.

John lowered his voice. "When you called to meet me here, you gave me the additional details on the suspicions you had. I did some follow-up and passed them along."

"You mean we're free to go? All of us? But . . ."

John tugged on his shirt sleeve, pulling Callan toward the exit. "Let's just go. I've told the sheriff where we'll be."

John gathered those who'd come from Chesterfield, including Penny, Glynis, and Mitchell. No one argued about a good breakfast, and the country diner nearby was nearly free of patrons. They sat around a large, round table off to one corner. They sat uncomfortably, exhausted mentally and physically. Conversations centered around the unusual events, but, for the most part, were subdued, lacking substance; that is, until Penny's curiosity got the best of her.

"What will become of Professor Banks, do you think?" she asked John.

"They'll be filing attempted murder charges among others here in Benton County," he said.

"What about Conner's death?" Glynis asked. "Do you think Banks'll be extradited to Vermillion to face charges for murder?"

John shrugged. "That's a little more complicated," he said. "I don't think the prosecutors have their hands wrapped completely around that case just yet. Everything's pending. With new evidence about the circle being discovered, we can expect some elevated charges. They'll work with Benton County, I'm sure."

"What about Logan's death?" Mitchell asked. "He was

killed here in Benton County. Won't they hold Professor Banks? Have they filed charges here?"

John didn't answer. Instead, he lifted a cup and pretended to be busy sipping his coffee, all the while peering over the rim toward Callan.

Callan lifted his head as if he hadn't been listening. "Hold him for what?" he asked groggily.

Mitchell was taken aback. "For murder. What else? Logan's dead too. Isn't Professor Banks going to be held accountable for that as well? Won't charges be filed for what he did to Logan?"

Callan shrugged. "I'm not sure what he did to Logan, Mitchell."

Mitchell held his breath. His eyes darted around the table. "I think it's pretty damn obvious. All the evidence points to him."

"Yes, I'll agree with you that all the evidence points to him, but it's circumstantial. Professor Banks was spotted at Mount Nebo during the day by two geocachers, searching for a cache on the prominence, but . . . was he there the night Logan was killed?"

"What are you saying?" Glynis asked. "I thought I heard that Logan and Professor Banks had a terrible row the day Logan was murdered."

"Yes, it's true, they did," Callan replied.

"Professor Banks almost killed him once before, the night Conner died."

"Yes, it's true, he did."

"Then, there you go!" Mitchell exclaimed. "Circumstances should dictate that Banks be charged for Logan's murder also, right here in Benton County."

No one moved. Time seemed to stop.

"Well, don't you think?" Mitchell asked confused, his

voice rising. "Don't you all think so?"

No one answered. Instead, their focus turned toward the restaurant's entrance where the sheriff and two deputies strode across the dining area and approached their table.

"More important than what we think, Mitchell," Callan said, pointing to the men in uniform, "is what these gentlemen think."

Terror replaced the exhaustion in the young man's eyes.

The sheriff glared at him and said, "Mitchell Dells, I'm placing you under arrest for the murder of Logan Allister." *Miranda* rights were read as Mitchell struggled, was pulled from his seat and was handcuffed.

"This is insane!" Mitchell cried. "This is a mistake! It's all a mistake. It must be. Someone please tell me what's going on."

CHAPTER FIFTY

All focus turned to Callan when the deputies led Mitchell away. Callan looked back at them; all had glassy eyes, swollen with surprise and despair.

"First of all," Callan said softly. "I want you to know that I didn't turn Mitchell in. All I did was provide additional facts and hypotheses that helped the authorities put the puzzle together with the evidence they'd already collected."

Glynis didn't know what to say. She stuttered briefly before finally asking, "What sort of facts were there? I don't understand." She inhaled and paused, shaking her head. "I didn't see any of this coming," she added, "and I sat with Mitchell for hours at the clearing in front of Randall Banks's cottage and tent, talking about everything under the sun to relieve us from our boredom, but I swear . . . there wasn't a hint of anything like this coming from our conversations."

"Mitchell's smart enough to know when to keep his mouth shut," Callan said. "I'm surprised he was able to. He was so despondent the day after Logan was killed. He wanted to talk and talk he did. He cast suspicion on Professor Banks. He made a plausible case."

"What did he say?" Glynis asked.

"He mentioned that Logan and Banks had an argument."

"I know that already, but that pointed the finger even more on Professor Banks."

"Except that Mitchell's story didn't add up," Callan explained. "He'd lied to me before about a conversation he'd had with Dana Weiss and Logan. The timing was wrong, and despite denying that he knew about Logan going to Mount Nebo, he did know it. Logan spilled his plans to Dana at the coffee shop in Vermillion when Mitchell was there. He knew all along that Logan would be at the prominence that night and why he'd be there."

"Did you suspect him then when he came into your office?"

"No, not at first. Mitchell killing Logan was the farthest thing from my mind. I just knew at that point that he was lying. I knew he had a propensity to lie even before that. When I first talked with him, he said he hadn't spoken to Marissa, but Marissa's mother told me otherwise."

That wasn't all. Callan remembered the exact moment he suspected Mitchell caused Logan's demise even though he didn't realize it at the time. "It was a statement Mitchell made, a careless, stupid comment to convince me that his head was on straight despite his emotions being so out of whack."

"What was it? What did he say?"

"That he didn't need to feel guilty about Logan's death because he wasn't the one who pummeled him."

Penny frowned. "Sounds reasonable. What was so alarming about it?"

"Because it was never mentioned how Logan was actually killed. Even I didn't know for sure. For him to say that Logan was pummeled was an odd and very specific cause of death. So later, when other clues came together for me, I called John to find out what the Benton County Medical Examiner discovered. A cause hadn't been determined. So how did Mitchell know?"

"Oh my God," Glynis said. "Then when I texted you that Mitchell was in love with Marissa, that provided a possible motive, didn't it?"

"It was a long shot, I'll grant you that," Callan said, "but it was an angle worth pursuing that we hadn't pursued before. All along, Mitchell believed Logan was in love with Marissa. He thought Logan was trying to vie for her affection, but Logan wasn't interested in Marissa at all. Mitchell had it wrong. Logan's affection was toward Dana. That's why Logan met her at the coffee shop; he wanted to ask Dana out to resume their relationship."

"And Mitchell, being Mitchell, cocky and self-assured, believing the world revolves around him, believed . . ."

"... that Logan was hitting in on his territory with Marissa," Callan said, finishing Glynis's thought.

John cleared his throat. "Like Callan said, he called me and asked if Benton County had found the murder weapon used to kill Logan. They hadn't. There was none."

"That's because the murder weapon was Mitchell's hands and feet, just like they were last night when he thwarted Banks's men on the path, saving Penny's and my life," Callan said. "Only, he wasn't out to hurt Logan. He meant to kill him, to permanently eliminate him as a possible suitor to Marissa."

"Oh my," Glynis said. "I can't believe it—all because of jealousy."

"I'm sure he thought he could get away with the crime because of the confrontation Logan had with Professor

Banks, hoping the authorities wouldn't look beyond Banks as a suspect."

"But one thing doesn't make sense to me," Glynis added. "Mitchell was lured to the same sweat lodge site that Conner and Logan were found at. Doesn't that put a wrinkle in your theory?"

"Not at all," John replied on Callan's behalf. "The lodge that we found Mitchell in was constructed much more crudely than the one Conner and Logan were in. Based upon what I saw, I knew that Professor Banks didn't build the lodge where Mitchell was found. Mitchell's lodge was poorly and hastily constructed. Even the materials used were different. That meant only one of two possible explanations: that the lodge was built by Banks's men and not by Banks, or that the lodge was built by Mitchell himself."

"That sounds unfathomable to me."

"It was all done to cast suspicion on Randall Banks," John said.

"But what Mitchell did last night in using martial arts to subdue Banks's men proves John's point that Mitchell was the one who built the lodge he was found in. At the lodge, Mitchell said the two men subdued *him* and knocked *him* unconscious until morning when we arrived."

Glynis frowned. "Couldn't that be the case if Mitchell was surprised?"

"Mitchell was trained to not be surprised," Callan said. "He's an expert, trained by his father, a Marine. In his own words, Mitchell said he arrived at the lodge under suspicious circumstances. If that was the case, he'd have been on his guard even more, unsurprised by being attacked."

With that, the conversation lulled. Glynis sighed with relief that the ordeal was over. Penny sat motionless, seemingly overwhelmed by what had transpired. John glanced at his watch, wondering where their order was.

"This was certainly one of the most complex, most baffling, and oddest cases I've ever been involved with," John said, looking up. "Odd from the beginning. Hard to believe the lives of two young men ended senselessly."

"One by a madman, playing God with an impossible fantasy," Glynis said.

"And the other, although shrouded by the complexities of that fantasy, was a simple case of the age-old murder-for-love triangle," Callan added. "Classic murder-for-love."

CHAPTER

FIFTY-ONE

After finishing breakfast, Penny Donnelly stood outside the diner staring awkwardly into the sun toward the cars in which they'd rode to Benton County. John had driven straight from Vermillion. Glynis had driven Mitchell to the Donnelly home from Vermillion and planned to head back from the diner. Callan had his car, but it would be a two-hour drive out of the way for him to return to Chesterfield. Penny objected to the diversion just for her.

"Not on your life, Penny, you're coming with me," Callan said. "You don't have an easy way of getting home without me. Besides, I want to update Rita on what happened. She deserves to know firsthand."

Goodbyes were short. Weariness wore heavily on everyone's faces. Callan and Penny stood in the diner's parking lot, waving farewell to John and Glynis.

"I've neglected to ask how Harry's doing," Callan said.

Harry. The recent events had overshadowed her poor husband, but she managed a cell call soon after her interview at the station. "Harry's fine," she said. "He's with Libby, my saint. He had a good dinner last night and went to bed early. More than I can say for myself, sitting in the sheriff's station."

They walked a few steps toward Callan's car. Random thoughts continued to ravage her mind. So many things she didn't understand or didn't grasp as the events unfolded. "You did a marvelous job unraveling the mess," she said. "I'm not sure I could've handled it with the patience and perseverance you had. I must ask you something though."

Callan stopped just short of opening the driver's side door of his car to climb in. "Please do."

"At the prominence, when we were standing there with Professor Banks as he held Marissa in his grip, you told him that what he was doing with the circle could be worked out. You also told him that even though his theories were flawed, all could be ironed out with a little more work in time for the winter solstice."

Callan nodded. "Yes, that's what I said. What of it?"

"You didn't mean it, did you?" she asked seriously. "You weren't really willing to let him go to rethink sacrificing a young woman so that he could predict the future."

He laughed heartily. "Oh hell no, Penny. Are you kidding?"

"Well, I didn't know." She laughed along with him. "You sounded very convincing to me."

"I said those things to give Banks a way out so that he'd drop the knife and let Marissa go," Callan said. "As it was, he didn't buy it. Of course, I could've promised him anything at the time, but in the end, it wasn't up to me. It was going to be in the hands of law enforcement. I was hoping Banks would be fooled by it."

"What about the drawing board?"

Callan rested his arms on the doorframe and peered over the top of the car. "There is no drawing board. I made that up. The circle is lunacy. It's over now. It'll be disbanded once and for all."

Penny smiled. "That makes me feel a lot better. For a while there, I thought you'd become delusional yourself."

"You're still probably not far off." He started to climb into the car.

"There's one more question that hasn't been answered, Callan," she said.

The serious tone of her voice made him pull his leg back out.

"What's that? Where pukwudgies come from?" he asked, half-joking.

"No," Penny said, laughing. "I pretty much have the pukwudgies figured out."

"Then you must be thinking of Arla May."

Penny sighed. "Yes, that dear little girl. What will become of her?"

Callan paused to let her think. "What do *you* believe?" he asked. "You must have a theory of your own."

Penny opened the passenger car door and gazed back at Callan. "I prefer to believe as we last discussed about her. Arla May is an angel whose mission was to watch over Marissa for as long as she could until Marissa was in better hands."

Callan smiled reassuringly.

"But what do you believe?" she asked. "I'm curious to know."

He looked away. Peace and serenity radiated from his face.

Penny didn't have to guess what his thoughts were about.

She realized he must be remembering all the times in his life when someone—or something—had been there for him at just the right time, at just the right place, to help him make sense of the difficulties.

Callan placed his foot back into the car, ready to move forward. "I believe," he said, expression soft and compelling, "there are some things best left to faith . . . and mystery."

A Note from the Author

They say you can't go home again, but I do every chance I get, through memories and contacts with dear friends. Raised in Chesterfield, Indiana, from 1959-1976, I know all about its whimsical folklore, superstitions, and old wives' tales. I didn't believe much of them, but I accepted them anyway because they were part of my community's culture. Camp Chesterfield was a focal point of that culture, nestled along the river's edge.

The beginnings of Camp Chesterfield started as early as 1843, when Dr. John Westerfield and his wife, Mary Ellen Bussell Westerfield, promoted speakers in mesmerism at Union Hall in nearby Anderson. Only a few years later, modern Spiritualism took hold in 1848 when two sisters, Maggie and Katie Fox of Hydesville, New York, changed the way people thought about life and death. When the Westerfields' only child, John Jr., passed at the age of fourteen in 1855, John and Mary delved deeper into clairvoyance as a way of dealing with their grief. It wasn't until they journeyed with other like-minded individuals in a spiritualist camp in Michigan that they decided to establish a camp of their own. They chose a grove on the banks of the White River in 1890 and opened what is now Camp Chesterfield on land owned by Carroll and Emily Bronnenberg (Ward, 2003).

At first, the gathering was only a tent-based church where visitors would camp, attend worship services, conduct séances, and receive readings. Their roots were faith-based, accepting the truth from a variety of all religions, including Christianity, and were far from what people would consider to be demonic or satanic (Leonard, 2014).

Camp Chesterfield soon emerged as a focal point for Spiritualism in the United States, drawing visitors to the area from around the world and garnering the support and enthusiasm of many. It thrives today as one of the most important, oldest and active communities for Spiritualism in the country, significant for its historic structures, landscapes, memorials, statues, shrines, museums, architecture, and culture. It exists today because of the commitment by the founding members of the camp to preserve tradition while embracing contemporary appeal. In 2002, the Chesterfield Spiritualist Camp District was designated historic and listed on the *National Register of Historic Places.*

But Camp Chesterfield isn't without its controversy and scandal over the years. On August 23, 1923, Virginia Swain of the Newspaper Enterprise Association escaped injury while investigating mediums at the camp, alleging that the mediums took money from people by conducting fake and fraudulent séances. Ms. Swain was nearly lynched while investigating the séances but came back to camp with members of the Anderson Police Department. Fourteen mediums were arrested but were released nine months later when it was determined that Ms. Swain's investigation constituted entrapment. Her findings, however, were published nationally in a six-part exposé on the subject (Anderson Public Library).

Since then, numerous other investigations have alleged and proven fraud and false practices at the camp. Some of the more notorious and interesting cases include:

The July 10, 1960, issue of *Psychic Observer* exposed fraud of a medium in the camp by investigator Andrija Puharich and editor and publisher of the magazine Tom O'Neill, even though O'Neill originally set out to prove that manifestations at the camp were genuine.

Paranormal author Allen Spraggett visited Camp Chesterfield in 1965 and was unconvinced that the séances he attended were valid, largely due to the voices of the deceased relatives sounding more like the medium herself.

Destructive evidence came in 1976 from the published book, *The Psychic Mafia,* by M. Lamar Keene, a former camp medium. Keene claimed that money was the root of the mediums' facade and called the camp "the Coney Island of Spiritualism." The book carefully described the various tricks used by them to conjure spirits, produce personal data of deceased loved ones, and entice people to spend money for information on their departed.

In 2001, Joe Nickell went undercover to expose various fraudulent techniques used during psychic readings, spirit writings, direct voice sessions, and the production of gifts which were nothing more than cheap trinkets purported to have come directly from the spirits.

Nickell followed up his visits at the camp in March 2002

with additional evidence of deceit obtained from a sting operation that was published in *The Skeptical Inquirer.*

Despite the controversies, Camp Chesterfield thrives among those seeking spiritual solace. Its camp meetings and festivals, held each year since 1890, draw hundreds, if not thousands, of followers. Whether one believes or scoffs at the camp's teachings and beliefs, the historic and spiritual significance of this peaceful park-like enclave, considered a utopia to many, cannot be denied.

~

I have Mary Jo (Stewart) McClure of Muncie, Indiana, to thank most of all for assisting me in bringing *Circle of Chesterfield* to life. She carefully tended to each page, sent me recommendations for improvement, edited terminology and phrases I overlooked, and encouraged me throughout each phase with my publisher. For that, I am very grateful. Above all, this story would not have been possible without my editor and publisher, Tahlia Newland, of AIA Publishing in New South Wales, Australia, who brought the manuscript to a professional completion with her candid expert advice and guidance. Of course, Rose Newland's cover design was stunning and captured everything about the story I envisioned. I'd be remiss if I didn't thank Roberta Basarbolieva-Stanisic of Ruse, Bulgaria, for her incredible attention to detail and expertise in editing and proofreading. She's an artist of words.

If you enjoyed this book, I would appreciate if you could write a review and publish it at your point of purchase. Your review, even a brief one, will help other readers to decide if they'll enjoy my work.

If you want to be notified of new releases from myself

and other AIA Publishing authors, please sign up to the AIA Publishing email list. In return you'll get a free ebook of short stories and book excerpts by AIAP authors. You'll find the sign-up button on the right-hand side under the photo at www.aiapublishing.com. Of course, your information will never be shared, and the publisher won't inundate you with emails, just let you know of new releases.

Gary Lee Edward Kreigh
Gulf Shores, Alabama
16 August 2023

REFERENCES

Anderson Public Library, "Camp Chesterfield", *Discover Indiana,* accessed August 15, 2023, https://publichistory,iupui.edu/items/show/517.

"Camp Chesterfield", https://alchetron.com/Camp-Chesterfield, 17 July 2002, accessed 15 August 2023.

"Inside Camp Chesterfield: The Psychic Retreat Made Famous by Whistleblower Lamar Keene", https://www.higgypop.com/news/inside-camp-chesterfield, accessed 15 August 2023.

Leonard, Todd, "Camp Chesterfield Serving the Midwest as a Spiritual Retreat for 128 Years", *Researching Hoosier History,* 31 October 2014.

Nickell, Joe, "Undercover Among the Spirits: Investigating Camp Chesterfield", *Skeptical Inquirer,* March/April 2002.

"Night News Summary", *Kokomo (Indiana) Tribune,* 24 August 1925.

Spraggett, Allen, "The Unexplained", New York: New American Library, 1967.

Ward, Rev. Yogi Willis W., "A Brief History of Camp Chesterfield", *Camp Chesterfield: A Spiritual Center of Light,* 2003.

ABOUT THE AUTHOR

Born in Anderson, Indiana, Gary Lee Edward Kreigh graduated with an accounting degree from Ball State University. He also studied at the University of Indianapolis for Computer Technology and the Gonzaga University for Organizational Development.

Gary uses his thirty-five years in the fields of forensic accounting, fraud examination, and internal auditing to write about corporate and social issues, and experiences that affect ordinary people in extraordinary situations. His experience spans the banking, retail, finance, education, and medical industries.

Gary is currently an operating officer with EEZY Productions in New Orleans. His own podcast, Mytality! is about persevering through adversity. He now juggles his time and residence between New Orleans and Gulf Shores, Alabama.

This is Gary's fifth mystery novel, and the third in *The Callan Morrow Mystery Series* along with *Why Birds Fall* and *Silence the Past*. His other two books, *Payola* and *Masquerade of Truth* comprise *The Reverend Fountain Mystery Series*. All Gary's books can be found in major online stores.